PRAISE FOR THE EDGE OF]

"**Absolutely brilliant!** We do put a lot of trust in our medical care providers. How far will technology go in the future to sustain life? This book kept me on the edge."

—Sharese Reese

Top-Notch Medical Thriller! As in his first book, *Adrenaline*, the author takes several subplots and connects them to bring you the full story in the end. The story is excellently written, with lots of action and a few "nail-biting" moments. The characters are well-developed, from bad guy Nick Chandler, to underdog Chip Allison, to creepy Frankenstein-ish Dr. Mueller, to *Adrenaline* alumni Doug Landry. Oh, and an ending that you'll never see coming! *The Edge of Death* **gets 5 well-deserved stars!**

—Kristen Chandler

Heart-pounding Medical Thriller! Oh my gosh, I got caught up in this book so fast, I just hated to put it down to get other things done. This was a page-turner from beginning to end as it kept me guessing and visualizing every scene and character. This fabulous book gets you thinking about and looking at people with near death experiences differently. Dr. Landry and his wife Laura along with Chip and Kristin go through one horrific ordeal after another in this spine-tingling tale. I definitely recommend this to anyone who loves thrillers, especially medical ones. **Hope there's another novel coming soon from the brilliant John Benedict!**

—PammySue

PRAISE FOR ADRENALINE:

"If you like **gripping drama, starkly effective description and almost unbearable suspense,** then this book is for you.

The characters and places are engagingly real. It has been suggested by readers that this book would lend itself to an engrossing film.

Throughout intertwining subplots, significant hints are provided to the reader—including one startling revelation. The ending is breathless. I found myself totally unprepared for the plot twists, even though they had been amply prefigured. The rhapsodic tone of lovely inner reflection of love and its beauty when juxtaposed with the ugliness of killing is particularly welcome.

I hope that many will read *Adrenaline*. Without question, it will jolt you to some interesting insights."

— **Leslie S. March**
Harrisburg Magazine Review

"**This guy can flat out write.** Benedict has a great grasp of the many ways language can be used in telling a story, paired with the skill to do it, which is the thing that makes him stand out… Add in a good feel for the basics of pacing the story and sentence structures, a superb eye for the role of detail, and the priceless ability to draw a reader in until they forget that they're actually reading the story they're in the middle of."

— **Poisonedpenpress.com**

"**Properly entitled,** *Adrenaline* **is a thrill ride from the opening chapter.** Dr. John Benedict has written a novel encompassing the intrigue of Michael Crichton's E.R. combined with the thrill of Crime Scene Investigations. This is a top-notch medical thriller and I hope it is the first of many from Benedict. **He could easily become the next Dean Koontz with a medical degree.**"

— **Robert Denson III**
Managing Editor of Sunpiper Press
www.sunpiperpress.com

"**Benedict has done an outstanding job** at creating scenes, as well as characters, using every detail no matter how miniscule to evoke clear images and emotional response from readers, thus allowing us to really care about what happens to these characters."

— **Betsie's Literary Page**
betsie.tripod.com/literary

"**Filled with accelerating suspense,** author Benedict builds the plot that moves *Adrenaline* forward with methodical and deliberate subplots and characters, each of which succeed to broaden the mystery and draw the reader deep into the workings of the operating rooms and administrative offices of Mercy Hospital. Characters are pleasantly humanized, his plotting is meticulous, offering a thrilling journey.

Adrenaline offers a new take on the term 'Medical Thriller' that offers a breath of fresh air to the meaning of the term."

— **Denise M. Clark**
Denise's Pieces Author Site & Book Reviews
www.denisemclark.com

"A series of mishaps and an accidental death at a Pennsylvania hospital raise suspicions of sabotage in the author's debut medical thriller.** Doctors in the anesthesia department at Our Lady of Mercy Hospital are worried about losing their jobs in an impending merger, so it doesn't bode well when a patient dies soon after anesthesia is administered. Dr. Doug Landry and others are unaware that someone in their department is intentionally setting up the anesthesiologists for failure in a series of desperate acts that will ultimately lead to outright murder. **Benedict's novel is a mystery story rife with suspense:** A killer, whose identity is concealed, creeps into dark operating rooms; med student Rusty, searching for his elusive past, finds his way to Mercy; and a patient awakens in the midst of surgery, unable to move but feeling every agonizing cut. There's a hefty number of subplots: Doug's temptation to stray from his marriage vows with a flirtatious hospital employee; sympathetic Dr. Mike Carlucci recalling patients he's lost and trying not to succumb to the pressures of the job; plus Rusty's training and the threat of a suit against the hospital. But through shifting perspectives and a focus on the darker side of medical care--Doug tells Rusty how easily anesthesia, inadvertently or not, can become lethal--ensure that the various plots are less sentimental and more in tune with the murderous saboteur. **Twists and turns abound as the story progresses, and they hit a crescendo in a scene of utter ferocity that's violent and intense."**

—**Kirkus Reviews**

By John Benedict

Adrenaline

The Edge of Death (sequel to *Adrenaline*)

Fatal Complications (coming: December 2014)

THE EDGE OF DEATH

by

JOHN BENEDICT

THE EDGE OF DEATH

by

JOHN BENEDICT

Printed in the United States of America.

Published by Createspace: November, 2013

ISBN-13: 9781492230946
ISBN # 1492230944
Library of Congress # 2013915484
CreateSpace Independent Publishing Platform
North Charleston, South Carolina

Cover Photo by John Dalkin   <johndalkin.redbubble.com>

To the beautiful girl I love,
My wife of thirty years, Lou Ann,
Who believes in me
And makes all things possible.

And to my three awesome sons,
Rob, Chip and Luke,
who inspire me and
are more than any father could hope for.

ACKNOWLEDGMENTS

*To my friends, Colleen Kruger and Dori Oneill
whose careful reading of the manuscript and
encouragement along the way was truly invaluable.*

*To my brilliant editor, Marg Wilks,
who employs her wizardry to transform my writing.*

PROLOGUE

Somewhere in Macedonia, AD 48

"I saw it with my own eyes."

"It was hot and dusty, Nicodemus. You were no doubt tired and thirsty. The mind sometimes plays tricks in the afternoon sun."

"Brother, I know what I saw," Nicodemus said.

Demetrius set the spindle down and looked up from his loom, tired patience tugging at his worn features. "So you're saying the holy man healed him?"

"Yes."

Demetrius rubbed his neck and sat up straighter on his wooden stool. "Healed Timon, who has been a raging lunatic his whole adult life?"

"Yes," Nicodemus said, struggling to tamp down his growing impatience.

Demetrius smiled and shook his head. "I've heard stories like this before. What proof do you bring?"

"Demetrius, do you not believe your own brother? Timon is sitting by the well in the marketplace." Nicodemus pointed down the rutted dirt road toward town. "He is having conversations with the townsfolk."

Demetrius chuckled. "Conversations? Or more ranting and spitting and gnashing of teeth?"

"Calm conversation. See for yourself, brother."

"I don't have time for this. I have work to do." Demetrius nodded toward the loom and picked up the spindle.

"The rug will wait."

Demetrius sighed. "It's a long walk. And the sun is high."

Nicodemus grasped a handful of Demitrius's tunic. "Come, brother. You must see this."

"All right, all right," Demetrius muttered, rising stiffly from his stool. "Let me fetch my stick."

The two headed off toward town, the dull flap of their sandals kicking up dust. Before they had gone far, Demetrius unslung the goatskin water bag from his shoulder and took a drink. "Do you remember Timon as a boy?" He swiped the back of his hand against his thick black beard, then handed the water skin to Nicodemus.

"Yes," Nicodemus said. "I used to play with him before— before the change." Nicodemus put the water skin to his lips and took several long swallows. The cool water felt good on his gritty throat. "You were there when it happened, right?"

"I remember it like it was yesterday," Demetrius said. "Tragic accident." He stared across the field, toward the rolling hills in the distance. A strange look—painful or haunted—came into his eyes. He looked older than usual and it had nothing to do with the seams of gray in his beard.

Finally, Demetrius spoke. "When Timon didn't come home that night, we went out to look for him. We found him lying under the big sycamore tree, the ground around him dark with his blood—he had been gored by a wild boar. We thought he was dead.

"Before we could carry his body home for burial, a freak storm blew in off the desert; a huge bolt of lightning cleaved the sycamore tree right down the middle and singed all the hair from Timon's head. Amazingly—and I'll never forget this part—he got up off the ground and walked home through the pouring rain, under a flashing sky that trembled with the booming thunder. We all kept our distance, terrified. Poor Timon. He came home, alright—but he came back a madman."

The two men walked on in silence, Nicodemus leading, Demetrius pausing occasionally to lean on his gnarled walking stick. The hot sun burned directly overhead, casting only tiny shadows. After thirty minutes, the outskirts of their small town came into view.

Demetrius paused to take another drink. "So the holy man cast the demon out of him? And you witnessed this?"

"Many others were there as well," Nicodemus said.

"And will likewise testify to this?"

"Yes, brother," Nicodemus said.

"What did he say, exactly? The holy man."

"He said, 'In the name of Christ Jesus, I command you to leave him.' And he threw his arms skyward and spat on the ground."

"So, he was speaking directly to the demon?" Demetrius asked.

"Yes, I believe so."

"And at that precise moment, Timon was cured?"

"Yes."

Demetrius stroked his beard thoughtfully. "I've heard of this man, Christ Jesus. They say he is a god. What was the holy man's name?"

"He calls himself Paul—Paul from Tarsus."

"I do not know him. But we must be wary of him." Demetrius glanced around and lowered his voice. "All this talk of demons and men who control them—"

"But this Paul, he seems a righteous man."

"And you say you actually saw the demon leave his body?"

"Well, that's the funny part."

"Ah, finally we get down to it." Demetrius fixed him with a hard stare. "So Nicodemus, what exactly *did* you see?"

Nicodemus cleared his throat. "Well—it looked like a shimmering bright light flew down from the heavens and went *into* his body."

CHAPTER 1

Tuesday, 5:00 p.m.

Consciousness crept slowly into Nick Chandler's brain, fingers of awareness snaking into his mind like shafts of sunlight penetrating the morning haze. Here, in the meadow where he lay, there was no time—or pain. He was content to bask in the warm sun and drink in the mingled scent of freshly mown grass and the heady nectar of honeysuckle. Such peacefulness was beyond his experience.

Voices that seemed miles away hummed lightly about his ears. Or was it just the sound of insects flitting about in the hedgerow? The only other sensation he felt was the rhythmic whoosh of air being forced into his mangled chest.

Thoughts began to coalesce, disturbing ones. Questions queued up for attention, threatening to perforate the fuzzy cocoon of his mind. *Where am I? What happened to me?* Then a stranger thought, more insistent, jumped the line. *Am I dead?*

Chandler shooed these thoughts away—he didn't want to deal with any questions right now. Answers usually brought pain and he preferred the tranquil limbo of his nonexistence. But one question buzzed back, like a pesky horsefly, refusing to be ignored: Was this what it felt like to be dead? He couldn't be sure—and, he realized, he didn't care. Deep down, though, he remembered that people were *supposed* to care about such things.

He sensed that something was different about him, changed somehow, though he couldn't put his finger on it; the feeling was way too vague. But he knew he was right.

Chandler sighed. Too much work for now—he was bone-tired. Besides, the sunlit meadow beckoned. He let his mind submerge again, bobbing just beneath the surface of consciousness.

An unknowable amount of time passed as Chandler drifted in and out, until the buzzing returned and grew louder, finally nudging him awake. He sensed other people around him, picked up bits of conversation.

"... congestive heart failure secondary to viral myocarditis ..."

" ... overwhelming sepsis with full-blown ARDS ..."

" ... multi-system organ failure with progressive renal and hepatic shutdown ..."

Later an older male voice, deep and resonant with a professorial tone, commanded his attention. "Lauren, bring us up to speed on what happened yesterday."

Chandler struggled to focus and stay awake to hear this part; the meadow would have to wait.

A young female voice, crisp and assertive, answered. "He coded around noontime and we consider it a miracle that we brought him back in the first place. An hour later, though, he arrested again and this time we couldn't get him back. He was pronounced dead. He was then rushed to PML."

"You mean Dr. Mueller's lab?"

"Yes. The postmortem lab."

"I assume you are all familiar with Dr. Mueller's groundbreaking research into resuscitation science?" the professor said, garnering quiet murmurs of assent. "Go on, Lauren."

"The patient was immediately placed on full cardiopulmonary bypass. His heart was infused with a hyper-cool cardioplegic solution, ultra-low oxygen therapy was instituted, and a slew of cerebral protective drugs and antithrombin agents were administered. After twenty-four hours of this treatment, combined with sufficient resting of the myocardium, they attempted to restart his heart. Amazingly, after several countershocks, his heart resumed beating and he was soon transferred here to the ICU. The patient hasn't regained consciousness, though."

That certainly answers a lot of questions, thought Chandler. *Carol Sue was right about the virus—should've listened to her.* And now that they mentioned it, he *did* remember signing some weird form dealing with resuscitation. It was from the Buchanan Med Center Bioethics Committee and was so chock-full of legalese, he hadn't been able to make heads nor tails of it at the time. But the gist of it was, if any of it came into play, you were basically fucked. And by signing it, you had just helped the hospital install an ironclad covering for their collective butts.

He had been so sick when he was admitted that this particular form and all the others he signed had been a complete blur to him. Except now, he could call to mind clearly the five-page experimental resuscitation protocol that dealt with the Mueller lab. He could page through the sheets in his mind, backward, forward, and zoom into any paragraph for a closer look. He had no idea how this was possible.

The professor spoke again. "So, what is his prognosis at this point?"

Prognosis? The word was delivered with such grave overtones. Again, Chandler fought off a wave of drowsiness.

"The patient is basically terminal and will be lucky to survive the night," Lauren answered, delivering her clinical assessment with a tasteful touch of sorrow.

Talk about your good news-bad news. He wasn't dead, but it didn't sound like he had long to live. Except again, Chandler *knew* they were wrong, as they'd been about the consciousness part. He couldn't say how he knew, or why, just that he felt certain. *But what was it the perky med student, Lauren, said? She considers it a miracle that I'm still alive.* A tiny smile curved his swollen, cracked lips and pulled painfully at the tape holding his endotracheal tube in place. *Miracle might not be quite the right word for it,* he thought, drifting back down into the narcotic haze of the soft meadow.

CHAPTER 2

Tuesday, 11:30 p.m.

Many hours later, Nick Chandler floated in that peculiar void between consciousness and dreaming, the drugs coursing through his veins only heightening the strangeness of the experience. His last intact memory played images through his mind. The fact that he recalled the exact details of that night, right down to the vibrant colors of Carol Sue's tattoo, went unnoticed.

* * *

Halfway through his graveyard shift, on a night that seemed as ordinary as countless nights before, Nick pushed his cleaning cart out of the ICU room, being careful not to bump the door-frame with the various mops and brooms bristling from his cart. He shook his head. The room still stank of death, despite all the industrial-strength cleaners he had used. He was happy to leave.

Nick yanked off his mask and cap. *Fresh air never tasted so good,* he thought, peeling off the flimsy yellow gown and the latex

gloves and chucking them all in the trash bin outside the room—
the red plastic one with the biohazard label on it. The laundry bag
hanging off the back of his cart was filled to the brim with dirty
rags; better take care of those.

Nick made his way down to the hospital basement and navigated the twisty corridors to the laundry with ease, something he
hadn't done two years ago, when he had first started working at
the med center—he used to get lost down here all the time. Now,
he knew the layout well—past the MRI machines with all their
funny magnet signs, and past the CAT scanners.

Nick hoped the laundry room would be empty, but his luck
was not that good; several other members of the janitorial staff
were taking a break, or trying to hide from their supervisors.
Carol Sue was there. So was Nasty Mike Kuzmich. Both were
seated on plastic crates tipped upside down on the dusty floor,
puffing away on their beloved cigarettes.

"Hey Nick," Nasty Mike said, sniggering. "What you got
there? A full load? Three bags full?"

"No," Nick said, "just one bag."

Nasty Mike snorted loudly and started laughing.

"Don't pay him no mind, Nick," Carol Sue said before taking
a long drag on her cigarette.

Nasty Mike continued as if she hadn't spoken. "Fuckin'
moron!"

Carol Sue belted Nasty Mike across his upper arm. "Shut up,"
she said, and made an ugly face at him.

Nasty Mike frowned and rubbed his arm for a moment. But
he wasn't done.

"What's that smell?" Nasty Mike stood and scrunched his
nose up something fierce. "What's that god-awful smell?"

"Leave him be, shithead," Carol Sue said. She got up and
walked over to Nick. He watched the bright pinks and greens in
her Tinker Bell tattoo slide in and out from under her sleeve as

her arm moved. Carol Sue's teeth were yellow and crooked, but he liked her and thought she was pretty, with her long black hair.

"Maybe you oughtta throw that stuff in a hazardous waste box," she said, eyeing his laundry bag. "It *does* stink," she added in a soft voice that only he could hear.

"Okay," Nick said. He looked around the room, then pulled a large flattened cardboard box off a stack in the corner. He tried to fold the preformed cardboard piece into a three dimensional box, but all the confusing flaps and arrows quickly turned into a jumbled mess in his mind. Carol Sue reached out to help him.

"Let me be," Nick snapped at her. "I'll do it myself."

Nasty Mike was staring at him. Nick felt his face heat.

"I seen it all now," Nasty Mike bellowed, shaking his head. "Outsmarted by a fuckin' box!" Nasty Mike bent over and mashed his cigarette in his Pepsi can. Then he looked straight at Carol Sue. "Just like I said, sweetcakes—a fuckin' moron."

Carol Sue glared at him. "You're the moron. Now, get the hell outta here." She pointed to the door.

"Don't worry, I'm leaving." Nasty Mike walked toward the door, bumping into Nick on his way. As he reached the door, he called back over his shoulder, "Bitch!"

Carol Sue turned to Nick. She had a nice smile on her face and touched his arm. "He's such an asshole. Forget about the box, Nicky. Those buggers can be tricky."

Nick felt ready to cry. He bit his lower lip.

She looked again at his cart and her smile faded. "Were you cleaning *that* room?" she asked. "The filthy ICU room with the patient who died? The one with the horrible smell?"

"Yeah, they told me to," he said meekly.

"You washed your hands, right?"

Nick looked at the floor. "I was about to," he mumbled. "I wore gloves."

"Shit," she said, shaking her head and looking plenty worried. "Go wash your hands. Now! And use the goddamn disinfectant."

Nick went over to the sink. "There was some serious bad shit in that room," Carol Sue continued, watching him wash his hands. "When you get home, take a good shower. Don't forget, now."

"I won't," he said, keeping his face turned away so she wouldn't see the tears.

CHAPTER 3

Wednesday, 11:45 a.m.

Tequila. What a cool name. He liked saying it—almost as much as drinking it. Chip Allison poured another shot glass full of *tequila*—his third, or maybe it was his fourth. *But who's counting, anyway?* No, this wasn't your Don Julio Anejo tequila, the stuff his dad liked to drink, aged for two years in oaken barrels and poured from the neat bottle with the fancy wooden stopper. And no, this wasn't even Jose Cuervo Especial tequila. Rather, this was the cheapest rotgut money could buy, complete with the chintzy metal screw cap.

Of course, let's be honest here. Honesty is the best policy, right? He wasn't really drinking it to savor the flavor. That much was clear. *And who gives a flying fuck that it's only twelve noon.* There was a celebration going on here—his twenty-third birthday—so he had every reason to get hammered. *And as long as we're telling the truth, it's not really a shot glass, either.* It was one of those mega shot glasses. You know, the three or four ounce jobbies—the true volume of which, only God Almighty knew.

He spilled a little tequila on the dingy white Formica countertop. *Shit. Can't even do that right.* But then, just as quickly, he came to his own defense: *Wait, hold on—no worries. Just a smidge, no need to panic.* His mom liked that word—smidge, that is, not panic. Short for smidgeon—whatever the hell that was. Although, truth be told, even dear old Mom wasn't too happy with him nowadays.

Retrieving a soggy washcloth from the pile of dirty dishes overflowing the sink, he swabbed up the spilt tequila. *There, clean as a whistle.* He tossed the rag back toward the sink.

Movement caught his eye and he peered out the little window of his third floor apartment's kitchenette, eyes following a sparrow fluttering down to join several others hopping around in the brown grass of his tiny backyard. Geez, when had the grass gotten *that* brown?

An unexpected wave of sadness came over him as he remembered when things had been different. Very different, in fact. Everything had been going well—really well—until that awful decision involving Michelle six months ago. How could he have been so stupid as to believe her? Was it really possible to fuck up your life so badly in such a short time? This line of questioning never failed to make his head hurt.

Out in the living room, Frodo was talking worriedly to Gandalf. Commercial break was over. Drink in hand, he sauntered back into the room and plopped down on his worn sofa, not five feet from the boob tube. The taco chips were there waiting for him. Salt always went well with tequila, right?

He checked his watch. He had to be at work in . . . let's see . . . nine hours. Or was it eight? His subtraction skills were suboptimal at the moment. *Taking a siesta. Wasting away again in Margaritaville. Whatever. Plenty of time.* He had experience in these matters. Besides, how alert did you have to be to watch the stupid cardiac monitors in the ICU? The newer computer-driven monitors had sophisticated dysrhythmia detection algorithms that rarely missed identifying a dangerous rhythm and then sounding the alarm.

Chip plucked his iPhone out of his pocket and set the alarm. Couldn't afford to be late for work; he'd never get back into med school that way. *So responsible . . .* Dad—or should he say the great and fearless Colonel Allison—would be proud. He was always big on responsibility. And integrity. Which explained why he was so disappointed when he found out about his delinquent son.

Chip tried hard to get his dad's face and stinging words out of his mind. Luckily, just then, the black riders rode across the screen, snorting and wailing, gnashing their teeth, blood dripping from their foaming mouths as they galloped down the road toward the Shire. Chip sat there mesmerized, crunching absently on some chips. Usually, he really liked this part of the movie. Today, however, Chip shuddered a little as he imagined the riders were somehow coming for him. He drained the tequila.

CHAPTER 4

Wednesday, 11:45 a.m.

The late-morning sun eventually cleared the nearby building and light poured in through the venetian blinds, bathing the ICU room in a garish, almost phosphorescent light, rousing him awake. Chandler squinted hard and cursed at the painfully bright horizontal stripes. But he quickly retracted his curse. The light was a wonderful thing, after all; it meant he had survived the night, something his good doctors had thought unlikely. Somewhere between his last conscious period and now, he'd discovered a will to live.

Chandler took inventory of his body. His heart had been ravaged by an especially virulent infection that had started it all. What had they called it—a viral myocarditis? They'd said his heart was ruined. Except he detected internal evidence that his immune system was rallying, locking onto the viral protein coat and taking out the virus. He could tell his heart was on the mend.

Similarly, his lungs were repairing themselves, the damaged capillaries starting to shore up their leaks and the oxygen exchange steadily improving across the delicate alveolar membranes. As the extracellular fluid diminished, the compliance of the pulmonary tissue improved, thereby decreasing the need for high pressures to ventilate him. Soon, he knew, the ventilator would not be necessary. His kidneys and liver were also responding to the improved cardiac output and no longer spiraled toward total shutdown.

He could see all these changes in his body as he had never seen before. How was that possible? He certainly wasn't a doctor. Besides, even a doctor couldn't see the inner workings of his own body. But it was more than that. He sensed that his brain was somehow directing these wonderful changes, manipulating his autonomic nervous system to improve blood flow here, tweak perfusion there, in a kind of intelligent design approach to healing by following the innate blueprints of his body, right down to the cellular level. Again, he sensed this was all a manifestation of the transformation he had somehow undergone.

The urge to sleep came over him again, but he resisted. He knew their goal was to keep him sedated, and to that end, he was on round-the-clock narcotics and a propofol drip. He'd have to deal with that before long.

He heard people entering his room and was careful not to open his eyes; no need for them to know he was conscious just yet. He was beginning to connect names with the voices. The attending doc, cardiologist Dr. Leffler, was speaking.

"Gorman, why don't you examine the patient and tell us all where the endotracheal tube is, instead of cutting corners and just saying it's in good position. Good for what? Medicine is not a field for sloppiness, young man."

One of the med students, presumably Gorman, leaned in close to him. Chandler felt a slight touch on his lips, then his tube was jostled a bit. He struggled to remain still and fought back an overwhelming urge to gag.

"Tube's at twenty-two centimeters at the lips," Gorman said, adding with a hint of irritation, "*Still* in good position." But the next part was not spoken aloud. Chandler saw the words form clearly in Gorman's mind, then heard them just as plainly in his own: *Doesn't really matter where the goddamn tube is, now, does it, Leffler, you frickin' asshole! This guy's toast!* This surprised Chandler so much that his eyes almost flew open.

When Gorman stepped back to join the group, the connection was broken.

CHAPTER 5

Wednesday, 7:00 p.m.

"You're late, Allison." Victor Cohen swiveled his chair around to face Chip. Behind Victor, EKG telemetry tracings from twenty-four very sick patients paraded across several banks of flat-screen monitors in high contrast green on black.

"Sorry, Victor," Chip said. "I had some things to take care of."

"Whatever." Victor's irritated expression grew serious. "I got a big micro test tomorrow and I need to get cracking."

"Okay, okay," Chip said. "How're things going?"

"Great—now that you're gone."

Chip sighed. "I meant with the patients." He nodded toward the monitor screens.

Victor's face morphed again—this time into a shit-eating grin. "I got the highest grade on the pharm midterm."

"Good for you." Same old Victor, annoying as hell. He never had much of a filter between his brain and his mouth. "Anything useful to report?"

"No, not really. They're all pretty much the same." Victor slid out of the chair and stood; he barely came up to Chip's chin and his thin face and skinny body made Chip think *weasel*. And of course, ever since Victor had joined the list of prime suspects who had ratted him out, the description seemed to fit all the more.

Chip tapped the bizarre-looking EKG trace from Room 237—super-wide QRS complexes that were going way too fast. "What's up with this one?"

"Oh—he's the new Mueller special. He's probably going to buy it tonight."

"Swell," Chip said.

"Ain't modern medicine grand?"

"Yeah, ain't it." Chip settled himself into the padded chair. "See you around, Victor."

Victor leaned in close, invading his personal space, and spoke in a lowered voice. "Chip, can I tell you something?"

Chip tensed. "What?"

"We used to be friends, right?"

"Uh-huh," Chip said warily, thinking Victor was stretching the definition.

"You need to lay off the sauce, man."

"What're you talking about?"

"For god sakes, I can smell it on you."

"Give it a rest, Victor. You sound like my old man."

"Look, Chip. I can only cover for you for so long. You know how it goes. Sometimes the people who know and do nothing get into more trouble than the ones actually screwing up. Remember all that Penn State shit?"

"Hey, you look, Victor. Don't do me any favors." Chip rolled his chair away from him in disgust. "I thought you had a test to study for."

Victor turned to leave, then stopped, his grin reappearing. "Heather's working tonight."

"So?"

"Don't pretend you're not interested."

"I'm not," Chip said.

"Sure—whatever you say." Victor's grin faded. "Anyway, that's probably a good thing. I don't think you have a chance in hell."

Chip didn't respond, struggling to contain the familiar anger welling up inside him.

"Just saying," Victor added.

"Go fuck yourself, Victor."

* * *

Three hours into the shift, Chip caught himself daydreaming again and angrily stifled a yawn, not for the first time. He was mad at himself for coming to work tired—and hungover. Chip rubbed his eyes and forced his attention back to the monitor screens he was supposed to be watching. Room 235 had frequent PVCs, but this had been going on for a week now and they were all unifocal. Room 242 was Afib/flutter that occasionally shot his rate up to 150 beats per minute—he'd have to keep an eye on that.

But the real money was on the new admission in 237. The trace had the dreaded red star taped next to it. Basically, it looked like shit. Victor had been right—this guy could go south at any moment. Chip knew he would spend extra time watching this room, but also knew it had nothing to do with the guy's rhythm.

Victor had also mentioned that 237 was a Mueller special— one of the poor saps that had been subjected to the new resuscitation protocol. So far, there had been three of them that Chip knew of over the past six months. Well, three that made it out of the lab, anyway. Word was that many more went into the lab, but never came out. The previous two lasted several hours in the ICU before dying.

Wheeling his chair to the right, Chip craned his neck around the monitor screens to get a look into room 237. He wasn't trying to see the patient, but rather hoping to catch a glimpse of Heather, the patient's nurse. Truth be told, he *was* interested in Heather—she was a real looker, like Michelle. No dice—she must be sitting in the corner, away from the door or window. After several minutes, Chip reluctantly rolled his chair back and refocused on the monitors.

The next hour passed by slowly, again lulling Chip into a trancelike state. Visions of making it with Heather paraded across his mind—until the tap of footsteps coming from his right interrupted another large yawn, and his head snapped up. He watched Heather walk by in a blur of blonde hair and fluid hips, swiveling his chair around in an attempt to make eye contact with her. Too late; she had already passed him. He did, however, get a blast of her perfume.

"Hi Heather," he called to her back.

She stopped and turned, giving him a half-hearted smile. "Oh, hi."

"How's your patient doing?"

"Fine. Well, he's really sick." Her shoulder-length blonde hair danced playfully about her pretty face as her eyes darted around the room, anywhere but on him. She took several steps toward him.

Chip's heart pounded even harder in his chest. "Yes, he's very sick," he said.

"Have you seen Dr. Donahue?" she asked.

"No."

"Listen, uh—" she glanced at his name badge "—Chip. If you see Dr. Donahue, tell him I need to talk to him, okay? It's important."

"Okay," Chip said. "But, I'm pretty sure he left."

"Darn." She rummaged around in her purse before yanking out a crumpled pack of cigarettes.

"Hey, your guy's complex looks pretty bad," Chip said. "Do you think he'll make it?"

"Can't say. Listen, I gotta go on break."

"Yeah, sure."

"See ya," she said as she walked away.

"Yeah, see ya," Chip replied, but doubted she heard him. *Damn.* He had to think of something a bit more clever to say when she came back.

A voice from the other side of his station startled him. "She's just not that into you, Allison."

He spun around to see Kristin, the radiology tech on duty, standing with her elbows resting on the wooden railing. She was sporting a large grin and toying with the end of her light brown, almost dirty blonde hair, which was woven into a complex braid.

"Huh?"

"Heather. I saw you talking to her."

"I was just asking her about her patient—you know, the Mueller special in thirty-seven."

"I saw the way you were staring at her." Kristin pushed off the rail and walked over to stand beside him.

"Come on," Chip drawled, forcing out a laugh even as he felt his face heat. He turned back to his monitors and pointed at the red star. "What do you think of *that* guy? Think he'll make it?"

"Don't try to change the subject, Allison. I mean, I can't blame you—she *is* hot. But she's kinda out of your league, don't you think?"

Chip glanced back at her. "What do you mean?"

"Well, she's got her sights set on *Doctor* Donahue. You know, cardiology fellow, MD after his name."

"Don't remind me."

"Have you seen him, by the way?"

"Oh no, you too?" Chip shook his head. "And to think I gotta take this abuse on my birthday."

"I need to ask him about a portable chest x-ray."

"Right. He's in the call room."

"Life sucks, huh?"

"Sometimes."

"Look on the bright side. I hear she's a royal bitch." With that, Kristin pirouetted and walked away, leaving him to digest her words of wisdom.

CHAPTER 6

Wednesday, 9:30 p.m.

"Finally, he's asleep," Doug Landry said as he walked into the family room. "I had to read him *three* books."

"I wondered what was taking so long," Laura said, smiling. She was seated on the couch, dividing her attention between her laptop and the TV. "Anthony loves when you read to him."

"We finished with *Two Bad Ants*—I like that one," Doug said.

"Yeah, me too."

"Teddy is still up, working on his English paper."

"He knows not to stay up past ten-thirty, right?"

"I told him," Doug said. "Do you want anything while I'm up?"

"No, I'm good." Laura threw a finger up before adding, "Actually, could you bring me an iced tea?"

"Sure."

Doug fetched an iced tea from the fridge before mixing a vodka tonic for himself, heavy on the Grey Goose. He balanced both drinks and his notebook as he returned to the family room.

Laura folded up her laptop and patted the seat next to her. "So, you all ready for tomorrow?" she asked.

"Yep. I have my slides all set." Doug handed her the tea and set his own drink down on the end table before settling next to her. "The lecture starts at nine, but I want to show up early to make sure everything works. It'll still seem like sleeping in, compared to going in to Mercy."

"What's your talk about?"

"Airway management in off-site locations," he said as he opened his notebook. He caught Laura's blank look. "You know, in places outside of the typical OR setting. Like the ER or CT scanner or MRI suite. I'm talking to some med students, respiratory therapists and x-ray techs."

"Oh. Okay." She gently patted his knee. "I think this whole thing is a good idea, Doug."

"Yeah, me too. I'm looking forward to a break from Mercy."

"You deserve it." She popped the tab and took a drink from her iced tea. "Hmmm, Professor Landry—it has a nice ring to it. Do you ever think of going to the med center to work full time? You'd be good at it."

"No. A six month sabbatical will be just what I need." He sipped his own drink, savoring the bitter taste of the alcohol.

Laura fiddled with putting her laptop away in its leather bag. "Maybe you'll sleep better, too."

"Right." He looked away.

She studied him. "Mike was a good friend. Grief is a slow business."

"Laura, he's been dead for over three years. How long does it take?" The ice clinked against the glass as he gulped a mouthful of vodka.

She set the computer bag down on the floor and grasped his hand. "Things will get better, Doug. I know they will."

"I'll be okay."

"Maybe you can try to make new friends; join a club or something."

He nodded. "Yeah, I will."

They sat for a while, not saying anything, listening to the TV. Laura was watching a Dateline special about teens and alcohol. Doug finished off his drink.

During a commercial break, Doug spoke up, forcing himself to sound more upbeat. "We can go for some bike rides, now that I'll have more free time."

"That'd be nice." She smiled and squeezed his thigh. "Maybe more time for ourselves, too."

"Sure." Doug closed his notebook and set it on the floor. He leaned over and nestled his head in her lap, looking up at her. "Do you mind?"

"No, not at all." She repositioned herself on the couch and began to stroke his hair. They sat that way for about twenty minutes, then Doug rose and retrieved his empty glass from the end table.

"Heading up?" she asked.

"Yeah."

She eyed the empty tumbler in his hand, worry clouding her features. "Didn't you have wine with dinner?"

"Yes."

She frowned.

"It helps me sleep, Laura."

"I know. It's just—I don't think it's the best example for the boys. Teddy will be driving next year and—"

"All right," he said, holding up a hand. "I get the message." He crossed to the stairs. "Night."

"Night," she replied.

"Love you."

"Love you, too," she said, but the worried look had not left her face.

Doug felt the familiar fear gnawing at him as he trudged up the stairs to the bedroom. Not good—tomorrow was a big day and he needed to sleep. His backpack was in the bedroom, where he'd left it. He pulled a small bottle of pills from an inner zippered pocket—his little secret, he thought as he swallowed one quickly. But he suffered the usual tangle of thoughts: sleeping pills on top of alcohol—you didn't need a medical degree to know *that* was a bad idea. Dangerous, even. Just ask Whitney Houston.

No, no, *he* was the expert in these matters—no dosage regimen too complex. Ironic, that one who spent his life putting others to sleep would have trouble putting himself to sleep. And strange, he had to admit, for the "Iceman" to be scared of something so intangible as sleep. Doug climbed into bed and tried hard to ignore the twinge of guilt he also felt; Laura definitely wouldn't approve of the pills, and she'd be right, as usual.

He wondered if Mike Carlucci, his former best friend and colleague, deceased three years now, had tried sleeping pills before getting hooked on drugs. And speaking of guilt, this always brought the same nagging questions to mind: Would Mike be alive today, if Doug had turned him in for his drug use, as Laura had told him to do? How had he missed the warning signs? Did it have anything to do with his preoccupation with a certain SICU nurse named Jenny Stuart? He welcomed the sensation as the sleeping pill took hold, pulling him down into oblivion.

* * *

Doug woke with a start, his heart pounding. Another damn nightmare. But it wasn't of the variety that had pockmarked his sleep for the last couple of years. There was no Mike getting pulled from the twisted wreck of his Suburban after the fiery crash on the interstate. Or the other deaths that had taken place at Our Lady of Mercy Hospital three years ago, when all the bad shit had gone down.

He sensed this nightmare was different, but the details had flown out of his brain so quickly, he'd been unable to snare them with his conscious mind. Something to do with Laura . . . Its very vagueness left him feeling unsettled, gripping his heart with a deep sense of foreboding.

CHAPTER 7

Wednesday, 10:30 p.m.

The alarm beeped shrilly and Heather Lindstrom glanced up from her magazine at the big flat-screen monitor suspended over her patient's bed. His blood pressure was drifting downward, triggering the alarm. BP from the arterial line trace read out as 85/63, a little below what it had been ten minutes ago. *Damn!* she thought. So that was how it was going to be. She hadn't been on the shift an hour and alarms were already going off. She sighed. Looked like it was going to be a busy night.

She reminded herself that nights in the ICU were like that—unpredictable. Sometimes slow as a graveyard; other times, complete mayhem. And she knew she thrived on the action in the ICU and, of course, working side by side with the residents. But tonight, she really wasn't into it. *Maybe it was the late night last night . . . or too many mojitos.*

Besides, she had other matters to attend to—like continuing her pursuit of Rich Donahue, senior cardiology fellow. Getting his full attention last night at the bar was the reason for those mojitos, and she'd been successful, but she needed to keep the pressure up—not give him a chance of wriggling off the hook. She was determined to reel this bad boy in.

Rich was definitely a looker, but Heather wouldn't deny that his financial future—he was less than a year or so from the big bucks—had something to do with the allure. *Okay, maybe a lot.* Rich had just agreed to meet her again tonight, this time at her apartment, where she would seal the deal. Heather smiled. *Poor Richard doesn't stand a chance.*

She jumped as the intercom came to life. "Heather, do you see the change in his complex?"

Her head snapped back up to the monitor. *Shit! Could those freakin' QRS complexes get any wider?* She looked out the doorway and saw the monitor tech, Chip or Chuck or whatever his name was, staring at her while pointing at his screen.

"Yes, of course I do," she said, not bothering to camouflage her annoyance. Although vaguely flattered that this guy was hitting on her, she certainly didn't need any more distractions or interference from him; he was always gawking at her. She recognized that was the price for being gorgeous, and even though he *was* cute in a nerdy sort of way, he had loser written all over him. *Who flunks out of med school, anyway? Once a loser, always a loser.*

Which brought her around full circle to her patient tonight. Why did she have to get stuck with this patient? She knew why, and it kinda burned her up. Her coworkers, her supervisor Bonnie in particular, had purposely dumped this one on her. She knew they didn't like her. Well, okay, hate was probably a better word. They were always jealous of her "luck" with the cute male residents. Could she help it if she was beautiful and had a killer bod, to boot? She *did* work out, after all, six or seven times a week at the University Fitness Center. And she was actually careful about her diet. Some of these lazy bitches—her esteemed coworkers— didn't bother. Hard to score with the McDreamys, if your butt was the size of Texas.

Heather cursed under her breath, set her magazine down and got out of her chair. She leaned over and inspected the art-line insertion site in her patient's wrist. No kinks or air bubbles in the tubing. She checked the waveform to make sure it wasn't dampened for some reason. It looked nice and crisp. *Guess the lower pressure's for real.* She silenced the squawking monitor and reset the BP alarm parameters.

Normally, Heather might have been more concerned about her patient's falling blood pressure or change in cardiac rhythm. But tonight, she knew her patient was terminal. In report, they said he might not make it through the shift. So a dwindling BP was not unusual—in fact, it was to be expected. He was a no-code anyway, so they wouldn't even try to resuscitate him. Still, she didn't want him dying on her watch—that never looked good.

Heather quickly reviewed her orders for her patient, trying to find some options to improve his blood pressure. She knew he was on a propofol drip to sedate him and she had standing orders to add Zemuron, a muscle relaxant, if he began fighting the ventilator. The propofol was already set low, because the guy didn't have much cardiac reserve and his liver and kidneys were shot as well. She decided to decrease the propofol even further, in an effort to boost her patient's BP. If he got too light and started to buck the vent, she would paralyze his ass.

She keyed in the appropriate changes on the IVAC pump. There, that should do it. She moved back and sat down and resumed reading about the latest, behind the scenes bickering of the judges on *American Idol.*

CHAPTER 8

Wednesday, 10:45 p.m.

Chandler smiled to himself. *She has no clue.* When his nurse had adjusted his propofol drip, he had gotten a whiff of her perfume. *Very nice.* He also had gotten a clear glimpse into her mind. Heather Lindstrom believed he was terminal and that the propofol was lowering his blood pressure. Neither was true. His vital organs—heart, kidneys, and liver—were now better than fifty percent functional and improving hourly. His BP was falling as a direct response to him vasodilating his arterial system and decreasing his heart's contractility and rate. A simple ruse. He had to be careful not to buck on the tube or she would "paralyze his ass," a complication he didn't care for at the moment.

Chandler next increased his liver blood flow three hundred percent, mindful of shunting blood away from the more damaged, less functional areas, to aid in metabolizing the propofol. That would allow him to act and think more clearly. He then increased the blood flow to his right arm musculature by five hundred percent and prepared his adrenals to release epinephrine. Not yet, or she would see his BP and pulse skyrocket. Timing was critical. He just needed to get her close to him one more time. He flexed his wrist slightly to kink the art-line catheter, creating an artifact in the trace.

He smiled again as the alarm sounded.

CHAPTER 9

Wednesday, 10:45 p.m.

"Hey Allison," Kristin said, giggling, "I have something for you." She pulled her arm from behind her back, presenting a Snickers bar on a small paper plate. There was a match clumsily taped to one side of the candy bar. "Happy birthday." She set the makeshift birthday cake on the countertop in front of him, her grin stretching wide.

"Wow, that's a surprise," Chip said.

"You said it was your birthday and I felt kind of sorry for you, working and all." She lit the match and several other ICU nurses materialized, although Heather was a no-show. Chip glanced over and saw her in Room 237, sitting in her chair, reading her magazine.

The nurses sang a butchered version of "Happy Birthday" and he felt his throat tighten with emotion.

"Make a wish," Kristin said, obviously enjoying herself. She pulled out a fancy camera and aimed it at him.

"Okay, got one," Chip said and blew out the match just as the bright flash of Kristin's camera lit up the room.

"Will you take one with my cell phone, too?" he asked. "You know—for Facebook."

"Sure." Kristin snapped one with his phone.

The small group quickly dispersed, leaving him alone with Kristin.

"Thanks," he said. "You didn't have to do that."

"It was fun," she said.

"A little embarrassing, too." He unwrapped one end of the Snickers bar.

"Sorry about that," she replied. "You can get me back—my birthday's coming up in a couple of weeks."

He smiled at her. "I'll remember that."

"So, what'd you wish for?"

"You don't want to know," Chip said, looking down.

"I'm sure I can guess," she said, her tone souring. "Hey, listen—if it makes you feel any better, Heather lent me the pack of matches for your birthday cake."

"Right. I feel much better."

An awkward silence followed while Kristin fiddled with her camera and Chip took a bite of the candy bar.

"Nice camera," he said. "What kind is it?"

"A Nikon. My dad got it for me for my birthday last year."

"Sweet. How many megapixels is it?"

"None," she said proudly. "It takes 35 millimeter film."

"You don't say," he said, genuinely surprised. "I have an old Minolta X-700 that uses film, too. I take pictures through my telescope." He didn't bother to add that his telescope was collecting dust in his closet and hadn't seen any use in over a year.

"Cool. Like wildlife or birds?"

"No. The stars and planets. Sometimes even comets."

"That's really cool," she said.

"Do you want a piece?" He offered her the Snickers.

"No thanks."

"What do you take pictures of?"

"Lots of stuff," she said, looking away.

"That's helpful. No, really—I'm curious."

Kristin's cheeks flushed. "You'll think I'm strange."

"Well, no real danger there." Chip softened that with a smile.

"Ha-ha," she retorted.

"No, seriously, what do you shoot?"

"My plants," she said matter-of-factly.

"*What?*"

"You heard me. My plants." Kristin turned to leave and her ponytail swished through a wide arc. "I told you you wouldn't understand," she said over her shoulder.

"Wait. You mean like macros of flowers?"

"No." She paused, apparently weighing a decision. She turned to face him, took a step closer, and asked, "Have you ever heard of Kirlian photography?"

Chip searched his memory. "You mean like ghosts? You take pictures of ghosts?"

"No."

"What, then?"

"All right, Allison—"

"Call me Chip."

"All right, Chip, you asked for it." Up close, he noticed what a pretty shade of light blue her eyes were and how they lit up as she spoke. "Every living creature gives off a life force that is visible as an aura on film, with special techniques."

"Even plants?" he asked.

"Yep. And I can tell how my plants are feeling from their auras."

"Feeling?" *Uh-oh,* Chip thought. *Major Earthgirl alert.*

"Happy. Content. Angry. Sad. Whatever."

"That *is* different."

Just then, they heard a lot of commotion coming from Room 237. Heather was screaming.

CHAPTER 10

Wednesday, 11:00 p.m.

The time had come.

Every sense dialed up to the max, Chandler didn't have to wait long. He heard Heather curse under her breath, then her chair creaked and paper rustled. A moment later, her heavy perfume stung his nostrils—she was standing beside him. Bingo. When she bent down close and touched his wrist, his adrenals squeezed a massive dose of adrenaline into his renal veins. Within seconds, he felt the effects of the hormone. He hoped his heart could tolerate the stress. The adrenaline raced through his brain, slamming his consciousness into overdrive like a pile-driver and obliterating any lingering effects of the sedative.

Chandler opened his eyes.

Heather's eyes went wide and she screamed. But not for long. He reached out and grabbed her, his hand easily encircling her slender neck. With a strength fueled by massively increased blood flow and the adrenaline surge, he squeezed, compressing her windpipe and abruptly silencing her screams. Her eyes shot open even wider as he lifted her off the floor. He sat up and slammed her head against the wall with a sickening thud. Her eyes rolled back in her head and she stopped struggling. Chandler released her limp body and it crumpled to the floor, blood spreading from her head in a growing pool.

He yanked the tube from his throat, gagging violently in the process. But it felt incredibly good to breathe normally; he paused to savor a couple of sweet breaths before jumping out of bed. He tore off his monitors and ripped out his IVs and arterial catheter. Blood spurted from his wrist where the art-line had been, splattering the white bedsheets in an arc of bright red dots. He ignored the bleeding, something he knew he could easily control, and strode out of the room.

Directly in front of him, blocking his way, stood a tall young man with a half-eaten candy bar clutched in his hand. "What're you doing?" the young man shouted. "You can't leave. What have you done to Heather?"

Chandler hesitated for only a fraction of a second before grabbing a fistful of the young man's shirt and flinging him out of his way as if he were a ragdoll—his adrenaline-enhanced right arm was still ridiculously strong. The young man hit the floor hard, his head banging against a cabinet.

To his right, a petite young woman made a run for it, ponytail swinging and the camera hanging around her neck bouncing off her chest. Chandler let her go. Stepping over the moaning young man, he went around behind the main desk and ripped all the phone cables out of the wall. Screams rang out from the far side of the room—another of the nurses. Ignoring her, Chandler scanned the room, found an exit sign, and trotted over to the stairway descending from the ICU.

He heard "Red alert" being announced over the hospital PA system as he made for the nearest door out of the hospital. He fled into the night, ignoring the pain as his bare feet pounded over the gravel-strewn macadam.

CHAPTER 11

Thursday, 2:00 a.m.

Nick Chandler lay on the mossy ground in a little clearing, huddled under a pile of leaves, trying to keep warm. He wondered again if he had killed that pretty nurse—Heather. Probably. He would never forget the sound her head had made hitting the wall—a thunk like a big-leaguer smacking one out of the park. His arm *had* been unbelievably strong. And then there was the blood. But he surprised himself by realizing he didn't really care. All that seemed to matter was that he was free.

He was vaguely surprised that they hadn't searched for him here in the woods behind the med center, right under their noses. Maybe his luck really was changing. He shivered again. Although he didn't think it would hit the freezing mark tonight, it would probably get close. He would have to find some shelter soon, or he would die from exposure out here. His home—a two-room, low rent shithole in the HiLo apartment complex just south of Hummelstown—was obviously off limits; they would surely be lying in wait for him there. Equally problematic was the fact that he had no food or water. Soon, he decided, after things cooled down a bit, he would have to risk being seen.

Chandler looked up at the dark sky and forgot momentarily about the cold. It was one of those super clear nights when the stars shone dazzlingly bright; he felt as if he could reach out and touch them. The starlit sky was a dead ringer for that fateful night so many years ago, when his life had changed. His mind drifted back to those earlier days, before he had dropped out of high school. Before his mother had finally left for good.

His best friend at the time—his only friend—was a medium-sized, scruffy mutt that had wandered into Nick's yard one day. He had named the dog Toby, after a favorite Nickelodeon cartoon character. The two outcasts had bonded instantly. Nick and Toby spent many a summer night camped out under the stars in the backyard. It wasn't exactly peaceful, with the big rigs rumbling down I-81, not fifty yards away, just on the other side of the concrete barrier. But it was nice, nonetheless.

Nick loved to look up at the stars or the moon and dream of better days ahead, or what it would be like to fly away and live somewhere else. Or even travel in a rocket ship to some alien world. And Toby was the perfect stargazing companion; he was always up for a night outside and never made fun of Nick or his dreams, like the kids at school did. The two would curl up together and keep each other warm. Dad would never let him build a fire—said he didn't trust a lame brain not to burn the fuckin' place down.

Then one beautiful summer night, things went bad—real bad. The stars were out in force that night. There was a gentle, warm breeze and Toby and Nick stayed up half the night, gawking at the sky. It was a night to remember, all right; they saw several bright shooting stars that zoomed halfway across the sky. Nick finally fell asleep with Toby's head resting on his belly.

Early the next morning, his dad kicked him awake. "How'd he get out of the yard?"

Nick shrugged and rubbed the sleep out of his eyes. "Huh?"

His dad kicked him again. "Goddamn barrier is a piece of shit."

Nick sat up, alarmed. Something was wrong—way wrong.

"Who the hell gave you permission to take *my* dog out with you?" his father demanded, towering over him.

Nick could tell his dad was awful mad, so he didn't say anything. He also knew better than to correct his dad and tell him it was he, Nick, who fed and watered and took care of the dog. And that he had spent many a night camped out here in the backyard with Toby. His dad had never shown any interest in the dog.

"That dog's been nothing but trouble." His dad waved a finger at him. "I warned you."

Nick looked around for Toby, but didn't see him anywhere. His mom was standing on the back porch in her robe with a sad look on her face. Was she crying?

"Well," his father said, "the goddamn police are here—showed up at the front door at seven in the morning and got my sorry ass out of bed—"

"Is he okay?" Nick asked, worry twisting his stomach.

"Okay?" his father said. "No, he's not okay."

"Where is he?" Nick pleaded. "Where's Toby?"

His father just stood there watching him—for once, he didn't have anything smart to say.

Nick turned and shouted, "Mom, where is he?"

His mom was silent too.

Suddenly frantic, Nick ran around the backyard, looking and calling for Toby. Toby was nowhere to be found.

Finally, his mom called out to him, "Toby's dead."

Nick's heart sank and he fell to his knees. He grimaced, fighting back tears.

Dad found his smart voice. "And what were you doin' while my dog was getting pancaked by that goddamn tractor trailer?"

"Nothing," Nick mumbled, his head down low. Tears streamed down his face. "I guess I was sleeping."

His dad walked over to him. "You ain't cryin' now, are you, boy?"

"No."

"'Cause I didn't raise no sissy."

"I'm fine," Nick said and roughly wiped the back of his hand across his face. He saw his mother go back inside.

"And how many times did I tell you?" His dad's voice rose. "You're not supposed to let him run free."

"I didn't," Nick said, finally meeting his father's eyes. "I tied him up. With that rope." Nick pointed helplessly to the rope lying on the ground.

"I ought to give you a licking." His dad raised his hand, about to hit him—as he had done countless times before.

Nick cringed and prepared for a blow—but it never came. Nick peeked up at the man. He would never forget the look of pure disgust on his dad's face.

"Do you even *know* how to tie a knot?" his father asked, slowly lowering his hand.

Nick hung his head again.

"All the lickings I done give you," his dad shook his head, "and they don't seem to make no difference."

The lump in Nick's throat was now big and painful. He didn't care about a licking; in fact, he would have welcomed one. And he wasn't sad for disappointing his father; he had long since given up on any kind words from the old man. All Nick could think of was Toby—poor Toby. And how much he'd miss him.

"The police have the dog's body," his father said. "What's left of it, anyway. You can bury it here in the backyard. I ain't paying those fuckin' township bloodsuckers to dee-spose of it." With that, his dad turned and walked back into the house, probably to fetch his first beer of the day.

A cold breeze swept through the trees, rousing Chandler from the memory, though the recollection of Toby and his father was still vivid in his mind as he tried to burrow down deeper in the leaves. Chandler rarely thought of his father these days; he had died of pancreatitis five years ago at the ripe old age of fifty-six—the alcohol had finally caught up with him. Funny, Chandler thought, he couldn't even pronounce the word "pancreatitis" five years ago. Now, thanks to some bizarro access to his own cellular blueprints, he believed he understood the physiological basis of the goddamn disease. Chandler shook his head and shivered again. One thing was certain—if his dad *hadn't* died, Chandler would be making a special trip to see him and put his super-strong arms to use, strangling the living shit out of him.

CHAPTER 12

Thursday, 9:10 a.m.

Chip squelched a yawn as he hurried toward the lecture hall. He hadn't gotten much sleep last night—he had spent half the night at the Hershey Police Department and the rest tossing and turning, trying in vain to get the grisly image of Heather's body out of his mind. He couldn't forget that look in Chandler's eyes, either—right before he tossed him into the cabinet. *Talk about chilling. And how could anybody be that strong?*

He paused and surveyed the lecture hall from the back door. The speaker had already started and the lights were dimmed for his slides, but Chip soon spotted Kristin's ponytail. Unfortunately, she was sitting way up front. He slunk in and slipped into the back row.

After briefly debating what to do, Chip pulled out his phone and texted Kristin's number. <Hi>

Her phone beeped and she jumped. She quickly silenced her phone and looked around for him unsuccessfully. It was hard to read her expression, but she didn't appear to be overly thrilled to have received his text. <What r u doing here?> she responded.

<Texting u>

She turned around again. She sure looked like she was scowling now as she searched for him. She couldn't find him in the darkened auditorium, against the glare of the slide projector's light, and soon gave up. <Haha No really?>

<Hoping 2 talk after lecture> he texted.

<K>

<Wat r u doing here> he texted.

<trying 2 listen 2 lecture>

<K sorry>

Chip pocketed his phone and tried to focus on the lecture, though it was difficult to concentrate on anything other than the horrendous events in the ICU last night. The speaker was some guy named Dr. Landry, an anesthesiologist from Mercy Hospital in Lancaster. Something about airway management; it seemed kind of boring, anyway. *But,* Chip thought, *you'd have to be pretty dull to go into a field like anesthesia. Not much patient interaction there.* If he ever got back into med school, he wouldn't make that mistake.

After the lecture, Chip waited for Kristin out in the hallway. She stomped up to him, arms swinging at her sides, her petite body moving mechanically. "Way to embarrass me in there," she said, planting one hand firmly on her hip. Even though she was nearly a foot shorter than him, she somehow appeared to be at eye level as she glared at him.

"Sorry," he said.

"What do you want?" she asked.

"Hey listen, I tried to talk to you last night, but you had already left."

"Yeah, go figure. Spending half the night at the Derry Township Police Department wasn't my idea of fun."

"When did they let you go?" he asked.

"Around one. How about you?" She relaxed her arm from her hip.

"A little after that," Chip said. "I gave my statement and then some detective—Markel, I think his name was—kept asking me the same questions, over and over."

"I know who you mean—the fat one. He talked to me, too. He made me feel like *I* was the suspect, not a witness."

"Exactly. So, what do you think?"

"You mean about Heather?" she said.

"I guess—Heather—everything."

"I feel *so* horrible for Heather." Her voice was a notch higher than it had been a minute ago. Her chin started to quiver and she blinked rapidly several times. "To think she's really dead." She began to cry.

"I can't believe he killed her." Chip reached out to touch her, to comfort her in some small way, then thought better of it. He ran his fingers through his hair instead.

"Did you see her body?" Kristin said through her tears.

"Yeah."

"And that look on her face?"

Chip nodded. "Uh-huh."

"And the blood all over the floor?"

"I saw it." He looked around helplessly while she cried.

After several minutes, she pulled a tissue from her pocket and blew her nose. "Sorry," she said. "This thing has me pretty shook up."

"Me, too."

She dabbed at her eyes with the tissue.

"What about the guy—Chandler?" Chip asked tentatively. "What did you make of him?"

"What do you mean?" she asked, visibly trying to get a grip on her emotions.

"Did you see the look in his eyes?"

"Sure," she said. "He came right at us."

"But, did you think he looked crazy? I always thought people like that—you know, someone who smashes someone's head against the wall—would have this crazed, bloodthirsty look or something."

"No," she said, eyes drifting as she thought back. "He didn't look that way at all."

"That's what I thought too. In fact, it looked like he was almost enjoying himself—he had this smirk . . ."

"Right."

"Did you see him throw me?"

"No. I guess I had already run. Sorry, I kinda panicked." She looked away.

"He picked me up with one arm and tossed me into the desk." Chip pushed his hair aside. "Check this out."

"Yikes—nasty bruise."

"I don't think they've caught him yet," Chip said. "It'd be all over the news if they did."

She grimaced. "I sure hope they get him soon. I'd sleep a lot better."

"Me, too."

They both started to walk down the hallway toward the main entrance, neither saying anything more.

Three-quarters of the way down the hall, Chip broke the silence. "But here's the real question. How do you explain that he was supposedly dying one minute and the next, he's pulling his tube out, strangling poor Heather, then running out of the ICU?"

"I can't," she said, eyes on the doorway up ahead.

"Hey, do you want to grab some coffee?" Chip asked. "I could sure use some."

She stopped walking and regarded him briefly. "I could too, but I have to get home and let my dog out. Thanks, though."

"Smokey?"

He watched her face soften. "How do you know his name?"

"You talk about him all the time," Chip said.

"I guess I do," she said, lips curving sheepishly.

"Well, some other time. Hey, I hear Mueller's giving grand rounds tomorrow on his resuscitation techniques. We should go and hear what he has to say. Maybe it will help shed some light on things."

"Yeah, maybe," she said. "Is it at nine?"

"Uh-huh."

"Okay, I'll meet you there. That is, on one condition."

"What?"

"No more texting," she said sternly.

"No problem."

"See you tomorrow," she said and turned to go, but not before he saw evidence of a tiny smile sneaking across her face.

CHAPTER 13

Friday, 7:00 a.m.

Gunter Mueller stared at the shiny MRI prints arranged neatly on the x-ray viewbox in his office and shook his head. There it was, in black and white—no sense denying it. A hint of a structure in the brain that shouldn't be there, right there in the hippocampal/amygdala region. What it was, he couldn't begin to imagine. A vascular shadow created by new blood vessels? A tumor? Parasitic cyst? Did this have anything to do with the strange EEG he had recently obtained on his most recent patient?

Gunter leaned forward for a closer look. Artifact? Maybe, but he didn't think so. This was, after all, the third subject in a row that had exhibited this shadow. Being a man of science, Gunter didn't really believe in coincidences. What Gunter *did* believe was that he was finally onto something extraordinary. His instincts told him this, positively screamed it at him. And it was about fucking time. After all, he'd put in his time, slogged out twenty years in the trenches of academic medicine in the decidedly *unglamorous* field of pathology. Anyone who needed further proof of this need only look as far as his office, which was plunked down in the basement, for god sakes, sandwiched between the morgue and the dog lab. That kind of said it all, didn't it?

He had long ago severed ties with his old med school classmates. His counterparts in clinical medicine—real medicine, as they liked to refer to it—were busy furthering their careers, putting feathers in their caps and, let's not forget, saving lives. He had long since wearied of their insults and believed he had heard them all. The favorite one went something like this: "Pathology—good field for you, Mueller. Can't kill 'em if they're already dead." Then they'd slap him on the back. Yuckity-yuck.

Gunter shook his head again. He had a big talk to give in a few hours and should be preparing. The press, TV cameras and all, would be there along with all his esteemed colleagues. And here he was, holed up in his little office, sidetracked by these stupid films and painful memories of earlier years. Should he add the MRI slides to his lecture? He had been wrestling with this decision ever since he had gaped in astonishment at the first MRI. Of course he should. Gunter was, if nothing else, a play-it-by-the-book researcher. Let the facts lead where the facts may lead.

Finally, surprising himself, Gunter stood and yanked the MRI prints from the viewbox. A loud grinding noise, louder than he would've thought possible and even sounding a touch accusatory, came from the heavy duty paper shredder as he fed scan after scan into the machine. He glanced guiltily around the room several times, ensuring there were no unwanted visitors. Gunter also wondered where Chandler was at this moment.

CHAPTER 14

Friday, 9:10 a.m.

Chip and Kristin trotted down the hallway toward the McKleester Auditorium, ten minutes late because Kristin hadn't shown up on time. Something about feeding her dog. As they approached, Chip's fears were confirmed—the lecture hall was packed, people spilling out the open doors at the back of the room into the carpeted reception area. Definitely standing room only.

"C'mon, let's go," Chip said.

"I'll follow you," Kristin replied.

Chip maneuvered through the tangle of people clogging the doorway, with Kristin right behind. Several people shot them glares as they pushed their way into the darkened auditorium. Once inside, they found a spot to stand on the back wall. As Chip's eyes adjusted to the dim light, he made out the usual assortment of med students, residents, and faculty. However, reporters from the various local newspapers, TV, and radio stations were also here, sitting down in the front row. A camera crew from WGAL TV-8 was off to the far right. Word had definitely spread about this event. But then, murder had a way of attracting attention. Even one of the cleaning staff, with her little cart, was perched just inside the doorway, presumably to hear what Dr. Gunter Mueller had to say.

The focus of all the attention stood hunched over the podium, light from the slide projector reflecting off his glasses and shiny bald head. Mueller was a short guy in his sixties with a noticeable paunch. "Next slide, please," Mueller said. His voice quavered slightly and Chip thought he seemed nervous.

"This slide is key," Mueller said in a monotone. "What you're seeing here is a high power micrograph of cardiac muscle cells." His presentation style was definitely not what you would call electric, and Chip wondered if this would turn out to be a complete waste of time. "The mitochondria are actively utilizing ATP molecules, the endoplasmic reticulum is busy synthesizing new proteins, etcetera." Mueller attempted to point these structures out with his laser pointer, but his hands shook, and the little red dot danced about the screen so badly that he quickly abandoned this technique.

"Notice that the cells exhibit clear signs of life." Mueller paused to wipe his brow with a handkerchief. "The point is that this slide was obtained from a patient who had been pronounced dead one hour previously." There was a collective gasp from the audience and a hush fell over the room. Boring delivery aside, people suddenly sat forward in their seats.

Mueller continued. "We simply don't see any evidence of cellular death. In fact, these cells don't actually die until several *hours* later."

Murmurs rippled through the audience. Chip shot Kristin a glance. "That's unbelievable," she whispered back.

"So, this begs the question, why can't we do a better job of resuscitating someone, if their cells survive for hours, not minutes?" Mueller said. "In med school, we're taught that if you deprive someone of oxygen for four or five minutes, irreversible brain death and heart damage ensues, rapidly killing the patient. This is simply not the case."

Dr. Alvarez, the current chief of cardiology and president of the medical staff, practically jumped out of his seat. "Excuse me for interrupting, Dr. Mueller, but what you're saying flies in the face of everything we *know* clinically. You're a *pathologist,* not a clinician." He delivered the word "pathologist" with a faint, but measurable, amount of disdain. Alvarez turned and scanned the audience, as if trying to enlist support before continuing. "When someone doesn't breathe, they die quickly—in a matter of minutes. Every med student knows this."

"You're absolutely right, Dr. Alvarez. Everyone knows this—and this might be the problem." Mueller stared down at Alvarez, a wry look spreading across his face. "What's the first thing *clinicians* do for someone in cardiac arrest?" Dr. Mueller paused for effect, then answered his own question. "Why, they try to re-establish breathing and administer oxygen, don't they? Pulse oximeters are rapidly applied. The oxygen saturation level is key and felt to be intimately tied to survival."

Dr. Mueller removed his spectacles and looked over the audience. "Gentlemen, ladies, what if we have all of this backwards?" He let that sink in before continuing. Chip had to admit the guy was fascinating. "What if our very efforts to save a life actually work against us? Perhaps we need to apply some creative logic here—think outside the box, if you will."

Now on a roll, Mueller no longer seemed hampered by nervousness. "Here we see a slide of a cardiac cell that has just been reperfused with blood and flooded with oxygen. What do you see?" He reached for the laser pointer again. "You'll note there is widespread evidence of cell death—degraded cellular proteins, lysosomal membrane ruptures and so forth, everywhere you look." This time, he successfully pointed out the structures. The audience was absolutely silent.

"What precisely is going on here?" Again, Mueller looked out over the audience. "In my lab, I have shown that mitochondria control a very important process known as apoptosis. Apoptosis is simply the programmed death of abnormal cells. It's the body's primary defense against cancer. When the mitochondria detect that a cell has undergone a cancerous transformation, they throw a switch that initiates cell death. What seems to be happening here is that the cellular surveillance mechanism has become confused and cannot tell the difference between a cell becoming cancerous and a cell being reperfused with oxygen. So the oxygen actually triggers apoptosis, or cell death."

"Preposterous," Alvarez blurted.

"Is it?" Mueller continued, unfazed. "Perhaps you recall the so-called diving reflex of mammalian systems? When a mammal holds its breath and simultaneously has its face subjected to very cold temperatures—such as immersing its head in icy water—the heart rate and metabolic rate slow down dramatically, allowing the mammal to stay alive without organ damage for twenty to thirty minutes. You've all heard stories of people being pulled from the freezing water after falling through the ice. They are miraculously revived an hour later with no significant brain damage. That, my friends, is the mammalian diving reflex at work."

Mueller paused to take a sip from his bottled water. "The reflex is felt to be an evolutionary holdover from more primitive cold-blooded reptilian or amphibian species. And this is what led us to examine the whole question of oxygen reperfusion in detail."

"So, you're saying oxygen is bad?" one of the residents asked.

"No, not at all," Mueller replied.

"You mean we shouldn't give oxygen at a code?" another resident said.

"No, no, of course not." Mueller shook his head vigorously. "I think I see the confusion here. Let me explain. It's not that oxygen is bad, per se. When it is given right away, it *is* life-saving, and this is what all you good doctors are referring to. What I'm talking about is the situation where there is first oxygen deprivation, say for five or ten minutes. This is then followed by a flooding of oxygen in a reperfused state. This is an entirely different clinical entity. Do you see the difference?"

Several in the audience nodded.

"So we're back to the original question. Can we do a better job resuscitating people? Next slide, please. Here you see in schematic form what we're doing in the lab. Basically we've slowed down the process of resuscitation. First, we cool the body down—way down—to 27 degrees Celsius. Then, just as the heart is beginning to fibrillate from the cold, we place the patient on a heart-lung machine, initiating cardiopulmonary bypass. Next, we infuse an iced cardioplegic solution directly into the coronary arteries, thereby stopping the heart. Up until this point, this is very similar to what happens when one has open-heart surgery." Several of the cardiac surgeons up front were nodding their assent.

"The difference is," Mueller said, "we now apply ultra-cool temperatures, especially to the head, to stimulate the diving reflex, and we administer oxygen only very sparingly. We also administer cerebral protective drugs, inducing a barbiturate coma to lower the brain's metabolism and hence its need for oxygen. We also give antithrombin drugs to prevent clotting of the cooled, sluggish blood. The idea here is to give the heart a chance to rest, repair some damage and clear toxic waste products that have accumulated. Then, after several days of this regimen, the body is slowly—and this is key—slowly brought back to normothermia. The heart is then restarted, and if all goes well, the heart-lung machine is removed."

The audience was still completely silent. Mueller took another drink and continued. "You may say this is impossible or that it contradicts every basic tenet of clinical medicine, but the fact of the matter is, I have demonstrated this technique in my lab. I am starting to see some amazing results that speak for themselves.

Something is going on here that we are just beginning to understand." Mueller took off his glasses, folded them up, and tucked them into his breast pocket. "I'll take some questions now."

A man in the front row immediately raised his hand; his Blackberry was clutched in the other. "Joe Singleton, Patriot News. If these patients are declared dead and you bring them back to life, aren't you playing God, doctor?"

"Nonsense," Mueller said. "Just trying to expand the envelope of science. Was saving someone's life with penicillin playing God?"

"How do you know when oxygen is a liability and no longer life-saving?" a familiar voice asked. Chip recognized Dr. Landry from the airway lecture the other day.

"Excellent question," Mueller said. "We are still trying to elucidate the precise timeline of this in the lab. Right now, it remains a judgement call."

Another reporter stood up and didn't wait for Mueller to acknowledge him. "What about *your* patient who murdered a nurse and escaped from the ICU last week?"

This one seemed to catch Mueller by surprise. He paled and gripped the sides of the podium. "H-how did you know about this? That information was not released."

Chip and Kristin exchanged glances again. Chip had read the account of Heather's unfortunate death in the local papers, but there had been no mention of Mueller's resuscitation lab.

"I can't reveal my confidential sources," the reporter said. "Did something go wrong with this patient's treatment? Did you make him violent?"

Mueller just stood there, looking increasingly uncomfortable. Several times he started to say something, but nothing came out. Chip thought of Heather and felt a wave of pity for her.

"Do you feel responsible for the nurse's death?" another reporter shouted.

"Should your lab be shut down?" a third called.

Chip looked over at Kristin and whispered, "Holy shit."

The quiet, respectful, academic atmosphere in the lecture hall had vanished, replaced by outbursts of conversation and the noisy confusion of cell phone beeps and texts as reporters called in with the breaking news.

A man in a gray suit hurriedly walked from offstage over to the podium and leaned over the mic. "I think that's all the time we have for questions at the moment. Dr. Mueller is a busy man. Thank you all for attending. We have press releases for all the journalists that summarize Dr. Mueller's lecture and cutting-edge research. You can pick these up in the back on your way out." He took Mueller's arm and escorted the rattled professor off the stage.

CHAPTER 15

Friday, 9:10 a.m.

Laura Landry pulled her Ford Edge into the parking lot at In Gear, the local bike shop in Hummelstown. She put the transmission in park and turned off the ignition, but didn't get out of the vehicle. Now that she was here, she was having second thoughts about going through with this. Fear shivered through her. She hated the dreadful little devices and had sworn she'd never use them.

She pounded the steering wheel. *Damn it!* She hated herself for being so weak. She thought of Doug, and how excited he had been to go on a bike ride with her today. He had acted just like a little kid when she had asked him. She needed to buck up and support her man, who needed her now. She just needed to firmly set her mind to it. She smiled; Doug liked to tease her that she would frequently set her mind—except he always added "like concrete." Well, she needed a little concrete right about now. Summoning her courage, Laura opened the car door and made her way into the cramped little store.

"You mean you're interested in clipless pedals?" asked the man behind the counter, a balding fellow with a big bushy beard who didn't really look like he belonged at a bike shop.

"No," Laura said, trying to keep the exasperation out of her voice. *Maybe he didn't understand.* She repeated herself, a little slower and louder. "I want the kind where my foot attaches to the pedals, like ski bindings, sort of."

"Right," the man said. "They're called clip*less* pedals."

"That's dumb," she said before checking her watch. This was turning out to be harder than she'd thought. "Who would call them that? Why not call them clip-*on* or something?"

"Look, lady, I didn't name them, okay? Do you want to see them or not?"

"I do."

"Road bike or mountain bike?"

"We'll be riding on the road."

"Okay, fine." He pulled out two boxes and set them on the countertop, then removed the box lids so she could see the contents. "These are the two most common brands we carry."

She fought the involuntary urge to cringe when she saw them. "And I need to use them today," she added.

He looked at her askance. "You'll also need bike shoes with cleats."

"Of course." Laura didn't admit that she was unaware of this small detail.

The man's eyes narrowed. "You know, you should practice some before you take these out for a spin," he said. "Like on the grass."

"I know—I will," she lied.

"Are you sure you want these?"

"Yes, I'm sure." Laura checked her watch again. "My husband uses them, so why shouldn't I?"

The man raised his eyebrows at this.

"Look, I know it sounds dumb," Laura said. "It's a long story, but I want to surprise my husband. He'll think it's really cool that I'm that into it."

"Whatever you say, lady," he said. "You're the boss."

"Besides," she said, "he says they make him go faster. I need to keep up with him."

This finally elicited a smile from the clerk.

Laura's phone rang; she fished it out of her purse and saw Doug's name on the display. "Hello," she said.

"Hi honey. I should be home around noon. You still good to go?"

"Absolutely," she said. "The weather looks perfect. It's a bit cool right now, but the sun is out and things are supposed to warm up nicely."

"OK, great," Doug said. "See you at home in a little bit."

"And I have a surprise for you," she said. *There,* she thought. *No turning back now.*

"Okay, cool," he said. "You know I like surprises."

"I'll be home shortly. I just want to stop at CVS and pick up some Chapstick and Gatorade." She pictured him smiling ear to ear as she ended the call.

CHAPTER 16

Friday, 10:00 a.m.

Chandler paced nervously in the parking lot of the CVS drugstore at the corner of Hockenberry and Chocolate Avenue in Hershey. He couldn't shake the feeling that maybe this wasn't the best idea. After all, the fricking Derry Township Police Department building was right across the street. But the store was relatively empty at the moment. Besides several employee cars parked behind the building, there were only two cars in the lot—an old Chevy Impala and a newer model Ford Edge. He walked around some more, chewing on his bottom lip.

Chandler shot one more glance at the police station—everything appeared copasetic, no cruisers with lights flashing or SWAT team vans mobilizing—and fought to calm himself down, think this through. First of all, they hadn't found him yet. The two nights he had spent hiding out in the woods behind the med center had done nothing to improve his disposition, but on the plus side, the downtime *had* bought his heart, lungs, and kidneys some valuable recovery time.

They would've searched his apartment by now, but they wouldn't have found anything of much use there—just a lot of empty beer and whiskey bottles, a small fritzy TV, and piles of dirty clothes. As he ticked off his possessions, a hard realization struck him like a bolt out of the blue: Was that how he really lived? Was that the total extent of his life? The answers were as painful as the pangs of hunger that gripped his stomach.

There *were* no framed pictures of him and his beautiful family with a golden retriever at their feet. Because, of course, he didn't have a wife or kids—or even a frickin' goldfish. There were no bookcases crammed with novels or books—actually, there were no bookcases, period. His only reading material consisted of a few crusty *Hustler* magazines strewn about the floor. They *would* find his med center badge and quickly figure out he was one of the night shift cleaning personnel—if they didn't know that already.

Chandler's hands balled up and he paced a little faster. He was done with that loser existence. No more cleaning up other people's shit, wiping it up, mopping it up, inhaling it, running his hands through it, until it seeped into his very pores. He shuddered. This was, after all, how he had caught the fucking virus that had laid waste to his heart in the first place.

Mueller's lecture had been a real revelation; although Chandler still had many unanswered questions, he now had a starting point and a frame of reference on which to build. He stopped himself and marveled, *Since when have I ever found any lecture remotely fascinating? Or even paid attention in a lecture? What's happening to me?* Clearly, he needed to pay Dr. Mueller a visit. This became his plan.

Plan? Another bolt of insight jolted him. For perhaps the first time in his life, he was aware of planning a strategy. Was this how other people lived and thought? *Is this how they always seemed to get the best of me? Lording their intellect over me and looking down on me like I'm a stupid pack mule, fit only for cleaning up their garbage . . .* He squeezed his fists so hard they ached. No, he would never go back to that dead-end job. Bigger things were clearly in store for him. He couldn't see the future, but he knew he was right on this score. Big changes were occurring inside of him.

His fists relaxed. Things were finally starting to go his way; he'd been given a second chance. The beginnings of a smile crept across his face. Head up, shoulders squared, Chandler marched directly up to the drugstore entrance. The automatic doors whooshed aside as if anxious to get out of his way. He knew one other thing: things would be different this time around.

CHAPTER 17

Friday, 10:15 a.m.

"Mommy's home," Kristin said, closing the front door behind her and tossing her purse on the foyer table in between the big Boston fern and glossy peace lily. Passing by the rest of her potted plant friends, she entered the cramped kitchenette, where Smokey lifted his head from between his paws, and thumped his tail. Kristin unlatched the crate's metal door (or the cage, as her father liked to call it) and Smokey squeezed out. She had to smile at the ridiculous sight.

A year ago, when Smokey had finally moved on from his prolonged puppy chewing phase, where he basically gnawed anything in sight, Kristin had figured it was time to retire the crate. Besides, the metal contraption was unsightly and took up precious floor space in her kitchen. So one day, while Smokey was tied out back, she had folded up the crate and stuffed it in the hallway closet. When she let had him back in, the poor thing had wandered through her small apartment, searching for the crate. He had looked so lost and befuddled, wondering how he could possibly have misplaced it. That was bad enough, but then he'd started whimpering and crying. When she'd told him, "You're a year old now. You don't need the crate anymore," he had responded with such sad eyes that Kristin had quickly caved, and put the crate back in the kitchen to keep the peace. Now, all grown up and tipping the scales at over a hundred pounds of pure muscle, the coal black Labrador retriever barely fit inside his crate anymore.

Smokey went through his stretching routine, then approached her for some hands-on attention. She knelt and ran her hands through his thick coat, pausing to scratch around his ears, which he loved. He looked up at her expectantly and started to pant, and she knew he wanted to go for a walk.

She eyed the door to the basement, where her darkroom was located. She'd hoped to spend some time there. She could lose herself for hours there, forget about the rest of the world—no crazed, murderous patients running about, no hideous dead bodies, no dead cardiac cells being revived. Then a wave of fatigue washed over her and she thought longingly of her bed. She hadn't gotten much sleep the past two nights—visions of Chandler killing Heather kept playing in her mind. But the gorgeous day, coupled with Smokey's insistence, ultimately won out. Besides, he threatened to break out the sad eyes. "All right, all right, we'll go," she said to him. "Go get your leash."

Kristin's tiredness soon evaporated in the sunshine and light breeze of a spectacular afternoon, and the first mile flew by. Kristin's sneakers barely touched the ground; she felt as if she and Smokey could walk forever.

They came to a fork in the road and she chuckled—when you come to a fork in the road, take it, her dad always said. He had a saying for every occasion. Some were witty and profound; most were just silly Yogi Bearisms, as he liked to call them. Smokey tugged to the right, toward the longer loop, but Kristin pulled back on the leash. "I can't spend my whole life walking you, you know.

People have to do other things with their lives. Like hold down a job. Pay the bills. Meet people—that sort of thing."

Smokey tugged harder on the leash. "All right, all right. It *is* a beautiful day. You win." She set off down the lane past the sheep farm, which added at least a mile to their standard three-mile loop. "So, let me tell you about this guy I met. His name is Chip. Actually, I've known him for a couple of months. He's kinda cute."

Smokey pulled hard to the side of the road and mashed his nose down in some leaves, picking up the scent of God-knew-what.

"Do you want to hear this or not?" Kristin said.

Smokey turned and gave her an indignant look, which she translated as "Do you think I can't sniff and listen at the same time?"

"Well, anyway, I think he's interested—a little bit. We've been talking recently at work. Because of the crazy guy. You know, the one I told you about yesterday, the one who killed the nurse. He asked me out for coffee—well, not actually *out*, but to get a cup at the med center. I said no, of course."

They paused at the edge of the sheep farm. Several lambs, some only a couple of months old, came out to greet them; most, familiar with the big black dog and his ponytailed companion, came right up to the fence and baaed. Smokey put his nose through the fence and calmly touched snouts with some of them, as if he were friends with them. Sometimes Kristin wondered if Smokey even knew he was a dog.

They continued down the empty lane. "The more I think of it, the more I think I should stop talking to him. You know, nip it in the bud. I don't need any more heartache in my life. Boys are nothing but trouble. He texted me right in the middle of a big lecture. Can you believe it?"

Smokey just tugged on the leash, catching the scent of something up ahead. "You remember cheatin' Andrew and how badly that went down, right? Chip seems different, though." Smokey pulled even harder. "I know, I know—I always say that. He *does* seem kinda lonely. They say he flunked out of med school."

Soon they passed through a wooded section composed mostly of maples and poplars, their canopy arching over the road and providing a bit of shade dappled with sunshine. The cooler air here added an extra spring to Kristin's step.

Suddenly, a fox darted out of the underbrush, running directly across their path. Kristin cried out in surprise and Smokey started barking and tugging so hard on his leash that she almost lost him. Gripping the leash with both hands, she planted her feet squarely on the macadam. "No way, honey buns," she grunted as she pulled him back. She peered after the fox as she knelt, tucked the leash under her knee, and rubbed the dog's ears and furry head. "I've never seen a fox on this trail before. He might have rabies or something, to come so close to us." Smokey stopped pulling but still craned his head in the direction the fox had taken, his panting interspersed with growls.

She cupped his big head with both hands and forcibly turned it toward her. "Listen you—I'm not taking any chances," she said, her face now inches from the dog's moist, jet-black snoot. "You're the only reliable thing I've got going, Smokers. Can't afford to lose you." The dog's neck muscles relaxed and he no longer strained to see the fox. He looked calmly up at her, then licked her cheek.

CHAPTER 18

Friday, 10:30 a.m.

Chandler strode through the doors of the CVS pharmacy then stopped abruptly, staring at the newspapers displayed on racks just inside the entrance. The headline on the *Harrisburg Patriot News* proclaimed *MED CENTER MURDERER STILL ON THE LOOSE*. Underneath was a blurry black and white picture of his face, presumably lifted from his hospital ID badge. *Guess that answers the question of Heather's fate.*

Chandler walked up to the checkout counter at the front of the store. A young woman, probably in her twenties, stood idly at her register, texting on her phone. She was pretty in spite of her round face and plump figure. "Can you tell me where your nutritional supplements are?" he asked, studying her closely.

"Aisle five," she said, barely looking up. "Over there, near the candy section," she added, waving her arm in the general direction.

He gazed into her mind. She had no idea who he was; there was no flicker of recognition—she was way too preoccupied worrying about her missed period and what the hell she would do if she were pregnant. And what her father would do. The only fleeting thought that registered about him was that he looked awful grungy and smelled bad, too.

Chandler mumbled a thanks and picked up a shopping basket.

Aisle five was a frickin' goldmine. He scooped lots of Powerbars and Zone bars into his basket, unconcerned with the few that fell on the floor. He hefted two six packs of Ensure protein shakes and chucked them into his increasingly heavy basket. Halfway down the aisle, he stopped at the vitamin section and grabbed some multivitamins and some extra B vitamins for energy and C and E vitamins for healing. As he approached the back of the store, he spied the energy drink section and crammed some Red Bull and 5-hour energy drinks into his overflowing basket.

If he'd had any money, he would've simply purchased the items. He supposed he could steal them easily enough, but he didn't want to create a ruckus—not yet, anyway. So instead, Chandler went into the men's room, ignoring the sign that read *No store items in the restroom*, and locked the door. He paused only long enough to inspect the room for surveillance cameras, found none, and began his feast. He tore into the Powerbars and devoured three of them as fast as he could. He popped a bunch of vitamins and washed them down with some Ensure shakes—chocolate, vanilla, and double-dutch chocolate. He almost gagged on the sweetness, but gorged himself anyway. Finally, he sucked down some Red Bull and 5-hour energy drinks until his stomach felt ready to burst. Finished, Chandler threw the wrappers and empty cans in the trash, flushed the toilet, and walked out with his basket, now considerably lighter.

Across the store, he spied an elderly couple standing in line at the pharmacy counter. *Perfect,* he thought, and sauntered over to them, stopping to pretend to read the self-help book titles in a rack nearby. He picked up *How Forgiveness Changed My Life Forever: A True Story* and leafed through it.

"May I help you?" the pharmacy tech, a skinny girl probably in her teens, said to the couple.

The old woman nodded. "We're here to pick up his prescriptions," she said, patting her husband's arm.

"Name?" the tech asked with all the warmth of an icicle.

"Ed Kopenhaver," the woman said.

"How many?" the girl shot back.

"Three," Mrs. Kopenhaver replied. "Blood pressure, diabetes, and heart medicine."

"Don't forget the sugar pill, Erma," Mr. Kopenhaver said loudly to his wife.

"I didn't," Mrs. Kopenhaver told him.

"What?" Mr. Kopenhaver bellowed. He had to be pushing ninety.

Mrs. Kopenhaver raised her voice. "I told her, Ed. It's all taken care of." The tech was busy rolling her eyes.

"Is there a problem?" Mr. Kopenhaver asked.

"No, everything's fine." Mrs. Kopenhaver shushed her husband with her hands.

The girl retrieved the prescriptions and rang them up. "That will be $104.65," she said, finally cracking a smile.

"Sakes alive." Mrs. Kopenhaver fussed with her wallet and produced a credit card. She handed it to the tech, muttering something about Medicare and donut holes.

"Did you say donuts?" Mr. Kopenhaver said.

Mrs. Kopenhaver shook her head and a sad smile crept across her face as she waited for her receipt.

Chandler had trouble suppressing his own smile. This would be a piece of cake. All he needed was a home address, which he easily obtained from Ed's befuddled brain.

The Kopenhavers moved so slowly toward the exit that Chandler thought they might never get there. He waited until they finally cleared the automatic doors before he followed.

Suddenly, a woman came out from a nearby aisle, walking fast, and almost collided with him. He was about to say something to her, but the angry words stuck in his throat. The sight of her jarred something deep within his mind. A memory? A dream? Something about her looked eerily familiar, but he couldn't say what. She had long black hair that reminded him of Carol Sue, but that wasn't it.

The striking woman headed to the checkout counter up front. He tried to follow her, but his feet seemed rooted to the floor, so he just stared after her. She paid for her items and left the store. Chandler broke his paralysis and practically bolted after her.

He stopped out in the parking lot, shading his eyes from the bright sun, and watched her drive away in the Ford. He couldn't shake the thought—the conviction—that their paths would cross again.

Chandler slowly turned toward the Kopenhavers, who were still there, working on getting Ed into the passenger seat of the Impala.

CHAPTER 19

Friday, noon

"You were right," Laura Landry called back to Doug, close behind her. "This road *is* sweet."

They were pedaling down Route 443 on their way to Fort Indiantown Gap. "Thought you'd like it," he shouted back.

The racetrack, with the new Hollywood Casino, flew by on the right. The roadway abruptly widened. Doug loved this new stretch of road; it had recently been paved and sported a shoulder wide enough for two bikes. He pulled his Trek road bike up next to Laura, careful not to crowd her; they were making better than twenty miles an hour on the flat. "We should check out the casino sometime," he suggested. "It looks pretty nice; might be fun."

"Yeah, sure."

Doug could tell Laura's heart wasn't in it. She didn't care much for the drinking/gambling crowd. He glanced over at the Appalachian ridge, several hundred yards to their left. It was still early October and the leaves were a blaze of reds and yellows. The stretch of nice weather continued, with temperatures in the seventies, low humidity, and barely a cloud in the sky. Laura had been right—the day was gorgeous. Perfect day for a bike ride.

"How much farther to the lake?" she asked.

Doug checked his odometer. "Three or four miles. We're making good time. Fifteen minutes at the most."

"Great."

"How're the pedals working out?" Doug asked, still marveling at Laura's "surprise" for him.

"I love them." She smiled at him.

"Just be careful," he said.

"I will. I feel like I really *can* go faster."

"You *are* really moving. I can barely keep up with you." Doug had to admit he was nervous when Laura greeted him with new clipless pedals on her bike. But she had insisted. 'Look,' she had said, 'If we're gonna do this biking thing seriously, I want to do it all the way. Besides, *you* use them. Why shouldn't *I*?' Checkmate. And now, seeing how well she handled her bike, new shoes clipped securely to her pedals, he began to relax about it.

A loud shriek overhead distracted him; it was followed by an even louder metallic burping noise. Doug looked up in time to see two A-10 Warthog jets dive over the ridge on their practice bombing run at the National Guard base at the Gap. The distinctive noise came from the A-10s' Vulcan machine guns letting loose at several thousand rounds per second. *Impressive. Glad not to be on the receiving end of that,* he thought.

Soon the entrance to Memorial Lake came up on the right and he and Laura turned in. They parked their bikes and strolled down to the lake.

"This is really nice," Laura said, taking his hand. "I'm glad we had time to do this."

"Me too. Gotta love a schedule with Friday afternoon off. I brought some snacks." Doug fished some granola bars out of his bike jersey. "Want any?"

"Sure."

They settled side by side on the top of a beat-up picnic table, munching on the granola bars and sipping on Gatorade as they gazed across the lake. Doug thought the term "lake" was a bit optimistic. The Army Corps of Engineers had constructed an earthen dam across a small stream and the resulting body of water was not much bigger than a large pond. But the name Memorial Lake had stuck with the local fishermen who frequented it. Their small rowboats dotted the lake, and he could even hear some of the conversations clearly, carried over the surface of the water. Doug knew some of these same fishermen would be out here ice fishing in mid-January. Talk about dedication.

"I'm glad your lecture went so well," Laura said. "This sabbatical of yours can really be a new start for us."

"Yes, it sounds good," Doug said, eyes on an adventurous teenager trying his hand at windsurfing. There wasn't any breeze to speak of, though, and the boy didn't get too far.

"We'll ride every Friday," Laura said. "And I'll make us a picnic lunch. We can spread out a blanket. It'll be just like old times. Do you think we can carry all that on our bikes?" Laura looked at him, eyes sparkling.

"Definitely," Doug said.

Laura sidled closer, wrapped one arm around him, and squeezed. "We're so lucky, Doug. Do you ever think that?"

"Yes, I do."

"I love you," she said.

"I love you, too."

They sat there a while in silence, Doug concentrating on the warmth and softness of Laura's body leaning against his. The only noise was the chirping of the birds and occasional squeals from small children as they played on nearby swing sets.

"Hey, I almost forgot," Doug said after several minutes, breaking their reverie. "You should've heard the lecture I heard this morning."

Laura eyed him quizzically. "Medical lectures usually aren't *that* exciting."

"This one was; it turned into a full-blown circus. Remember that nurse who was killed in the ICU earlier this week?"

"Yes, of course."

Doug related the details of Mueller's lecture and the audience reaction afterward.

"Sounds creepy, if you ask me," Laura said, scrunching up her nose.

"We'll have to watch the news tonight. I think the whole thing's going to hit the fan. The press were all over his case. I'm going to try to talk to Gunter Mueller—he's the pathologist in charge of all of this resuscitation stuff—and see some of his protocol in more detail."

"Sounds fascinating," Laura said, feigning a yawn.

"No, really, it is. The whole oxygen/reperfusion thing intrigues me. Remember, I make a living out of ensuring proper oxygen delivery."

"Whatever you say, dear."

"But I guess I'd better see Mueller before they shut his lab down."

"Would they do that?" Laura asked.

"They might." He jumped off the table. "Why don't we head back before the boys get home from school."

The two walked back to the bike rack. "You know, Doug," Laura said as they put their helmets on, "maybe they should shut his lab down—I mean, what if his stuff *does* make the patients violent?"

"That seems a little far-fetched, Laura."

"I'm just not a big fan of tinkering with the dying process."

"He's trying to save lives," Doug said.

"Yeah, I know. But if these people are really dead, what happens to their soul?"

"I don't know; never really thought about it." Doug squeezed his tires, checking for proper pressure.

"Sometimes that's the trouble with research."

"Yep."

"Did they catch the person responsible yet?" Laura asked as she prepared to mount her bike.

"I don't think so. But I'm sure they will soon. How hard could it be to track down a near-dead patient on foot?"

CHAPTER 20

Friday, 11:30 a.m.

Particularly energized by his morning meal in the CVS men's room, Chandler walked briskly down Caracas Avenue, feeling as if he could break into a jog. He didn't want to push his body too fast, though; another couple of days with some decent, regular meals and some sleep, and he'd be ready to tackle anything. He focused on walking, his thoughts returning to the woman he had seen in the drugstore; he still couldn't place her.

Soon Chandler saw the vintage Chevy Impala parked on the street in front of a two-story brick house and knew he'd reached his destination. He walked up the narrow cement walkway and onto a large wooden porch. A sign by the door read: *The Kopenhavers. All Friends Welcome!* Chandler smiled and knocked on the door. No answer. They had to be home. He knocked louder.

Finally the door opened several inches before being stopped by a security chain. Mrs. Kopenhaver's wrinkled little face peeked out at him. There was no recognition in her eyes. "Yes, can I help you?" she asked. She seemed a bit frazzled, no doubt from encountering a stranger at her front door.

"Hi, I'm Bill from the drugstore," Chandler said, working to smile as widely as he could. "I have one of your medicines." He held up a little plastic bag with the CVS logo on it. There were several Powerbars in it. "You must've forgotten it."

"No, I think I have everything," she said. "We only went to get some prescriptions for my husband." Mrs. Kopenhaver's eyes narrowed and she regarded him suspiciously.

"The pharmacist didn't have the heart medicine ready in time," Chandler said, improvising.

"I could have sworn I got that one."

Chandler studied her briefly. "I have Mr. Kopenhaver's Lanoxin right here." He held the bag higher.

She reached out through the gap to take the bag.

Chandler pulled the bag back. "I need you to sign for it, Mrs. Kopenhaver. Sorry. You know, Medicare rules."

"Oh, all right," she said, sounding exasperated. She closed the door and he could hear her struggle with the chain for a moment. Finally she opened the door wide and said, "Come in, please. Let me just go and get a pen."

Chandler entered the foyer and looked around. The hardwood floor creaked under his feet. A little peekapoo came out of nowhere and began snarling at him.

"Don't mind the dog," she called out from the dining room. "He won't hurt you—he's a real scaredy-cat."

Chandler knelt down and reached out to pet the dog, who promptly nipped him on the finger. Mrs. Kopenhaver returned with pen in hand. "Duchess and I are getting along great," he said, hiding his bloody finger.

"I see," she said. "Now, where do I sign?"

Chandler hesitated, then pulled a receipt from the bag and handed it to her.

She took the paper and made room on the small end table to write on, pushing the lace doily and empty flower vase out of the way. "This doesn't look like a Medicare form," she remarked, worry tugging at her eyebrows. She looked up at him. "By the way, how did you know the dog's name?"

Shit! Before she could react, Chandler put his hand over her mouth and pushed her against the wall, knocking over the end table. The flower vase shattered on the floor. She struggled harder than he would've thought possible.

"Erma," came the voice of Mr. Kopenhaver from the living room. "What's all the fuss about?"

She bit his hand.

Damn!

He pulled his hand back and she let out a blood-curdling scream that hurt his ears.

Damn it!

She tried to slip out of his grasp, but he grabbed her tight and slammed her body to the wall. Her head smacked against the doorframe and she let out a moan. Her gray wig slanted crazily, halfway off her head. He overpowered her easily and pinned her arms tightly against her body. This time, he clamped his hand securely over her mouth and nose. Her mind radiated massive amounts of terror with undertones of anger.

Chandler could hear the old man grunting, and a chair creaked in the other room. "I'm coming," Mr. Kopenhaver said.

Erma's struggling dwindled and then ceased altogether. He watched her eyes with fascination as her pupils began to dilate. Seconds later, he sensed a strange, invisible force brush up against him. He shuddered, and it was gone. He lowered her lifeless body to the floor, his eyes avoiding the horrified expression frozen on her face.

Duchess was barking fiercely and scrambling about, but she kept her distance.

Hearing footsteps approaching, Chandler quickly moved over and stood against the wall, out of sight.

Mr. Kopenhaver finally shuffled into view, huffing with the exertion. He almost tripped over his wife's body before he noticed it. He immediately knelt down at her side. "Erma, what's the matter?"

Chandler came up behind the old man and twisted his head sharply to one side. He felt the old man's neck snap as easily as a dry twig and the man went limp. Once again, Chandler sensed the presence of a spiritual being floating by him. This time it touched him as it went by. Chandler was a bit unnerved by this, but couldn't deny what he had felt—twice now.

He took several moments to calm himself before carrying the bodies to the basement, one by one. He laid them side by side on the cement floor, thinking it fitting that they be together in death.

As the adrenaline haze started to clear, Chandler waited for the bad feelings to come—but remarkably, they never did. No sorrow. No guilt. No remorse. Nothing.

Chandler climbed back up the basement stairs, the gray wig now poking out of his back pocket. He hadn't intended to kill these two, it just happened. The old lady had bit him and then screamed, triggering some primitive survival reflex in him. His mind drifted to the invisible things that had touched him. Had he actually sensed the souls leaving the newly dead bodies? Since when did he have the ability to sense these things? *More gifts from the transformation?* he wondered. *More questions for the good Dr. Mueller.*

A wave of drowsiness suddenly washed over him as he reached the top of the stairs, and he staggered. He realized the boost from the energy bars was fading and his caffeine level was dropping along with his blood sugar. He could easily regulate his own blood sugar by suppressing his pancreas's insulin output, but a little snack would sure fit the bill. And a nice nap in a real bed with sheets seemed mighty tempting as well. He was still far from full strength and his body could use the down time. Finding answers and furthering his goals could wait.

He didn't think the Kopenhavers would be missed for a while. Their house would make a suitable safe house where he could recuperate. Tomorrow would be a new day—he would make a fresh start.

Once again, Chandler was quite taken by the novelty of making a plan. He smiled. Things were definitely going his way. There was no question he was smarter, more intelligent than he had ever been.

He checked the refrigerator and found half a roasted chicken wrapped in aluminum foil on a plate. An oversize serving fork with two sharp tines was also on the plate. Over to the side was a small Tupperware container of mashed potatoes. Perfect. Add some milk to wash it all down with, and he had a proper feast! But he had one more task to attend to before he could indulge in his meal and luxuriate in his new bed.

He tore off a piece of chicken with one hand and held the fork behind his back with the other. "Duchess! Here, girl. Want a treat?"

CHAPTER 21

Friday, 2:00 p.m.

"The view's even better from this side," Laura said, nodding toward Memorial Lake from the top of the dam.

"I think you're right."

She and Doug dismounted from their bikes and stood surveying the serene water. The picnic table they had been sitting at earlier was visible on the far shore.

"Thanks again for a lovely day." Laura leaned over and kissed him.

Doug smiled. "Sure, anytime." He glanced at his watch. "It's two o'clock—we'd better get moving."

"Right," Laura said. "You can sure lose track of time out here."

They biked along the edge of the lake to the park exit, where the little one lane road T'ed up to the main road. They braked to a halt at the stop sign and looked and listened for traffic. The visibility to the left was very limited—only about fifty yards or so as Route 443 disappeared into a sharp curve. Doug got off his bike and leaned it against his hip. He pulled off his helmet and fiddled with the mirror attached to it. "You go on," he said, frustrated. "I'll catch up. I just need to fix this blasted mirror."

Suddenly, two motorcycles came powering around the bend; an ear-splitting roar from their unmuffled pipes shattered the placid silence of the afternoon. The motorcycles sped off down the straightaway to the right and quickly disappeared from sight. Soon their engine noise also faded, restoring the tranquil quiet of the woods. Several birds twittered nearby and the cicadas resumed their rhythmic song.

"Be careful," warned Doug, glancing up.

"I will," Laura said, clipping her left foot into her pedal.

Doug watched her from the corner of his eye as she started across the road. He cursed under his breath at his fussy little mirror, wanting to join her while the road was clear.

Seconds later, he heard the throaty growl of a revved-up V8, before a pickup truck careened around the bend—directly toward Laura. It had to be going at least sixty around the curve. Dropping his helmet, Doug let his bike fall to the ground and stepped forward, waving his arms wildly at the Dodge Ram while shouting, "Laura, watch out!"

Laura didn't see the truck bearing down on her; head down, she was focused on trying to clip her right foot into the pedal.

It was all happening so fast—

Finally, after an eternity, she looked up, drawn by the roar of the truck or him shouting—who knew. *Pedal, Laura, pedal!*

A loud *screech* as the driver jammed on the brakes. The truck went into a vicious skid, tires screaming on the dry pavement. Doug yelled, "Laura!" just before he heard an awful, sickening thud as the truck slammed into her body. She and the bike flew ten yards from the impact, landing on the far shoulder of the road.

Doug sprinted across the road to her. Laura was tangled up in her twisted bike, one foot still clipped into her pedal, the other leg caught between the frame and the bike chain. She was scraped up pretty badly from sliding across the asphalt. His eyes fell on the jagged white of splintered bone—her femur—sticking out from a ragged hole in her bike shorts. *Shit—not good.* Blood seeped out around the bone onto the pavement. But amazingly, her eyes were open. *Thank God for her helmet.* "Laura, are you okay?" he asked breathlessly.

"I don't know," she mumbled, sounding dazed, eyes unfocused. "What happened?"

"You got hit. Your leg's broken."

The truck driver, a big, bearded man in a plaid flannel shirt and jeans, lumbered over to them, wheezing with the effort. "Hey lady, you okay?" he called, then, "Oh, shit." He recoiled. "Her leg!" He ran a meaty hand through his reddish hair and turned away.

"We have to get her to a hospital," Doug said.

"She pulled out right in front of me," the driver said, turning back to face Doug. He shook his head and held his hands palms up in a helpless "what could I have done" gesture. "I hit the brakes as soon as I seen her."

"Can you call for an ambulance?"

"Yeah, sure." He whipped out his cell phone.

Doug turned back to Laura. "Here, let's get you untangled from your bike."

"My leg hurts badly," she said.

"Your left leg is broken—we'll try to be real careful with it. Anything else hurt?"

She thought for a moment. "I don't think so."

"Good," Doug said. "Help is on the way."

He worked carefully to free Laura from the wreckage of her bike. He noticed that her leg was bleeding more freely now. *Shit.* "Laura, your leg is bleeding. We're going to have to put a tourniquet on it."

She nodded.

"Where's that ambulance?" Doug said to the driver.

"On the way. Ten, fifteen minutes, they said."

"Can I have your belt?" Doug asked.

"Huh? Sure."

Doug wrapped the man's belt around Laura's upper thigh and cinched it tight. *Hopefully that will stop the bleeding.* "Laura, how are you doing?" he asked.

"Okay, I guess." Pain pinched her eyebrows together.

"Did you hit your head?"

"No. My side really hurts, though."

Doug gently touched her left side, where her biking shirt was torn over her rib cage. This looked like another point of impact with the truck's bumper.

Laura grimaced in pain. "Ow, that's really sore."

"Shit," Doug said. "You may have fractured a rib, too."

"It kinda hurts to take a deep breath."

"Just breathe easy, honey."

Laura was now leaning forward, propped up on one arm, her other hand holding her side. "Doug, it feels harder to breathe," she said, looking up at him, pain and fear now glazing her eyes.

"It'll be okay, Laura. Help is on the way," Doug said, but he watched in horror as she struggled to take in a deep breath. The muscles in her neck worked as she strained to inhale. "Just try to take slow, easy breaths, Laura."

"Why is it so hard?" she asked. "What's happening?"

"I'm not sure," Doug said, but he began wondering about her fractured ribs. About how a jagged rib might easily have punctured and collapsed her lung.

Doug looked over at the truck driver. "Lemme have your phone."

The big man tossed him his phone and Doug dialed.

"Buchanan Med ECU," came the reply.

"Put me through to whoever's in charge," Doug demanded.

"This is Dr. Sorenson. Who is this?"

"This is Dr. Landry. Listen, I've got a critical situation here. You need to send the Life Lion out to Memorial Lake. We're at the park's east exit, along 443. My wife was hit by a truck and can't breathe. Please hurry."

"Roger that, Dr. Landry. We're mobilizing now."

Doug turned back to Laura. "How's it going?"

"Bad, Doug." She was panting, eyes wide with fear. "I can't catch my breath. Help me."

"Laura, help is on the way. They're sending the helicopter. Hang in there."

"Okay," she said, but her breathing only worsened.

Suddenly, the idea of a tension pneumothorax flashed across Doug's mind—one of the most dreaded complications of a traumatic rib fracture. That would explain a lot. With every breath she took, air would leak out of the punctured lung into the chest cavity, causing a buildup of intra-thoracic pressure that would choke off all venous return to the heart and drop her blood pressure to zero. If that were happening, she would die in a matter of minutes—long before the helo got there.

She reached up and grabbed his arm and fixed him with a look that verged on panic. "Help me." She was gasping now.

There was only one treatment for a tension pneumo. If he were wrong about the diagnosis, he would likely kill her. He had no CXR to go on, no pulse ox, no EKG, nothing. Not even a frickin' stethoscope. Not to mention, he didn't have any surgical equipment on hand.

Laura's eyes rolled up in her head as she lost consciousness. She slumped forward into his arms. He felt for a carotid pulse—it was very weak. And her jugular veins were horribly distended. All this fit with a tension pneumo.

"What's wrong with her?" the truck driver asked.

"Not now," Doug snapped, frantically searching for ideas. "Do you have any knives or sharp things," he said, speaking so fast, his words ran together.

"I don't think so."

"In your truck?"

"I'll go look." The man ran to his truck.

"Hurry," Doug called after him. He gently laid Laura down on the gravel shoulder. "Laura, hang in there—don't you leave me." But clearly, she wasn't hearing him right now.

The man came back with a fishing tackle box. "It's all I could find."

Doug opened the box and rummaged through it. Not much of use. Lots of fishing lures and weights and bobbers and hooks and fishing line. No knife, though. Finally, on the bottom, he found needle-nosed pliers. He grabbed them.

"Will that work?" the driver asked.

"I don't know." Doug wiped some black grime from the pliers. With his left hand, he quickly searched around Laura's side for a place in between her ribs where the most damage was. "Laura, this is gonna hurt a bit." No response. He readied the pliers in his right hand.

A large hand fell on his right arm. "What are you fixing to do?" the driver asked, voice taut with fear.

"Leave me alone," Doug said, staring down the man. "Haven't you done enough harm for one day? I'm a doctor—I know what I'm doing."

"I sure hope so," the driver said and released his arm.

Me too, thought Doug. He inserted the tip of the pliers into her side and pushed hard until he felt a distinctive pop as he cleared the chest wall musculature. Nothing happened. Laura groaned, but this still wasn't what he was looking for. Could he be wrong about his diagnosis?

With the pliers still buried in her side, Doug opened them and twisted them back and forth, trying to make a bigger hole in her chest wall. This was the part that would either fix her or kill her.

"Are you crazy, man?" the driver exclaimed, and looked away.

Doug ignored him and continued to work with the pliers. Finally, there was a loud whistling noise as the trapped air came rushing out, confirming his diagnosis. Thank God—there *was* a tension pneumo and he had just relieved it.

Thirty seconds later, Laura opened her eyes. Her blood pressure must've improved enough to allow her to regain consciousness. Her breathing also seemed much easier.

"Well, I'll be damned," the driver said.

Relief washed over Doug, but it was short-lived. *Where's that chopper?* He knew Laura needed some real treatment—like a chest tube, for starters. He also knew the tension pneumo would just re-accumulate in short order.

Several minutes later, he heard the thumping of helicopter blades in the distance, followed by the distinctive whine of the Life Lion's enclosed tail rotor. Soon he made out the navy blue copter's shape as it cut through the air toward them.

"Hang on, Laura. Help is on the way." She was laboring to breathe again and her eyes showed renewed fear and pain.

The driver ran out onto the road and waved his arm, signaling the chopper. It set down in a nearby field. Two paramedics hopped out and ran over with a litter. They loaded Laura onto it. She had slipped back into unconsciousness.

Doug accompanied them as they carried her to the chopper and loaded her on. "We'll take it from here, sir," one of the paramedics yelled to him over the engine's roar. He started to close the helo's side door. "Meet us at the hospital."

Doug grabbed the door. "I'm not leaving her side. She's got a tension pneumo and a bad femur fracture with a tourniquet. She needs oxygen and a chest tube."

The older paramedic stared at Doug, then at Laura. "Bring him," he barked. "We gotta move."

Doug climbed in and they shut the door. The pilot pushed the throttle to the max and the Life Lion spun its mighty rotors up to speed. "Hang on!" the pilot yelled back to them above the roar of the turbo-charged engine. He pulled back on the cyclic and the helo leapt into the sky. The trees and grass blew wildly in the fierce downdraft and Doug could see the driver below, shielding his eyes, looking up at them. Once they attained sufficient altitude, the helo tilted forward and the blue devil began its sprint to the med center. Within the chopper's belly, Laura Landry fought for her life.

CHAPTER 22

Friday, 3:00 p.m.

Doug tried to ignore the queasiness he felt in the pit of his stomach. The Life Lion rocketed forward and the ground below sped by at an alarming speed. *Best not to look out.* The aircraft's intense vibrations shook him to the core. He held Laura's hand, but his eyes were glued on the pulse ox. It read a lousy 83%.

Bob Kruger, the chief paramedic on board, also glanced worriedly at the monitor. He was talking over his helmet radio, but Doug couldn't hear him. Kruger turned to him. "I'm afraid I'm going to have to intubate your wife," he said loudly.

Doug could barely hear him above the whine of the turbine jet engine and thump-thump of the rotors. "I don't think that's a good idea," Doug said, trying to project his voice toward Kruger.

"Her sat. is dangerously low," Kruger said, nodding at the portable pulse oximeter. It now read 80% and was blinking in alarm status.

"I see it." Doug knew Laura was running out of time. He looked out the window and tried to get his bearings. Up ahead, not far, he spied the distinctive twin turrets of the Hotel Hershey. "We're almost there," Doug said, a glimmer of hope forming.

"Look, I follow orders from my doc on the ground." Kruger tapped his fingers to his radio headset. "And he's telling me to tube her. Tube her now." The paramedic reached for his intubation equipment.

Doug grabbed his arm. "Listen to me!" he shouted. "You've got to listen to me."

The paramedic glared at him. "You promised not to interfere. That's why I—"

"I'm pretty sure she's got a tension pneumothorax," Doug said, leaning in as close as he could to Kruger. "If you tube her and give positive pressure ventilation, you'll kill her. The tension will get worse."

"Tension pneumo . . ." Kruger became still, staring back at Doug. "If you're wrong and I don't tube her, she may die."

"I know," Doug said. "Give her as much oxygen as you can— put her on a non-rebreather, if you have one. And tell the pilot to hurry and land this damn thing."

Kruger gave him a thin, grudging smile. "Sure hope you're right."

CHAPTER 23

Saturday, 8:00 a.m.

Chip navigated the confusing layout of the radiology department, following signs to the basement where the MRI suite was located. He could tell he was getting closer because the signs began to change. They now contained the stark warning, *DANGER: HIGH INTENSITY MAGNETIC FIELD*, coupled with pictographs of a cell phone and a pacemaker with red null icons over them. Looked serious.

Finally, he found the MRI control office. He peered through its small window and saw Kristin, clad in a white lab coat, seated at the console. The door was slightly ajar; he knocked and stood in the doorway.

Kristin turned to him and smiled. "Allison. Come on in. I'm almost finished."

Chip walked into the small control room. "You were right, this place isn't so easy to find." His eyes were drawn to the monitor, displaying high-resolution coronal slices of someone's brain. "What're you working on?"

"Emergency CVA scan."

"Stroke?" He looked at the black and white video observation monitor, saw a patient's legs sticking out of the huge circular magnet in the scan room.

"Right," she said. "Trying to determine if it's hemorrhagic or not, to see if they should anticoagulate the patient."

"Sounds important." Chip studied the images on the screen to see if he could draw on his rudimentary neuroanatomy knowledge to identify familiar structures or abnormalities. Of course, he reminded himself, he hadn't completed that course. He could make out the cerebral cortex and ventricles, but that was about it.

"The scan should be complete in—" she checked the console "—about ten minutes."

"Good. Mueller's expecting us at nine o'clock."

"What do you think he wants?" she asked.

"He didn't say exactly, but I'm sure it has something to do with his patient."

"Chandler, you mean?"

"Yes, and what we saw," Chip said.

"Let me just set up the final scan protocol." She fiddled with some knobs on her console.

Chip studied her as she worked. Her face was serious and it dawned on him that she wore no makeup—this would explain why sometimes he thought of her as plain. But other times, like when she smiled, he thought she had a natural, fresh-faced look with pretty blue eyes and nice skin. He leaned against the front wall and absently examined the weave of her braid; the pattern seemed different from what he recalled. Did she change it every day?

"Hey, Allison! Be careful what you touch."

Startled, Chip stood up straight. "Sorry."

"That's the emergency quench switch." She pointed at a circular, palm-sized push button mounted on the front wall close to where his hand had been.

"Does that turn it off?" he asked.

"Yes, but it's not the normal power down switch. It's a safety cutoff used only in dire circumstances."

"Dire circumstances? Sounds a bit dramatic."

She flashed her blue eyes at him. "Look, I know the machine looks like a CAT scanner, but it's really very different. Dangerous, in some respects." She pointed at the observation monitor. "The big arched structure you see there houses the superconducting magnet; it's cooled by liquid helium to just about absolute zero." She tapped the temperature gauge mounted on the wall—it registered minus 270 degrees Celsius. "That's the magnet temperature."

"That's cold, all right," Chip said. "What's the redline indicate?"

"The temperature above which superconductivity is lost. If the quench switch is thrown, the helium is vented to the roof and out to the atmosphere. Without the liquid helium to cool it, the ferrous/niobium magnetic core quickly warms up and is no longer superconductive. The resulting electrical resistance generates a tremendous amount of heat, causing the magnet to partially melt or suffer irreparable damage. The liquid helium itself costs $5,000 per charge. If the magnet is damaged, the expense may run into the hundreds of thousands."

"Holy crap!" Images of explaining that one to his father ran through Chip's mind.

"Exactly," she said.

"Hang on, though; back up a step. Why bother to use a *superconducting* magnet in the first place, if it's so much trouble?"

"It produces a much stronger magnetic field," she said. "This one is rated at five Tesla—that's about as big as they get. The bigger the magnet, the better the scan."

"All right, I get that," Chip said. "But I still don't see the big danger."

"Two things, really. There's the helium itself. And then there's the missile effect."

"Did you say *missile*?"

"Yes," she said. "If a ferro-magnetic object is brought into the magnet room, it will accelerate rapidly and fly through the air toward the magnet, becoming a high speed projectile, or missile."

"Yikes," Chip said.

"The patient or tech might be in the way and get pinned to the scanner—or worse, crushed."

Chip looked from the monitor to her. "Are you serious?"

"I'll show you pictures sometime. That's what the emergency quench switch is all about—to deactivate the magnetic field as quickly as possible. But it's only to be used in life-threatening situations."

"All right. But you said the helium is dangerous too." Chip couldn't help smiling as he added in a high, squeaky voice, "Makes you talk funny?"

"Ha-ha. No." She looked at him sidelong, her lips compressed as if she'd eaten something sour. "Remember, it's *liquid* helium—it's a completely different animal than gaseous helium, like in a kid's balloon. First, it's extremely cold—almost down to absolute zero. If the helium reservoir"—she pointed to the tank-like structures on either side of the magnet—"develops a leak or the vent malfunctions, the helium will rapidly boil out and lower the temperature drastically, potentially freezing anyone in the room. Second, a small quantity of boiling liquid helium will produce large amounts of gaseous helium, enough to displace the oxygen and asphyxiate anyone in the room. It also generates high pressure—enough to seal the door shut."

Chip gazed thoughtfully at the door. "Nasty."

The console beeped and Kristin hopped out of her chair. "Good, the scan is done. I wasn't sure the patient would hold still enough, but he did. Want to help me move him back onto the litter?"

"Sure."

Her expression turned serious again. "You can't go into the magnet room with any metal."

"I'll take my belt and watch off. And my cell phone."

"Cell phones are pretty useless down here anyway. There's permanent magnetic shielding built into the walls, plus when the scanner is active, high level radio frequency interference is produced. You don't have any internal metal clips or wires from surgery in your body, do you?"

"Not that I know of," Chip said, placing his metallic items on the desktop.

"Pacemakers or defibrillators?"

"No," Chip said, but then he saw her smirk.

Kristin swiped her badge and opened the thick metal door, which swung on oversize hinges. She led him into the magnet room and closed the door behind them. Chip heard a lock engage automatically and raised his eyebrows at her.

"That's so no one can wander into the magnet room by mistake when I'm in here tending to the patient," she said. Kristin pushed one of the buttons on the magnet housing and the gantry with the patient slowly retracted from the magnet. Chip fought off a wave of claustrophobia as he noticed how snugly the patient's body fit into the tunnel inside the magnet. Finally, the patient—an old man with a grizzled growth of beard—completely emerged. He stared up at them with unseeing eyes, drool leaking from one side of his mouth. Chip shuddered and looked away.

The two transferred the frail old man back onto the litter; it was easy—his body was rigid and he couldn't have weighed more than 120 pounds. But, as far as Chip was concerned, he couldn't leave this nasty place soon enough. Maybe it was just the tight quarters, packed with the whirring hi-tech equipment that he had gained a newfound respect for—or maybe it was the sickly smell wafting up from the man. He couldn't put his finger on it, but something about this MRI room was definitely unsettling.

CHAPTER 24

Saturday, 8:00 a.m.

"You gave me quite a scare back there." Standing by her bedside, Doug squeezed Laura's hand; it felt limp and cold within his fingers. The ventilator continued to hiss and whoosh regularly, her chest rising and falling in time with it. Multiple monitors beeped quietly in the background. Wan light seeped through the window as the eastern sky brightened with the approaching dawn.

They would be coming for her soon.

Doug's eyes kept sliding back to Laura's monitors; the art-line registered a beautiful pressure waveform and the pulse ox was also a reassuring 98%. He massaged his sore neck—collateral damage from his earlier attempts to catch a few zees on the cramped foldout recliner bed.

The events of the last twelve hours were little more than a nightmarish blur in his mind. The helicopter ride had been especially tense; Doug had been terrified that Laura was going to die. In the ER, he'd watched a number of surgical doctors attend to Laura in rapid succession, starting with one of the CT surgeons, who confirmed the diagnosis of a tension pneumothorax secondary to fractured ribs. He placed a chest tube, which finally stabilized Laura's breathing, and pulled Doug aside afterward.

"I've never seen a tension pneumo diagnosed in the field and treated successfully with a pair of fishing pliers," the veteran trauma surgeon told him. "Gutsy move, man. Hope she doesn't die of infection."

The vascular boys came in next, and determined that Laura had a lacerated femoral artery that needed immediate attention. They did remark that the belt around her thigh had been life-saving. The orthopods also evaluated Laura's leg and said they would book the case first thing in the morning to repair the fractured femur after her vascular issues had been addressed.

Then Laura had been whisked off to the OR and spent half the night in surgery while they performed the delicate femoral artery repair. She'd been returned to her bed in the ICU around three in the morning. Doug had been waiting for her. She was still heavily sedated, intubated, and on a ventilator. She also sported a new art-line and central line. Blood hung alongside wide spectrum antibiotics. The medical doctors said she had lost a fair amount of blood and they were transfusing her. But her BP had stabilized, her kidneys were responding and she was making good urine. All in all, things had gone about as well as could be expected. They'd told him she had a good prognosis. All that remained was to fix her fractured femur.

The sun peeked above the distant ridge, bathing the valley in golden light. Doug squeezed Laura's hand again. "You need to get better, Laura. Don't worry about the kids. I've got it all taken care of. Teddy said he'll do all the housework and Steven promised to keep his room neat." Doug felt a lump growing in his throat. "And Anthony said he'd take care of the cooking as soon as he gets home from kindergarten." He bent over and whispered in her ear, "I don't know what we'd do without you." The tears came now, but he wasn't finished. "I don't know what *I'd* do. You know I love you." His voice broke and he squeezed her hand tightly.

Several folks in OR garb had joined him in the small ICU room. One of the nurses, a woman with a kind face, put a hand on his shoulder. "Is it time already?" Doug asked, turning to look at them. She nodded and gave him a warm smile.

One of the other OR nurses, more businesslike, said, "Don't worry, we'll take good care of her."

"I know you will." Doug wiped his eyes.

A young man with a Steelers OR cap stepped forward, hand outstretched. "Hi. You must be Mr. Landry. I'm Dr. Novacinski—one of the anesthesia doctors."

Doug shook the man's hand. He looked so young.

"How'd this all happen?" Novacinski asked as he readied the Ambu bag for transport.

"Biking accident," Doug said woodenly, watching them hook up Laura's EKG and art-line pressure tubing to the transport monitor.

"You don't say. I bike a fair amount myself," Novacinski said. "It's a jungle out there."

Doug was hoping he was at least a third year resident. *Please God, not an intern.* "Who's your attending?" he asked.

Novacinski's jaw tightened at this. "Zimmerman. But I'll be taking direct care of her."

"Zimmerman's a good man," Doug said.

"Do you know Dr. Zimmerman?"

"Yes," Doug said. "I'm on staff here."

"Oh." Novacinski failed to completely hide the surprise in his voice. "What department?"

"Anesthesia."

Novacinski's face reddened. "Gotta go," he muttered and started to wheel Laura's stretcher out of the room. "Mustn't keep the surgeons waiting."

"Wait," Doug said and grabbed the side rail of the stretcher. He took Laura's hand and squeezed it gently. "It'll be okay, Laura. I'll be right here waiting for you. I love you."

Doug could've sworn he felt a weak squeeze in return this time, and he thought he saw her eyelids flutter a bit, as well. He felt the burn of new tears as they wheeled her out.

CHAPTER 25

Saturday, 8:20 a.m.

The woman's vitals were surprisingly stable despite what she had been through recently, Dennis Novacinski observed as he hooked his patient up to all the monitors. He reached for the propofol syringe, then thought better of it. *Better use Amidate,* he thought. *This lady's pretty sick and just my luck, her husband's a frickin' anesthesia attending.* He drew up 20 ccs of Amidate.

"Why are you using that?" asked the nursing student on rotation with him.

"How about you tell me," Dennis said, never failing to miss an opportunity to pimp the students. Kind of like his attendings would grill him. "I'll give you a hint. The generic's etomidate." He didn't want to be *too* much of a prick with her—she *did* have a nice ass, after all.

"Is it a new muscle relaxant?" she asked in her high, squeaky voice.

"No . . . I'm going to give it *first.*"

"A narcotic?"

"No." How she ever got into nursing school, he didn't have a clue.

"I give up. I never heard of it."

"Didn't you read the chapter in Miller on induction agents?"

She hit him with her big brown eyes. "I was busy," she said, and then looked sheepishly at the floor.

"Look, Miss, uh—"

"It's Tara."

"Look, Tara, we don't have a whole lot of time to talk right now. After we get things settled, I'll try to teach you some stuff. Emerick's gonna come storming in here any minute, wanting to go."

"Emerick?"

"He's the ortho attending. You haven't heard of Emerick?"

"No, not really."

"Well, here's the skinny." Dennis glanced around furtively. "Orthopods are basically all cut from the same mold. They're always in a goddamned hurry and then they're cranky to boot, because they feel everyone is trying—on purpose, mind you—to slow them down. As if *their* time is more precious than anyone else's. Of course, that's when they even realize there *is* anyone else. And Emerick's got a bad case of it."

"Great," Tara said with zero enthusiasm.

The door flew open, ending their exchange. Dr. Emerick stomped in, his oversize orthopedic wader boots clumping on the floor. "Jesus, Novacinski, put her to sleep, for chrissakes! I've been watching you through the window at the scrub sink for the last ten minutes. Quit yakking it up with your lady friend there and get to work. Who's your attending and where the hell is he?"

"Zimmerman," Novacinski said, glancing over at Tara. "But I'm an R3 and can induce on my own."

"Well, by all means then, do it. Just hurry the eff up."

"Sir, yes sir," Novacinski fired back with a crisp military salute. He injected the syringe of etomidate into his patient's IV.

Thirty minutes later, with Mrs. Landry playing by the book and things proceeding smoothly, Dennis Novacinski started to relax. Time to make good on his promise to teach his nurselet something.

"So, Tara, what do you think?"

"Cool," she said. She was seated on a little metal stool next to Novacinski, who sat on the more comfortable chair at the controls of the anesthesia machine. He noticed her pretty brown eyes again.

Novacinski stood and offered her his seat. "Want to drive the bus?" he asked.

"Sure," she said with glee. "If it's all right?" she added in a lower voice, shooting a look over the drape toward Emerick.

"Yeah, it's fine. Don't worry, I'll help you."

They switched seats. Emerick seemed preoccupied with the large power drill he was using to ream out the central shaft of Mrs. Landry's shattered femur. The drill made a horrible racket only to be outdone by the Rover machine as Emerick suctioned the blood pouring out of her bone.

"Want to squeeze the bag?" Novacinski said.

"Definitely," Tara replied.

Novacinski reached around her to turn off the ventilator control, his arm brushing against her bare arm as he did. He squeezed the two-liter rubber bag a couple of times. "Here, you try." He guided her hand to the bag.

She looked up at him. "How hard?"

"Not too hard," he said, scooting his stool closer so he was only inches away from her. He put his hand over hers and helped her squeeze the bag. "Just like I was doing."

"Like this?"

"Perfect. I see you have a good gentle touch."

Tara giggled but kept squeezing.

Novacinski reached out with his other hand, so that his arms now encircled her—the patented Novacinski squeeze play, perfected over years of residency with many female nursing students—and pointed to the monitor screen. "Here, you see? You're breathing for her. That's the end-tidal CO_2 waveform. Every time you relax on the bag, the patient exhales and we get a CO_2 wave."

"Very cool," Tara said. "It's reading thirty-six. Is that good?"

"Yes, perfect," he said, sampling the fragrance of her dark hair. "It means you're squeezing the bag just right."

"Thirty-six what?" Tara asked. "No wait—don't tell me," she said excitedly. "Centimeters of water, right?"

"You got it." No need to correct her and tell her it was millimeters of mercury. What's a little metric system difference between friends?

Emerick was now grunting as he hammered a long flexible rod up the proximal end of Mrs. Landry's busted femur.

"What's he doing now?" Tara asked as she stood on her tiptoes to peer over the drape.

"He's placing the IM rod—intramedullary rod," Novacinski said, admiring her tight ass again.

"Seems like he's banging it awfully hard," Tara said.

"I was thinking the same thing," Novacinski said, and chuckled. "Well, that's ortho for you. Hey, are you going to the med student party in the kennels tonight?"

"Yeah, I think so. Are you—"

One of Novacinski's alarms rang out, interrupting her.

"What's that?" she said.

The end-tidal CO_2 monitor was registering a low value of 25.

"Am I doing something wrong?" Tara asked nervously.

"Probably just squeezing the bag a little too much," Novacinski said. "Let's put her back on the vent." Novacinski flipped the appropriate switches and the ventilator came back to life. "There, that should fix it."

"It's now fifteen. Is that better?" she asked.

"No, of course not," Novacinski said, nettled. An end-tidal CO_2 of 15 was definitely an odd reading. Perplexed, he stood and

Tara quickly vacated her seat at the controls. He looked closely at the screen to make sure he wasn't missing anything. He still had a waveform, it was just markedly reduced. EKG and oxygen saturation still looked normal. But the CO_2 now read 10!

"What's wrong?" Tara said.

Novacinski shushed her with one hand and quickly followed the sample line from the patient's breathing tube that carried the exhaled gasses to his monitor. Sometimes these little tubes got kinked or became disconnected, leading to bogus readings. The sample line looked fine. *Shit!* The patient's endo tube also looked fine—again no kinks, secretions, or disconnects. Novacinski heard her pulse rate rising—she was now definitely tachycardic, with a rate of 120 bpm and climbing. *Shit again.* He cycled the BP monitor, hoping for some sign of stability. Thank God, her O2 sat. was still 100%.

Novacinski's mind raced. What could possibly have caused her end-tidal CO_2 to drop that fast? He drew a blank. Then it dawned on him—an air embolus. She could easily be sucking air into her bloodstream via her shattered femur. That would lead to a drastic fall in CO_2. But his monitor was equipped with a mass spectrometer system as well as infrared gas detection. Novacinski quickly pushed some buttons on the monitor and studied it for the presence of nitrogen in her exhaled gasses—the hallmark of an air embolus. The mass spec read out only the three gasses he was using:

Oxygen: FiO2—.50
Nitrous Oxide: FiN20—.42
Desflurane—.08

No nitrogen. This effectively ruled out an air embolus.

The sat. started to drop. 95%. Novacinski quickly shut off the nitrous, thereby boosting the inspired oxygen to 100%. What was happening?

He surveyed the operative field. Emerick continued to hammer away viciously at the IM rod and alternately take C-arm x-ray pictures. Blood was spattered everywhere. Novacinski felt a wave of nausea descend upon him. What should he do? BP came back as 85/50. Not horrible, but down significantly from what it had been minutes earlier.

"Did I do something wrong?" Tara asked, her voice even more high pitched. "I'm sorry."

"Not now," Novacinski snapped at her. "I'm trying to think."

"Should we call for help?"

"Shut up," he said forcefully. Tara started to cry. Novacinski gave ephedrine to treat the lower BP and turned down the ventilation, then threw in a couple of Hail Marys. He hoped things would turn around soon. He didn't want to hit the panic button just yet and have all the residents laugh at him in Morbidity and Mortality conference. He cycled the BP machine and watched the sat. monitor intently, hoping against hope for a good sign.

The oxygen sat. began to drop precipitously.

CHAPTER 26

Saturday, 8:45 a.m.

"So, he called you at home?" Kristin asked.

"Yes, early this morning," Chip said.

"What did he say?"

"He said that it was vitally important that he talk to us—he used that word, vitally. But he said he didn't want to get into it on the phone."

"How would Mueller even know your number?" she asked.

"I'm a hospital employee, I guess." Chip pushed the button for the basement and the elevator door slid shut. "He said he wanted to talk to you too, but didn't know your name. I told him—hope you don't mind?"

"No, no, that's fine."

"Thanks for coming, by the way."

"Sure," she said. "Sorry about the emergency scan."

"No problem. It was interesting—especially the MRI stuff."

They got off the elevator and headed left, down a narrow corridor, their footsteps echoing loudly on the concrete floor.

After several minutes, Kristin asked, "You sure this is the way?"

"Yes. I know it's in the basement . . . somewhere."

"That's comforting." She frowned at him. "I didn't know this place was so big. Or had so many stupid hallways."

"Relax, I know where I'm going. I used to pass his lab on the way to the animal research facility."

She stopped walking. "Animal research? What were you doing there?"

"Nothing—just basic grad school stuff."

"They don't have dogs, do they?" Her voice definitely sounded accusatory.

"Naw, just rats and mice," he lied. Chip figured he wouldn't bother to mention that some med students—including himself—practiced surgery on dogs. "Let's keep going—I think we're close."

"It's kind of spooky down here," she said.

"Well, I don't want to creep you out, but we just passed the morgue."

"Great, thanks for sharing. That accounts for the yucky smell, I guess."

"Yep," Chip said. They walked a bit farther in silence. "And here it is," he announced, stopping before a glass door stenciled with frosted white letters identifying the room as:

Postmortem Laboratory
Director: Gunter Mueller, MD, PhD

Chip opened the door for her and walked in behind her.

Dr. Mueller was standing behind what appeared to be his secretary's desk. He looked up and came around the desk to greet them. "Thanks for meeting me." He extended his hand.

After they shook hands and introduced themselves, Mueller ushered them back to his office. "Have a seat," he said, gesturing to several chairs as he walked behind his desk, which was piled high with books, manila folders, and mail. He didn't sit, but immediately began to pace.

Chip pulled up a chair for Kristin, then took his own seat. Mueller kept running his fingers across his bald scalp while pacing, but remained silent.

"That was a very interesting lecture," Chip finally said.

"Thank you." Mueller stopped and studied them with hazel eyes that danced behind his spectacles. He cleared his throat and started to speak, but abruptly stopped.

"How can we help you, sir?" Chip asked.

Mueller walked over to the large bookcase behind his desk, then turned toward them. "I'm told you two were the last to see Chandler—the patient in Room 237—before he . . . uh, before he left the hospital."

"Yes, we saw him run out," Kristin said.

Mueller stared at them; his eyes appeared larger than normal, magnified by his thick glasses. "Let me be blunt," he said. "Are you sure he—Chandler—was the one who overpowered and killed that poor nurse? I mean, he was literally on death's door. His heart was basically ruined and so were his kidneys and lungs."

"It was him, all right," Chip said.

"Last I saw him," Mueller said, "the day before the incident, he was unconscious and on full life support."

"It was definitely him." Chip whipped out his phone and started pushing buttons. "I think I might even have a picture."

"What?" Kristin asked incredulously. "What are you talking about?"

"*You* took it," Chip said.

"Huh?" Kristin rolled her chair closer to Chip and leaned over his cell phone. "Let me see that."

"Here, look." Chip held his phone out.

"Oh, right," Kristin said, relaxing. "The birthday picture."

"Watch. Let me blow it up." Chip fiddled with the phone some more. "In the background, you can clearly see Room 237. And through the window, you can see Heather standing at the bedside. And you can see Chandler sitting up in bed. The resolution's not that good, but it sure looks like his eyes are open."

"That's amazing," Kristin said. Chip handed the phone to Mueller.

"Hmmm," Mueller said as he studied the picture. "Okay, I see he's awake. But he still should've been weak as a pussycat."

"Dr. Mueller, he was far from weak," Chip said. "He tossed me aside with ease—I'm close to two hundred pounds—and threw me into the countertop. Look at this bruise on my head."

Mueller peered over his glasses at Chip's forehead. He sat back down and ran his hand over his head before continuing. "Look, I couldn't say this in front of the press—you saw how it went out there. They're like sharks in the water when they smell blood."

"Say what?" Chip asked.

"This treatment could save thousands, potentially tens of thousands of people every year. People that don't need to die." Mueller's eyes were blazing. He stood again and resumed pacing. "I can't let them shut me down now. Now that I am so close. You understand."

Chip exchanged a worried glance with Kristin.

Mueller continued. "I had some misgivings about this one—this Chandler."

"Misgivings?" Kristin said.

"No one was ever as far gone as he," Mueller said.

"What do you mean?" Chip asked.

Mueller stopped and fixed them with another intense stare. "He was dead, I tell you. Dead!" He slapped his hands down on his desk.

Chip began to have a bad feeling about this. "So, shouldn't you be happy with your technique? I mean, isn't that the point, to keep people alive?"

"Yes, yes." Mueller waved the comment away. "But his *EEG and*—" Mueller stopped; his brow furrowed, then a pained expression crossed his face.

"What about his EEG?" Chip asked.

"Protocol dictated we get pre-procedure and post-procedure EEGs on each successive day, looking for any changes in brainwave activity. I've always insisted on proper documentation—I'm a stickler for details. A researcher must be thorough, if nothing else."

"*What* did it show, Dr. Mueller?" Chip said.

"I've never seen an EEG like Chandler's. Very strange."

"In what way?" Chip coaxed.

"It showed something abnormal in the ultra-high frequency range—the gigahertz range—that I'm completely unfamiliar with."

Suddenly Kristin leaned forward in her seat, head slightly cocked. "Can you describe it?" she said, a coolness coming into her voice.

"Well, yes." Mueller stroked his chin. "Actually, there was a dead zone—pardon the expression—an *absence* of signal in one particular band of the high frequency range where normally there is substantial activity. Most peculiar. I have several literature searches pending, but so far as I know, this has never been described before."

"And its significance?" she asked.

"I have no idea."

"Did any of the other subjects show this?" Kristin said, her eyes shining with an intensity that Chip had not seen before.

"No," Mueller said, and looked away.

CHAPTER 27

Saturday, 9:30 a.m.

"Hey, what was that bit about the electroencephalogram back there?" Chip asked as they headed back down the concrete hallway from Mueller's office.

"What do you mean?"

"You got all weird when Mueller mentioned the EEG part. What do you know about EEGs?"

Kristin abruptly stopped walking and gave him a strange look, as if she were focused on something distant. "Nothing—it's just a hunch," she said. "And it has more to do with photography, not EEGs. I need to get home."

"What's your big hurry? Smokey?"

"There's something I gotta do."

"Listen, I've been thinking and—" Chip paused and tried to read her expression. She still had the distant look in her eyes. "Well, since you're into photography and I'm an amateur astronomer—I may have mentioned that."

She smiled politely at him and fidgeted with her ponytail, but he could tell she wasn't paying attention.

"Well," he continued, "there's this meteor shower this weekend. We should take pictures or something, and—"

"Yeah, sure," she said.

"The weather's supposed to be good. Wait, you really want to?"

"What?" she said.

"Take pictures."

"Huh? Yeah." Kristin was definitely preoccupied.

"You know," he said, struggling to keep the irritation he felt out of his voice, "you just agreed to sleep with me."

"*What?* Are you crazy?" She grimaced. "Listen Chip, I gotta go."

"Okay, okay."

"Besides, I have plans with Chris this weekend."

"Chris?"

"My roommate."

"Oh."

She hesitated a moment, then looked away. "We're going to celebrate our one-year anniversary. He's taking me out to El Sol, downtown."

"Terrific." He should've seen this one coming.

"Talk to you later," she said and continued down the hall. "See you Monday."

"Yeah, whatever," he muttered.

Kristin walked away so fast that she almost decked the gray-haired cleaning lady who was mopping the floor outside of the morgue.

CHAPTER 28

Saturday, 9:30 a.m.

The hospital-wide intercom blared to life. "Code Blue, Main OR complex, Room 16. Code Blue, Main OR, Room 16."

Doug had been fitfully dozing in the cramped lounge chair and the page startled him awake. He didn't know which OR room they had taken Laura to, but he had a bad feeling about the page. He checked the clock on the wall. She'd been gone about an hour and a half—just enough time to get into trouble. He knew he shouldn't assume the worst—the med center was a busy place with lots of operating rooms; they worked on very sick patients around the clock. Nonetheless, Doug got up and raced toward the main OR.

It didn't take Doug long to figure out where the emergency was; Code Blues have a knack for attracting lots of people, especially at a teaching hospital. Doug pushed open the door into a scene of controlled chaos and his worst fears were confirmed in an instant. Laura's surgeon, Emerick, was there, blood smeared all over his gown and dripping from his gloves, screaming at the ortho resident. The resident was doing chest compressions. Novacinski and his attending, Zimmerman, were at the head of the bed, pushing drugs. The patient on the operating room table was his wife.

A hush came over the room as Doug entered and everyone stared at him.

Emerick turned to face Doug and cleared his throat. "Everything was going smoothly—I just about had the IM rod in place," Emerick said, his speech uncharacteristically halting. "Here, look at the x-ray. Rod's in perfect position." He pointed to the monitor of the portable C-arm machine. "We were thinking about closing. And then all hell broke loose." Emerick shook his head, then nodded to the head of the table. "See if Zimmerman can tell you what happened. I'm still trying to figure it out."

Doug made his way through the throng of med students and nurses to the anesthesia end of things. One of the nursing students appeared to be crying; Doug ignored her. He gave Novacinski a quick glare before turning to Zimmerman. "What happened, Chuck?"

"She arrested several minutes ago," Zimmerman said. "Not exactly sure why yet. Look, Doug, maybe you should leave." Zimmerman dropped his eyes. "We're in the middle of a code here."

"Keep running it, Chuck. I'll stay out of your way." Doug pushed by Novacinski, to the head of the table. He tried to take in the totality of the situation. He did his best not to look down at Laura's face; it was critical that he not view the patient as his wife. He focused on the monitors. The EKG was flatline. Pulse ox wasn't registering and the A-line wave showed weak pulsatile flow with each chest compression. *Shit—not good.* Doug turned to Novacinski. "What happened first?"

Novacinski hesitated, scratching his head.

"Think, damn it," Doug snapped at him. "What was your first sign of things going bad?"

"Her CO_2 level dropped," Novacinski got out. "Dropped fast."

"Probably a fat embolus," Doug muttered.

"Yeah, that's our working diagnosis," Zimmerman said. "But you know it's a bear to treat."

"Acute right heart failure is the problem," Doug said.

"Right," Zimmerman said. "Novacinski, go get the transesophageal echo probe."

Novacinski looked relieved to have an excuse to leave the OR; he made a rapid exit.

The monitor's alarm sang out. The EKG now showed V-tach. Doug noted that it was a pulseless V-tach—again a very bad sign.

"Shock her again," Zimmerman shouted to the ortho resident.

The resident applied the paddles to Laura's chest and fired them; her body jumped off the bed like a ragdoll. Doug turned away from the sight and stared at the EKG monitor. Thankfully, the V-tach broke into a rapid sinus rhythm.

"We need to get the pulmonary artery pressure down," Doug said, feeling sick to his stomach.

"Yes, I know," Zimmerman said. "We're running Nipride and just started vasopressin. We also sent for prostaglandin from the pharmacy—should be here shortly."

Several minutes later, Novacinski came back, wheeling the portable ultrasound machine. "I have the prostaglandin, too," he said, holding up a small IV bag.

"Good. Run the drip," Zimmerman said as he placed the long, snake-like black probe into Laura's mouth and shoved it deep into her esophagus. He adjusted some controls on the unit and a ghostly image of Laura's heart appeared on the monitor screen. Her right ventricle was massively dilated, consistent with a pulmonary embolus.

The ultrasound could not identify the source of the embolus, but Doug believed that fat globules—not the standard blood clot—were the culprit. The fat globules could've been released from the marrow of Laura's femur when Emerick had hammered the IM rod into place. The only good thing was that her left ventricular function appeared to be OK.

The next ten minutes saw the prostaglandin drip started, several more doses of epinephrine given, and multiple additional countershocks applied. Doug couldn't shake the feeling of hopelessness settling over him. Laura's right heart was still failing due to sky-high pulmonary artery pressures caused by a presumptive fat embolus. All the medical maneuvers in the world would be unlikely to overcome this.

And then a flash of insight blazed across Doug's mind. He grasped Zimmerman's shoulder and locked eyes with him. "Chuck, she *needs* to be on bypass."

"Doug, I already thought of that. You know we can't get her to a heart room, crack her chest, and insert all the cannulae in time."

"How about percutaneous cardiopulmonary support?" Doug said.

"I've read about it," Zimmerman said, looking doubtful. "But I've never actually *tried* it."

"Me either. But do you have the necessary equipment?"

Zimmerman paused, his brow furrowing deeper. "Yeah, I'm pretty sure we do. We can access the femoral artery and vein quickly and place her on peripheral cardiopulmonary support to decrease the strain on the right heart. It just might work."

"We need to do it fast, though," Doug said.

"Novacinski," Zimmerman shouted. "Go to the workroom and tell the techs to bring us all the peripheral bypass equipment—femoral cannulae, membrane oxygenator, and mini-pump. Move your ass! And go find Dr. Moyer, too."

An hour later, Laura's pressure was still 50/30, despite being on full PCPS and receiving massive dose pulmonary artery vasodilators. Even with the assistance of Dr. Moyer, the facility's expert on extracorporeal membrane oxygenators, they were running out of tricks. Doug began to face the inevitable. He blinked back tears.

Someone tapped Doug on the shoulder. He turned to look into an older man's hazel eyes. The man looked familiar, but with his surgical mask up, Doug couldn't place him. However, he soon recognized his voice.

"We need to talk, Dr. Landry. My name is Gunter Mueller."

CHAPTER 29

Saturday, 10:45 a.m.

"There's only one way I'll sign your form," Doug said as they pushed the litter with his wife on it down the long hallway through the basement corridors, past the morgue.

"You're hardly in a position to bargain, Dr. Landry," Mueller said.

Doug met the pathologist's gaze. "I can help you. She's extremely critical and I am familiar with her physiology."

"This is highly unorthodox." Mueller returned his stare. "Family members generally are a great hindrance and usually do nothing but get in the way."

"I *need* to be with her," Doug insisted.

"You may cause us to *lose* her. Do you understand that?"

"Yes," Doug said. "I'll take that chance."

Mueller hesitated. "All right, Dr. Landry," he said with a sigh. "But I give the orders here. Understood? I'm in charge."

"Of course," Doug replied.

"There will be no committee or group discussion here."

"I understand completely," Doug said.

They came to a stop in front of the glass doors with the frosted lettering. The Postmortem Laboratory. "Here we are," Mueller said and reached out to unlock the door.

"One more thing," Doug said.

Mueller gave him an exasperated look. "What now, pray tell?"

"Call me Doug."

Mueller cracked a thin smile at this as he swung the door open. "Okay, Doug it is."

They wheeled Laura Landry into the PML.

CHAPTER 30

Saturday, 11:30 a.m.

Kristin tossed her purse on the kitchen table and went directly to the crate. "Sorry that took so long," she said as she unlatched the door.

Smokey emerged from his crate, stretched briefly, and made his way to the French doors leading to the backyard. "Now, go pee," she instructed him as she opened one and Smokey walked out onto the small flagstone patio.

Smokey hesitated and looked back at her.

"Hurry up." She waved a hand at him.

Smokey stood his ground and sniffed the air.

"No—don't even go there. I know it's beautiful out and you've been cooped up all morning, but there's something I have to do."

Reluctantly, tossing his head in indignation, Smokey padded down the cement steps into the yard to do his business.

Kristin marched over to the closet to get her camera bag. Her Nikon camera felt particularly weighty in her hands.

Smokey was soon scratching at the back door to be let in. She opened the door and Smokey sauntered by, brushing up against her thigh. "Don't you give me that look," she said, but Smokey did anyway. "Oh, you're impossible." She set her camera down on the kitchen table, sighing. "All right, you win. Go get your leash. I'll get my sneakers." Smokey scampered away to the laundry room.

As she knelt on the tile floor to tie her sneakers, Smokey returned with his leash in his mouth. "You should've heard what I heard today. About the crazy man. If I told you, you wouldn't believe it. And guess what. Chip asked me out again—to stargaze, I think. Interesting, huh? I said no, of course. I still don't think I'm ready for any of that."

She stood up and looked at Smokey, who was now staring at her. "What? You think I'm being stubborn? What would *you* know? You've never had your heart broken, have you?" She paused to regard him. "I didn't think so."

Kristin and Smokey set off down the driveway, Smokey tugging on the leash with extra exuberance. "Hold your horses there, bucko. Listen, just a short loop today. And promise me, no more sad eyes, okay?"

* * *

Several hours later, tingling with excitement, Kristin stood in the small room in her basement that functioned as her darkroom, her gloved hands bathed in the soft red glow from the safelight in the corner. Three large plastic trays partially filled with her developing chemicals were lined up on the countertop before her, next to her enlarger. The time had come.

Her hand trembled as she grasped the photographic print paper with sponge-tipped plastic tongs and dipped it into the first tray—the developer. She agitated the paper gently in the solution and bent over to take a closer look. As if by magic, a ghostly image appeared on the paper, intensifying and darkening with each passing second. Kristin never grew tired of this part. Soon, she could make out Chip's face as he blew out the makeshift birthday candle.

She dunked the paper into the next tray—the stop bath—that would stop the darkening process. Finally, the print went into the fixer to arrest the developing process. After thirty seconds, she retrieved the glossy print and clipped it on a wire strung across the sink. Again she leaned in to take a closer look at the wet print. Even in the dim light, she could clearly make out Chip's handsome face. Her eyes fixed on his hair. Soon she saw a distinctive aura radiating from his head.

Smokey growled upstairs, cutting her inspection short. She cocked her head to listen. The black Lab growled again. Then he was silent. *Probably just annoyed at squirrels scampering about in his backyard.* Kristin turned her attention back to the new print.

Bingo! Her intuition *had* been right. Her heart pounded. She could make out Heather through the window for Room 237 in the background of the photo. She studied Heather's image. There, rising from Heather's blonde hair, was her aura—faint, but clearly visible.

Chandler was visible as well, sitting up, eyes open. At first glance, she didn't think she could see any aura around him. But here in the dim, weak light thrown off by the safelight, she couldn't be sure. Maybe his aura was hiding in the shadows or obscured by the white bedsheets? She yanked the print from the wire and held it up close to the safelight. She tilted it back and forth, hoping for a better angle, then put her nose right up to it. Searching. Searching for any hint of an aura coming from Chandler. Her blood ran cold as it finally hit home. There was no aura.

She would have to examine the print under a bright white light and probably use her magnifying glass to be sure, but she felt sick with foreboding. What did it mean?

She recalled hearing about this phenomenon many years ago in a lecture she had attended on Kirlian photography. She had pretty much forgotten about it, relegated it to the weird science folder in her mind, until Mueller had stirred up her imagination. What was it he had said this morning? "An absence of EEG signal in the gigahertz range." She had never imagined in her wildest dreams that she would ever be holding a photograph like this in her hands, let alone one she'd taken and developed herself. Let alone knowing the subject in the photo and what they suspected he was capable of. Chills raged up and down her spine.

Kristin reached down to her hip and fumbled with her phone case. Damn—it was empty. She must've left her phone upstairs. Her mind raced. Should she run up and call Chip? Or should she dry the print and examine it with a magnifying glass in the daylight first?

And then she heard the cellar staircase creak.

CHAPTER 31

Saturday, 1:00 p.m.

Three flights of stairs to his apartment—seemed like four or five today, Chip thought as he trudged up them. After much coaxing and cursing, he finally got his key to turn the persnickety lock and release the deadbolt. One of these days, he was sure, the key would simply snap as he twisted it. This image nearly brought a smile to his face. *Then there'd be a real fuck-storm,* he thought. *You wouldn't want to be around to hear that.*

He tossed the keys onto the floor inside the door and they skidded several feet across the nondescript gray surface before coming to rest at the base of an old iron radiator. The landlord had insisted the flooring was hardwood, but it could have been made of anything. The only noteworthy thing about it was that it was slightly tacky.

Chip flopped down on the sofa, sinking deep into its soft, lumpy bulk, and swung his feet over the sofa's threadbare arm as he flipped on the TV. He had the whole weekend off for a change. No goddamn work. No goddamn school. What wasn't to love? He should've been on cloud nine, except he wasn't—because he had no goddamn plans, either.

Did every girl *have* to have a boyfriend? Was that, like, an immutable physical law of the entire universe? Because it sure seemed like it. He tried to push his sneakers off by pushing on the heels with his toes; one got stuck and he had to pry it off with his hands. He flung it across the room. Oh well, he reasoned. Better he found out about Kristin now, before he got all wrapped up in her. *One-year anniversary! What's up with that? That's like practically being married.* Chip couldn't recall ever going out with a girl for a year. Maybe six weeks. In fact, the last relationship he'd had, with Michelle, lasted only about six days.

Chip had first noticed Michelle about a year ago; she'd been at the Hershey Fitness Center, working out like nobody's business—a regular dervish on the elliptical machine. She was gorgeous by anybody's standards. He remembered being completely mesmerized by the sight of her—her long brunette hair bouncing gracefully as she pumped her thighs up and down; her tight-fitting gym suit; her skin glistening with a light sweat.

He had attempted to catch her eye, but it was difficult; Michelle always had lots of male attention. So he had contrived to use the lat pulldown bar just as she was finishing with it. But the best he could come up with was some lame small talk and all he discovered was that she was a PSU nursing student who hailed from somewhere around Pittsburgh.

Finally, out of the blue, several months later, she actually spoke to him. He had been busy sucking down brewskis at a Christmas party in one of the student nurses' dorms. He still recalled pretty much the entire conversation, even though he had been half loaded.

* * *

"Hi Chip, it's good to see you."

Chip fought the urge to turn around and look behind him for another Chip; he was shocked Michelle knew his name. "Hey Michelle. Great party."

"Thanks," she said. "Haven't seen you much at the gym."

"No." Chip knew Michelle didn't miss many days at the gym. "It's finals time and I've been hitting the books pretty hard."

"That's good."

They both had to talk fairly loud to be heard over the stereo that was blasting out Christmas tunes along with the usual rock and roll. Right now, the Trans-Siberian Orchestra was cranked up.

"Yeah." As usual, Chip was at a loss for words around beautiful women. "Uh, the keg's still going strong." He nodded toward the sliding glass doors; beyond them, on the patio out front, the keg rested in a large metal bucket filled with ice. "Do you need any more beer?"

"No, I'm good."

"I think I need a refill." Chip turned to head for the sliders.

"Hang on, Chip." She lightly touched his arm. "There's something I want to ask you."

Chip froze in his tracks. "Huh?"

"I've been studying hard, too," she said. "We have a pharmacology final coming up this Tuesday and—"

"I have one, too," he said.

"I'm having a tough time with it—you know, all the stupid drug names sound alike. It's very confusing." She tilted her head slightly and gave him a little lost girl look. She also proceeded to brush her fingertips up and down his arm.

"Yeah, I know what you mean," he said, swallowing hard.

"Maybe you could teach me? You know, tutor me?" Her face brightened adorably.

"I'd love to—I mean, I'd be happy to." Chip wondered whether he was dreaming or maybe just had had too many beers. "Just tell me when."

"That's *so* nice of you." She took a sip of beer from the plastic cup she held, its rim smudged with her lipstick. "Hey, if you hear anything about our test, maybe you could let me know that, too?"

"All right. I'll keep my eyes and ears open."

"It would mean a lot to me." She was now standing really close to him. She leaned into him—so far that he had to reposition his feet to keep his balance. He felt the softness of her breast pressing against him. Her fragrance washed over him. The room felt very hot. She caressed his arm again and stared seductively into his eyes. Then she whispered into his ear, "I really suck." She pulled back briefly and pursed her lips into an oval. Then, smiling mischievously, she added, "At pharmacology, that is."

* * *

Alone on his living room sofa, Chip massaged his forehead, now pounding painfully; by now he should have known better than to stroll down *that* particular memory lane. Someday he would get that blasted memory out of his head. It always led to the inevitable, *How could I have been so stupid?* or, *Did I really think she was into me?* or, *Am I really that weak?*

He distracted himself by trying to come up with something to do; anything to take his mind somewhere else. He ignored the siren call of his "friends" under the kitchen sink. Let's see, what else? The meteor shower didn't interest him anymore. He had seen every movie on TV. You could only watch *Lord of the Rings* so many times. Then he remembered it was playoff season and the Phillies were still on the hunt for a postseason berth. Last year, he'd followed baseball religiously, knowing all the latest player trivia and scores and standings. A lot of things had changed since last year. This summer, by contrast, the season was a complete blur to him. He checked his phone—the Phils were playing the Cards this afternoon at four-thirty. Perfect.

Maybe he'd head over to Arooga's and watch the game on the big screen? Kinda lame going alone, though. He could call Victor or Steve. But Chip didn't feel much like hanging out with his old med school buds right now. They would still call from time to time and invite him to parties, but let's face it—most didn't want to associate with him anymore. And who could blame them?

His new friends called to him again. He'd been seeing a lot of them recently. They weren't very talkative, but what they lacked in social skills, they made up for in dulling pain and blurring memories. He sensed they were bad news and knew he'd have to part ways with them at some point. Just not now; he still needed their camaraderie. So it was decided: he'd settle in, have a couple of refreshments, and watch the game here in the cozy comfort of his apartment.

His phone rang. Caller ID said it was his mom. "Hello."

"Hi, honey. Guess what? Your father and I are on the turnpike heading to Hershey."

Shit! Double shit! Images of recent ugly family scenes came to mind, with painful words like disappointment, disgrace, and embarrassment being hurled about.

"We thought we'd take you out to celebrate your birthday."

"Oh."

His mother continued in her happy tone, completely unfazed by his total lack of interest. "It's okay if you have plans. Let's see—we'll be there in about an hour. We can probably make a late brunch or lunch and have you back home by three. Or if you have a date, you're welcome to bring her along. So, what do you say?"

"Sounds great, Mom," he said, resigned to his fate.

Chip hung up and cursed his bad luck. Could the weekend get any worse? Soon, though, he realized he had some business to attend to in the kitchen. The half-empty bottles clinked accusingly as he retrieved them from underneath the sink. He carried his precious load to his bedroom, where he stashed the tequila, vodka, and whiskey bottles in the back of his closet—way back, behind his neglected running shoes and beat-up telescope—and tossed an old Phillies sweatshirt over them.

Returning to the sofa, he flipped on the TV and hunkered down, waiting for his parents to arrive and hoping his dad would be in better spirits than the last time.

CHAPTER 32

Saturday, 2:00 p.m.

"So son, how's life treating you?" Chip's dad was a big man; he served up a crushing handshake when Chip took his extended hand.

"Good, Dad," Chip said, extricating his hand.

"Give your mother a hug," he ordered.

Chip hugged his mom, then led them into the living room.

"Your place looks nice," his mom said, although Chip could see her eyeing the plates stacked up on the end table. He and his mom sat on the sofa while his dad remained standing.

"Job going well?" his father inquired.

"Yep," Chip replied.

"Your mother told me about that nurse getting killed and you being a witness and all." His father started walking about the room with his hands clasped behind his back.

"Yeah," Chip said. "Very freaky."

"Did you know her?" his mother asked.

"No, not really," Chip said.

"Did they catch the son-of-a-bitch?" his dad asked, his square jaw set.

"I don't think so," Chip said.

"Hmmm." His father paused, appearing uncomfortable. Apparently he was at a loss for words, which was unusual. "Hey, I've been talking to some people and, uh—"

"That's good," Chip muttered.

"They might be able to help you get back into school. Med school. You know, next year, after all this blows over."

"Sure." Chip didn't share his dad's feelings that a cheating scandal like his would blow over anytime soon.

He stared at Chip and looked as if he wanted to say more, but again, uncharacteristically, he held his tongue. Finally he said, "I need to use the head."

"It's down the hall, to the right," Chip said.

After his dad left the room, his mother, never a big fan of open confrontation, said in a hushed voice, "Why is it so hard for the two of you?"

"I don't know, Mom."

"Can't you at least try to get along?"

"I am."

"He's trying to help you. Don't you see that?"

"Yes."

"You hurt him quite a bit when you—"

"Yeah, I know, Mom."

"Your father loves you, Chip."

"I can tell."

His mom frowned, then changed the subject. "Meet any new girls yet?"

"I'm working on it." Chip cracked a fake smile for her.

"Well, Auntie Jean just told me about a niece of hers—Jennifer. Sweet girl. And unattached. We have to get the two of you together, when you come home for Thanksgiving. You *are* coming home, right?"

"Yes, Mom, I'm coming. You don't have to fix me up with girls, you know."

"I'm just trying to help."

His father returned. "So, did you two decide where you want to go for dinner? I'm partial to the Hershey Country Club, myself."

"Sounds good," Chip said, fighting back a yawn.

His mother nodded. "Sure."

"Helen," his father said, "why don't you go down and wait in the car. Chip and I will be down in a minute."

Oh shit, Chip thought. He watched his mom's face squirm with anguish, but Chip knew he was on his own here. She would never try to intervene when his father used *that* tone of voice. She shot Chip a worried look as she left. Chip figured he was in for it; his dad would surely lay into him without his mother around to be the buffer. At least it looked like Chip wouldn't have to wait long to find out the particulars.

His father straightened to his full six foot two height, leveled a stare at him, and cleared his throat. He tried and failed to sound nonchalant. "You're not drinking anymore, right?"

There it was, right out of the blue, on the table. His dad had never been one to mince words. He was one of those "say what you mean and mean what you say" kind of guys.

"No, Dad. I'm good."

"I mean, we talked about this, right? I don't want to go sticking my neck out for you, if you're—"

"No. It's not a problem anymore."

His father cleared his throat again. "I saw some beers in the fridge."

Chip looked at the floor and squeezed his fingers together so hard they hurt; he was intent on not smiling. His intuition had been dead on, concerning his dad's snooping habits.

"Do you think this is funny?" his dad asked.

"No," Chip said, biting his lower lip.

"No more hard stuff, right?"

"No, Dad. Just a little beer now and then." Chip lifted his head and locked eyes with his father. "To go with the Phils."

Several expressions played across the older man's face as he worked to digest this. Finally he settled on a weak smile. "We should go to a game. Just the two of us, like old times."

"Yeah, sure," Chip said, trying to add as much sincerity as he could muster.

"If the Phils make the playoffs, I'll buy us some real sweet seats on StubHub and we'll go."

"Sounds good." Chip breathed a sigh of relief—ugly family scene averted. "That is, if I can get off from work. I can't screw up this job."

"Right." His dad dropped the hard stare and took a seat across from the sofa. "Look, Chip, I can see that you're hurting. Things will work out. It's time to move on—time to stop beating yourself up over this."

Now Chip was at a loss for words. He sat there and played with the loose stuffing in the sofa arm. He didn't think he had ever seen his dad in this caring father mode. But his dad wasn't finished.

"I understand that a woman can be hard to resist—almost impossible. I get it. You may find this hard to believe, but I was young and foolish once."

Chip had to admit he *did* have trouble imagining this.

"Let me tell you a little story. Once, a long time ago, I snuck off the base—I was stationed at Fort Bragg at the time—in the middle of the night to meet up with your mother. We went out for a midnight drive and then grabbed a late night snack at a downtown bar. I was lucky—we didn't get caught. They would've thrown me in the brig and probably court-martialed me."

"I never heard that story before," Chip said, genuinely impressed.

"There was a time," his dad continued, a distant look coming into his eyes, "I would've done anything your mother asked of me."

Chip wasn't sure, but it seemed that his dad's eyes were becoming moist. Or maybe it was just the light? Chip *was* definitely sure he had never heard his father open up like this before.

"Luckily, we were never tempted to do anything else against the law." They shared a smile at this. His father placed his hands on his thighs and stood. "Well, we need to get going—can't keep your mother waiting forever. She'll think I'm beating the tar out of you, by now."

"Right," Chip said, rising.

"One last thing, Chip," his father said as they headed toward the front door. "Next time, just make sure you're in love."

CHAPTER 33

Saturday, 2:00 p.m.

Kristin tensed and held her breath, straining with every fiber of her being to listen. Another creak of the steps. Was it Smokey? No. It sounded like a person—no clattering of nails on the wooden steps. Besides, the dog would scamper down the stairs, not slowly descend. Kristin tried desperately to keep her cool and figure out what to do. She reached out and locked the door, but didn't feel much safer, cooped up in a darkroom not much bigger than a large closet. She heard footsteps approaching and the hair rose on the back of her neck.

There was a loud knock on the door. She jumped and a small cry escaped her lips. She stood there motionless.

"I know you're in there," a man's voice said on the other side of the door. She didn't recognize the voice. "Open the door. I just want to talk."

The voice sounded mellow, not the voice of a crazed house intruder bent on murder. "About what?" she said, trying hard to keep the tremor out of her voice.

"Your interest in photography," he answered. "I share your interest."

What? How bizarre is this? Let's just have a casual conversation about hobbytime with the man who broke into my apartment. "What do you want?"

"I want your film." The doorknob rattled. "Open the door, Kristin."

"No, I won't. Go away. How do you know my name?"

"We've met before. Don't you remember? In the ICU."

The ICU? Could it be? "I'm calling the police," she lied. "Who are you?"

"I think you know."

"Just go away," she said, her trembling now uncontrollable as her fear amped up exponentially.

"I will. But first, I need the photograph you just developed—the one with me in it."

Holy Mother of God! Kristin could hardly believe her ears. *It's Chandler. How is that possible? How could he possibly know what I'm doing here? Am I going crazy?*

"I'm waiting." His voice no longer sounded mellow.

She frantically looked about the room for a weapon.

"We need to talk," he said.

"Just like the nurse in the ICU," she said, her voice ranging into the hysterical. She picked up the enlarger and hefted it.

"I won't hurt you. Now, open the door."

She didn't answer, but adjusted her footing and gauged the distance to the door. She wasn't going down without a fight.

"Suit yourself," he said.

A fist smashed through the door, splintering the old wood.

Kristin screamed.

His hand groped for the handle and locking mechanism.

She swung the enlarger, still plugged in, and whacked his hand with it as hard as she could. Glass lenses smashed and blood flowed from his hand. Chandler howled in pain, but amazingly didn't withdraw his hand. She hit him again. Somehow, he still managed to unlock the door and then turned the handle. She screamed again.

He was in the room. His bloody hand grabbed the enlarger and flung it aside. He stared at her menacingly.

She reached wildly for one of the plastic trays. Somehow, he beat her to it and swatted it away, the stop bath splattering all over the wall.

He was on her in an instant, wrapping his hands around her neck and driving her against the wet wall. He towered over her and outweighed her by at least a hundred pounds. His face was bathed in the red light and his eyes looked like glowing coals, radiating evil. She knew it was over.

Suddenly, there was a vicious snarling noise and in a blur of fur and fangs, Smokey leapt onto Chandler's back. The dog buried his fangs into the nape of his neck. Chandler shrieked in pain and released his death-grip on Kristin. He groped behind him, trying to get a good hold of Smokey. When that failed, Chandler spun around and slammed Smokey into the wall, knocking him off his back. The dog sprawled on the floor. Chandler's hands went to the back of his neck and came away dripping with blood.

Smokey quickly scrambled to his feet and came at him again, jaws snapping ferociously, saliva flying. The dog's ears were flattened down and his lips were stretched back in a frightening grimace that Kristin had never seen before. Smokey went straight for Chandler's throat. Chandler threw up his arms to protect his face and neck, warding off the dog's attack as he maneuvered for position. Keeping Smokey at bay with his mangled hand, Chandler reached down with his other and grabbed the ruined enlarger. He swung it hard right into Smokey's teeth; the dog yelped in pain.

Kristin grabbed the tray of fixer and flung the contents at Chandler's face. The liquid scored a direct hit to his eyes; he howled and rubbed them furiously. Smokey leapt again. This time, he found Chandler's soft throat and clamped his jaws tightly together. Bright red blood spurted out from between Smokey's clenched teeth. Chandler's scream was quickly squelched by the dog's viselike grip, but Kristin saw his eyes detonate with pain. Turning away from the gruesome sight, she ran out of the darkroom and raced wildly up the stairs. The steps were slippery—with blood? She went down hard and smacked her right knee, sending bolts of pain through her leg.

In the kitchen, she grabbed her cell phone from the table and dialed 911. She could hear Smokey growling fiercely as the struggle continued downstairs.

"Nine-one-one operator. State your name and the nature of your emergency."

Kristin was breathing so hard, she could barely speak. "There's a man trying to kill me," she got out in gasps. Just then, she noticed a bloody serrated knife on the floor under the table and shuddered.

"Calm down, ma'am. What is your name and address?"

Kristin told her.

"Does he have a weapon?"

"No. I don't think so." She glanced again at the bloody knife, striving to comprehend its meaning.

"Do you know him?"

"Are you sending someone now?"

"Yes. Officers are on the way. Do you know the intruder?"

"Sort of. His name is Nick Chandler. He was a patient at the med center."

"Where is the intruder now?"

"In the basement. Fighting with my dog." Although, at the moment, she didn't hear any growling.

"Sit tight. Help is on the way."

"I have to go check on my dog."

"Ma'am, do not go back to the basement! Under any circumstances. Do you hear me?"

Kristin tossed the phone down and reached for the knife.

CHAPTER 34

Saturday, 2:30 p.m.

Kristin's hands were shaking so badly, she almost dropped the steak knife. Fear swelled within her, threatening to engulf and incapacitate her. The only thought that drove her on was that Smokey was downstairs with that monster. And he might need help. Wiping the wooden handle of the knife on her jeans so it wasn't so slick, she walked to the top of the basement stairs and listened.

Silence. No more growling. No sounds of a struggle. Nothing. *Maybe I should wait for the police? Or just get out of the house?*

She crept down the steps, trying hard not to make a sound, the knife held high, her breathing accelerating. The liquid on the stairs—definitely blood—was becoming tacky and her sneakers made a squelching noise, no matter how quiet she tried to be. She paused at the bottom of the stairs and listened again. Still nothing—other than the rushing of blood in her ears.

The door to the darkroom was closed.

A cloying, musty smell hung in the basement air. She almost slipped on the smooth cement floor; it was covered in blood, making footing treacherous. She couldn't be sure, but didn't remember so much blood being here on her way out. She approached the door and put her trembling hand on the doorknob, knife held in the other. How long had it been since she had called the police? Five minutes? Ten? Her time sense was all screwed up. *Should I wait?*

She turned the knob gingerly and tried the door. It didn't budge. She pushed and the door grudgingly began to open, but only inches. Something was blocking it. She peered in through the gap and, as her eyes adjusted to the dim light, she realized Smokey lay on the floor with his back up against to the door. He wasn't moving. She couldn't see anything else in the room.

Kristin pushed on the door again, sliding Smokey's body farther across the floor. The door was now open a foot, but she still couldn't see behind the door. She took a deep breath, her heart hammering painfully in her chest, and squeezed into the darkroom, knife ready as she carefully stepped over Smokey.

No sign of Chandler.

She quickly knelt down beside Smokey. His fur was all matted down and looked particularly eerie in the red safelight—it looked wet, but not red, as if he had just taken a dip in the creek. But she knew it was blood. She hoped to God it was Chandler's blood.

She set the knife down and ran both hands gently over Smokey's body. She could feel faint evidence of breathing in the dog's chest, but it was very shallow. She felt his heart fluttering beneath his ribcage; it was beating ridiculously fast. Soon, her hands discovered a large gash wound in his belly, and her heart sank. The bloodied knife now made sense.

As her eyes adjusted further, she could see Smokey was looking up at her. She could read the fear and pain in his eyes. She gently put his big head in her lap and stroked his soft ears and face. She felt the tears come. "You're going to be all right. You're going to be all right, Smokers."

Smokey let out a faint whimper.

"You saved me, Smokey. You saved me."

Smokey's breathing became increasingly labored; he was taking only tiny breaths now.

Where are the police? Shouldn't they be here by now?

"Hang in their buddy. Help is on the way."

Smokey gave her a sorrowful look, then closed his eyes.

She caressed his big head.

"I'll take you for a walk," she said softly.

Smokey's one eye opened a little at this.

"As far as you want to go," she said, her tears flowing freely. "You can chase whatever you want."

Smokey's eye closed.

"Even the fox," she blubbered.

The dog let out a shuddering exhalation and then stopped breathing altogether. "Don't go, Smokey," she pleaded, her face touching his. "Please don't go."

His head went limp in her lap.

"I love you, Smokey. I love you." She hugged his big furry body tightly and wept uncontrollably.

CHAPTER 35

Saturday, 5:00 p.m.

"Why don't you take a break?" Mueller asked.

"I'm fine," Landry said.

"You don't look so fine. And I caught you dozing right now."

"I was just resting my eyes."

"Listen, Dr. Landry—Doug." Mueller touched his shoulder and pointed to the monitors. "Everything is stable right now. I've got this. Besides, you haven't slept in God knows how long."

"Really, I'm fine. I just need some more coffee."

"Listen, I have a sofa in my office. It's right around the corner. You can lie down, just for a couple of hours. I promise to call you if anything changes or I need you." Mueller took Landry's elbow and escorted him to the door. Landry hesitated, worry still clouding his features. Mueller felt genuinely sorry for Landry and his predicament. He again put his hand on Landry's shoulder. "We'll be able to take better care of her if we both get some rest," he said with as much reassurance as he could manage. "I'll take a break after you," he added, although he had no intention of doing so. "We can spell each other."

Reluctantly, Landry let himself be led to Mueller's office.

Before Mueller could disengage from him, Landry turned to face him. "Do you think it will work, Dr. Mueller? Do you really think she has a chance?"

Mueller saw the fear in the man's eyes and again pitied him. What it must be like to have such a relationship, he could only imagine. He weighed his words carefully, not wanting to give the man any false hope. "She's a strong woman, in good health. If anybody has a chance, she does."

Landry appeared satisfied. Mueller turned to go.

"Dr. Mueller, wait—one last question."

"Yes, Doug," Mueller said, trying hard to remain patient.

"You don't think she'll turn out like the last one, do you?"

"No. I think he was—uh . . ." Mueller searched for the right word. "An aberration. His MRI was quite unique."

Landry was already lying down on the couch. "Okay, good."

Returning to the lab, Gunter Mueller took a generous sip of coffee from his mug, adjusted his bifocals, and examined Laura Landry's monitors. She had gone on cardiopulmonary bypass around noontime and things were proceeding smoothly—in spite of her husband's unwanted presence. Her core temp was now registering a frosty 25 degrees Celsius. Dark blood drained from her right atrium via large clear tubes as big as garden hoses—the venous cannula—and flowed into the heart-lung machine. Here, a series of centrifugal pumps acted to generate sufficient pressure to perfuse her entire body. Finally, Mrs. Landry's blood passed through the membrane oxygenator, and the resultant bright red arterial blood, freshly resupplied with oxygen, was pumped back into her body via the aortic cannula.

These next twenty-four hours would be critical; Mueller would not leave her side for a minute, no matter what he had told Landry. The pathologist drained his coffee. The daunting task that lay ahead, with the prospect of many more cups of coffee, didn't bother him in the least. Nerves tingling with excitement, body brimming with energy, he was fully engaged. To say he loved this part would not have been far from the mark. This was no dull autopsy report detailing the cause of death. He was, for the first time in his life, practicing real medicine where the results actually mattered. Hopefully, if all went well, he could begin the rewarming process tomorrow afternoon. And then would come the tricky wean from CPB and the attempt to restart her heart.

What Mueller didn't need was any interference—however well-intentioned—from Dr. Landry, who was proving to be one stubborn fellow. Health care providers and their families always made the worst patients. With any luck, Landry—who looked totally exhausted—would soon be fast asleep and out of his hair for a while.

Mueller turned away from the monitors and gazed at the patient in front of him. She appeared very peaceful, but he knew this was not the case. She was actually deeply unconscious in a thiopental-induced coma; her brainwave monitor was practically flatline. However, all the tubing and equipment could not hide the fact that she was a striking woman. Landry was a lucky man, Mueller thought. Or at least he had been.

CHAPTER 36

Saturday, 6:00 p.m.

Chip walked into the smoky, dimly lit room and was immediately assaulted by the familiar noise level—all standard fare for this establishment. *Welcome to Arooga's Sports Bar and Grill,* he thought, and paused to let his eyes adjust while he looked around for Victor.

"Hey, Chip," Victor called, rising from a nearby table to wave him over.

"Hey, Victor," Chip replied, walking over to slide into the booth across from Victor.

"Good to see you," Victor said.

"Yeah, you too."

Arooga's was doing its usual brisk business—cheap beer by the pitcher never failed to draw a crowd, all ostensibly there to watch sporting events on the multiple TVs mounted around the room. The Phils and Cards were going at it on the high definition flat-screen on the near wall.

"Wasn't sure you'd show," Victor said.

"You said it was important," Chip said. "Besides, you rescued me from my parents."

"Glad to help out."

"So, what's the big news?" Chip asked. "You ace another test?"

"Very funny," Victor said, frowning. "You're gonna want to hear this. Trust me."

"Let me be the judge of that."

"Just listen. I was here this past weekend with a couple of buds watching a Flyers game. It was Anderson's birthday and we were doing shots."

"Fascinating," Chip said. Ryan Howard was up to bat.

"Well, your old anatomy lab partner shows up at the next table."

"Gorman?"

"Yes, Gorman. So anyway, he joins us and we drink some more."

"Okay," Chip said. Victor never could tell a short story. A waitress with some hard to ignore cleavage came over and Chip ordered a beer from her.

"Well," Victor continued, "Gorman gets pretty drunk and starts talking."

"That's different."

"Just wait. Guess who he's seeing now?"

"I dunno," Chip said, seriously rethinking his decision to come here. "The man in the moon?"

"No. Michelle."

"How nice," Chip said, hiding his surprise. "I'm happy for them."

"He said he's really into her."

"Victor, so what! Tell me something I care about."

"Okay, try this. Remember Jill? Michelle's roommate?"

"Of course I do," Chip said.

The waitress brought his beer and leaned over more than necessary to set it on the table in front of him. Chip obliged her with a stare. "Need anything else?" she asked.

"No, we're good." Chip turned back to Victor. "Jill and I both got tossed. For cheating."

"And you might also remember," Victor said, "that Jill got a hundred on the pharm final. How do you think *that* happened?"

Chip shrugged. "Beats me. Look, I've been through this a thousand times." He took a large gulp of his beer, hoping to ward off a headache.

"Humor me here," Victor said. "First off, why don't you tell me what you recall from that day."

"All right," Chip said with resignation. "The day before the nursing pharmacology final, they passed out the test to the med students to let us see it. Then they collected them at the end of class."

"Right," Victor said. "That's the way I remember it too."

"Not realizing they had numbered the copies," Chip said, "I foolishly decided to keep mine, so I could show it to Michelle."

"So you could sleep with her."

"You don't *know* that," Chip said, quickly becoming irritated. "I admit my intentions weren't the noblest. Do you want to hear this or not?"

"Go on," Victor said, his smile a tad smug.

"I gave her the test that same night and—"

"Did she sleep with you?" Victor asked.

"No."

"Blow job?"

"No."

"I heard she gives *monster* blow jobs."

"Give it a rest, Victor. Anyway, the next day, after the final, thanks to an anonymous *tip*—" Chip paused to stare at Victor "—I get called into the dean's office. They find a copy of the test in my anatomy book and I get tossed. End of story."

"Except you haven't explained how Jill got a perfect score."

"I'm guessing that after I gave the test to Michelle, she must've shown it to Jill."

"Wrong," Victor said emphatically.

"What do you mean, *wrong*? How would *you* know?" Chip's head was starting to ache.

"Turns out, I *do* know," Victor said. "Gorman told me."

Chip digested this. "What did he say?"

"That *he* gave the test to Jill."

"*What?* Why would he do that?" Chip exclaimed, although the implications were beginning to sink in.

"Getting the picture?" Victor said. "Turns out, you weren't the only one who lifted a copy of the test that day."

"So, let me get this straight," Chip said. "Gorman feeds Jill the test—she's dumb enough to memorize the answer key exactly, including the bogus cheater question. Then Gorman plants the test in my anatomy book—would've been easy enough to slip it in during a lab session. He tips them off and I get caught red-handed. Jill and I both get tossed. The rest is history."

"You got it," Victor said. "Told you you'd be interested."

"That fucker," Chip said, shaking his head in disgust.

"Guess what Michelle got on the test?"

"I don't know," Chip said. "How would *you* know?"

"God, you can be dense—try to keep up, here. *Gorman* fucking told me. She got a 92, just making the cutoff for an A."

"Holy crap," Chip said. "Man, was *I* played. Michelle gets her A, Gorman gets BJs for life, and Jill and I take the fall."

"Clever, huh?" Victor said. "Answer me this, though. How come you never turned Michelle in?"

Chip thought for a moment. "Good question. I've asked myself the same thing—many times. It wouldn't have changed anything. I mean, the fact is that *I* cheated. And I got what I deserved."

"I guess you're right."

Chip took another large swig of beer. "And here, all these months, I thought *you* were the one who ratted me out."

"You didn't really, did you?" Victor said, sounding fairly earnest.

"I wasn't sure what to believe or who to trust."

"But, I *told* you I didn't do it," Victor said.

"Who's dense now, Victor? *Why* would I believe you, if I thought *you* were fucking me over? Besides, who's getting the highest damn test grades now?"

"Good point." Victor paused, his brow furrowed in thought. "How about this, smartass: if I wanted to get you so bad, how come I haven't turned you in for coming into work fried?"

"What're you talking about?" Chip's head was thumping now, with this trip down memory lane. "Oh, get off it—just that once."

"Jesus, Chip. You come in wasted all the time."

"I do not."

"Yeah, you do." Victor took a drink of his beer. "Even your new pal, Kristin, says you do."

Chip didn't respond; he focused on playing with his beer bottle.

"What's up with *that*, anyway?" Victor asked, peering up from his mug.

"Nothing. We're just friends."

"Are you *seeing* her?"

"No. Why?"

"Just wondering."

"I mean, I wouldn't mind," Chip said absently.

"Are you *kidding*?"

"She has a boyfriend, anyway."

"What happened to your *standards*?" Victor said, affecting a look of horror.

"What're you talking about?"

"I mean, she's got a nice little bod, but she's no Michelle or Heather. Just saying."

"I think she's cute," Chip said, determined not to sound defensive.

"She's a bit bohemian."

"What do you mean by that?"

"You know, *hip-pee* girl."

"Whatever."

"They say her dog is better looking."

"Go fuck yourself, Victor," Chip said and stood up to leave.

CHAPTER 37

Saturday, 8:00 p.m.

Doug jolted awake. The dim light and unfamiliar surroundings were disorienting, but he soon realized he was lying on the couch in Mueller's office. He checked his watch and saw he had only been out for about an hour. His alarm wasn't set to go off for another hour. He sat up and massaged his stiff neck. What little sleep he had gotten didn't make him feel any better; in fact, he felt worse, if that was possible.

Doug resisted the urge to run back to the lab; Mueller had made it clear he preferred to work solo. Instead he lay back down on the hard sofa and tried hard to relax. It was impossible; his mind was engaged in a heated internal argument.

The logical part of his brain, the medical, rational, unemotional part, kept whispering to him like some infernal devil inside his head, not giving him a moment of peace. *Look, she suffered a massive fat embolus, went directly into right heart failure, was pulseless for twenty minutes while they did CPR. Not to mention her rib fractures and recent tension pneumothorax. Patients don't survive that stuff. You know that. Yeah, she's in good shape and all, but still. Patients just don't survive that.*

Yet his emotional side refused to listen, clinging to hope. That was why he had agreed to the PML protocol in the first place. Sure, he and Laura had had conversations about death, as most couples do. They always said, "Don't put me on life support if it's hopeless. Just let me die, rather than end up as a vegetable on a ventilator in some ICU, languishing and lingering and dying a slow, agonizing death." Easy stuff to say when everything's honky-dory. Things were different now. Mueller *had* given him some small shred of hope—something to cling to. He simply couldn't bear the thought of losing her.

He put his head back down on the pillow, stared at the ceiling, and began to pray.

CHAPTER 38

Sunday, 7:00 a.m.

"C'mon in," Kristin said, holding the screen door open for him. "Thanks for coming so early."

"No problem," Chip mumbled, immediately struck by Kristin's appearance—face puffy, eyes red, hair all askew—not bundled up securely in the usual ponytail. She had on a pair of faded jeans and an old Penn State sweatshirt. Her affect was way off, too—not the usual happy-go-lucky Kristin. He stepped onto the shiny wooden floor of her foyer. Real hardwood, he noted. A pleasant scent permeated the apartment; it was clear he had entered a female's territory.

"Let's go sit," she said, gesturing to the living room. "There's something I've got to ask you." Her intonation was flat—flatter than he'd ever heard it.

"Sure."

Chip sat down on the leather sofa. It was new and clean; you could smell the leather—definitely several notches above what he was used to. Its soft texture proved irresistible. Chip began rubbing his hand over the arm of the sofa.

Kristin took a seat in the wooden rocker across from him. "My dad helped me move my stuff out last night," she said. "There's no way I can stay here. I'm gonna stay with him in Halifax until they catch this guy."

"Makes sense," Chip said, trying hard to imagine the extent of her ordeal, but also wondering why she had asked him here.

She fell silent and stared at the oval throw rug, playing with her hair as she gently rocked.

"Are you okay?" Chip asked. "I can hardly believe what you told me over the phone."

"Yeah, I'm okay," she managed, but her chin started to quiver.

"You don't look it," he said softly.

"Thanks. Flattery will get you nowhere." She cracked a thin smile, the first real sign that anyone was home. She absently brushed wayward strands of her long hair out of her face. Out here in the better light, she looked like she had been crying for a week.

She took a deep breath. "I wanted to talk to you because you're the only other person who's seen what Chandler can do."

"You're sure it was Chandler?" Chip asked.

"Yes, of course I'm sure." She met his gaze, and in her reddened eyes, he glimpsed a flare of anger. "I'll never forget his face or his silver-flecked gray eyes."

"Me either." Chip shook his head. "He definitely was one strange dude."

"What do you *mean*?" she shot back, leaning forward in her chair, shoulders rigid.

Her tone startled Chip, momentarily confusing him. "Well, one minute he's like, dead, then he runs out of the ICU. And his eyes—"

"No," she interrupted, staring at him intently. "You said *was*."

Chip processed this for a moment, wondering where he had gone wrong. "I thought you said Smokey killed him—you know, ripped his throat out, blood spurting everywhere."

"I never said he was *dead*. Smokey *did* rip his throat out and there *was* blood everywhere, but—"

"You mean he's *not* dead?"

"No. I mean, I don't know."

"Where is he?" Chip shot several glances around the apartment.

"I don't know. He's gone." Her voice started to quaver. "There's only one thing I know for sure—poor Smokey's dead." She began to cry.

Chip absolutely hated when girls cried; he felt so helpless. "God, that's awful. I'm really sorry about your dog." An uncomfortable silence followed. Chip had no idea what to say to console her. *Besides,* he thought, *isn't that someone else's job?* Finally, with one hand running across the smooth leather and his eyes directed downward, he said, "I thought you were going out—you know, anniversary weekend and all."

"I told you," she said, sniffling. "Chris's mother got sick and he had to go home for the weekend—last minute."

"Right."

She stood and dabbed her eyes with a tissue. "Maybe this wasn't such a good idea."

Chip was thinking the same thing. "Look, I just don't want to intrude, that's all."

"You're not." More crying. "I needed someone to talk to," she blubbered out.

Chip wrestled with this for a moment. "Kristin, I'll stay and talk as long as you need."

She blew her nose and relief washed across her face. "Thanks, Chip. You're a good friend."

"Thanks," he said. *Story of my life,* he thought. "I'm always a sucker for scary stories."

She sat back down on the rocker and folded one leg under the other. "I didn't even tell you some of the bizarre stuff yet."

"What're you talking about? What else could you possibly add?"

She blew her nose and said, matter-of-factly, "He took the prints."

"What prints?"

"That's what I was doing in the darkroom—developing my film."

"Oh."

"I think he came for the film."

"I'm not following you," Chip said.

"Remember? I told you I might have a picture of Chandler and I wanted to play a hunch."

"When you bugged out of the med center yesterday?"

"Yes. Well, it turns out, I *did* have a picture of him. When I took a picture of you blowing out your birthday candle, I caught Chandler in the background."

"So, *that* was your hunch?"

"No. I wanted to look at a *Kirlian* photograph of him."

Chip scratched his head and then it slowly dawned on him. "Because of what Mueller said about his weird EEG?"

"Yes, exactly."

"So, what'd it show?"

"Chandler didn't have an aura."

"No aura. Is that bad?"

"Of course it is. Everyone has one—unless they're dead. You have one."

"Can you show me?"

"I told you—he took the prints." She ran her fingers through her hair, attempting to impose some sort of order. "I'm convinced he came for them."

"What? That's ridiculous. How could he possibly have known you were developing these pictures? You weren't even sure you *had* any pictures of him."

"I don't know." Kristin began braiding her hair. Several rubber bands had appeared from nowhere, and were now held in her mouth. "But there's more," she mumbled.

"Go on."

Her ponytail quickly took shape; she took the rubber bands, one by one, out of her mouth and snapped them into place. "You know the part where I tried to throw the solution at him?"

"Yeah," he said. "You said he pushed it out of your hands."

"I didn't tell the police this—or my dad—but he frickin' smiled at me right as he pushed the tray away."

"So what? He's got a sense of humor?"

"No, don't be silly. It's almost as if he *knew* I would grab for it."

"What're you saying?"

"I'm saying, something weird happened."

"Like what? Like he saw the future??" Chip said incredulously.

"Maybe, or else—" She stared across the room.

"Kristin, I think your imagination's getting the best of you."

"Or else, he saw the intention in my mind before I acted."

"*What?* He read your mind? Look, I know you've been through hell here, and I get that, but—"

"Chip, you're not listening to me. I know I'm upset, but I'm not kidding or delirious."

Chip didn't know what to say.

"I'm telling you," she said, "he *knew* I was going to reach for the tray and he was showing off—taunting me."

"Maybe it was just a lucky guess. I mean, what else were you going to use as a weapon?" Chip *did* know he wasn't ready to buy into her crazy mind-reading theories.

"I'm serious, Chip. Look, I gotta show you this part—that's why I wanted you to come over here." She took his hand and led him over to the basement door. She stopped at the yellow crime scene tape crisscrossed across the doorway and looked up at him. She was trembling. "Now, all of a sudden, I'm scared to go back down there."

"We don't have to."

"Yeah, we do. I have to show you this." Her face was set with determination.

"All right. How about I go first, make sure it's okay."

"Okay," she said. "Sergeant Markel said we shouldn't go down there—that they'd be back today to do more forensic crime scene analysis."

"I can hear him saying that." Chip took her hand. "We'll be careful not to touch anything."

They ducked under the tape and he led the way down the stairs. Chip had to admit the basement was plenty creepy. And he was pretty sure he could still smell the blood on top of all the Clorox.

She pointed up to the small, shattered basement window. "There," she said. "He climbed out that window." The window was at least eight feet off the ground with no obvious objects to stand on. She fixed him with a hard stare. "How do you explain him climbing out of that window after Smokey ripped his neck apart? He lost a ton of blood."

Chip had to admit he couldn't really explain how anyone could reach the window, let alone break it and climb out. "Look," he said, scrambling to come up with something, "sometimes a little bit of blood looks like a lot. I've seen traumas in the ER and—"

"Damn you!" she screamed at him. "You frickin' med student know-it-all!"

Her reaction surprised him and he took a step back. "I'm just saying, sometimes—"

"You flunked out, Chip. Remember?"

That one stung and he just stood there, looking at the floor.

"I saw Smokey's jaws clamped around his neck, all right?" she said, the shrillness in her voice intensifying. "Blood was pouring out of Smokey's mouth. And I'm talking bright red blood— arterial blood—must've been from his frickin' carotid artery. He should be dead!" She came up to him and started pounding his chest with her balled fists. "He should be dead." She began to sob and buried her face in his chest.

"You're right," he said and awkwardly put his arms around her shaking body. "He should be dead. It doesn't make sense." Up close like this, he couldn't help but notice the scent of her hair; it was clean and fresh and had some meadow flower overtones— lilac or something. "Hopefully Chandler wandered off and died in a ditch somewhere."

"I don't think so," she said, her breaking voice muffled by his shirt. "I have this creepy feeling that he's alive. I just *know* it somehow."

Chip disagreed with her again, but this time decided to keep it to himself.

"Poor Smokey," she said. "I can't believe he's gone. I miss him." She broke down into fresh sobs.

"He was a great dog—we'll sure miss him." Chip wasn't quite sure what to do with his hands, so he gently patted the small of her back while she buried her face deeper into his chest.

After several minutes, she pulled back and looked up at him, eyes swollen and face tear-streaked. "You know," she said, her voice trembling, "Chandler tried to kill Smokey before he came down to the basement to get me. He stabbed him with a damn steak knife."

"*What?* I wondered how Chandler got by him—Smokey's a good watchdog." Although Chip didn't actually have a clue what kind of watchdog Smokey had been, it seemed like the right thing to say. "Wait—so you mean Smokey attacked him down here, *after* he was stabbed?"

"Yep," Kristin said, tremendous pride radiating from her. But her face also bore the look of a freshly broken heart. "Smokey came back down to protect me."

"I'll bet Chandler didn't expect *that*."

"You got that right." She smiled weakly through her tears, but when she spoke again, she sounded stronger, almost defiant. "You should've seen the look of surprise on that bastard's face when Smokey jumped on his back and sank his fangs into him."

She put her head back on his chest and stayed that way for several minutes, arms loosely surrounding him. Finally, she pulled her head back and looked up at him. "Chip, I'm sorry," she said softly.

"What? About the tears?"

"No," she said, sniffling. "The med student comment."

"It's okay. Really, I don't mind."

She disengaged from him. "You didn't deserve it."

Chip studied his sneakers. "It's okay."

"Thanks for listening."

"No problem," Chip said and smiled thinly. "That's what friends are for, right?"

CHAPTER 39

Sunday, 7:30 a.m.

Dr. Gunter Mueller made himself another cup of coffee from the Keurig coffeemaker installed in his lab. He added a generous amount of half-and-half from the lab fridge and tossed the empty Dark Magic K-cup into the trash. Although he was physically tired, his mind remained alert. He didn't have that much longer to go—hopefully this afternoon they could start weaning Mrs. Landry from the heart-lung machine. He had just sent Dr. Landry on a breakfast run to the hospital cafeteria.

A noise from behind startled him. Was Landry back already? Mueller turned. An elderly cleaning lady stood in the doorway, staring at him. Why was she here now? There was something odd about the woman, besides the red bandanna she wore over her gray hair. There was also something familiar about her.

"Do you know who I am?" the woman asked in a deep voice, coming closer to him.

Sudden recognition sent chills through him. "Yes, I believe I do." He could never forget those gray eyes with the silver flecks in them—Chandler. "W-what are you doing here?"

Chandler took another step toward him, mouth open to answer, but then collapsed onto the floor. Mueller quickly knelt by his side and felt for a radial pulse—it was very weak and thready. A makeshift bandage clumsily wrapped about Chandler's neck was saturated with blood. Mueller carefully removed the bandage and gasped. There were several large, hideous gashes practically encircling his neck. Some still oozed fresh blood. He looked closer. *Are those bite marks?* In any case, the wounds looked like they should've been fatal; he was surprised Chandler had been able to walk in here under his own power. "What in God's name happened to you?"

Chandler murmured incoherently.

Mueller retrieved some supplies from a nearby supply cabinet and frantically worked on starting a large bore IV. This man desperately needed fluids before irreversible hypovolemic shock set in—if it hadn't already. Chandler's lips were very pale and he looked chalk white. No doubt what he really needed was blood. But Mueller didn't have time to wait for a crossmatch from the blood bank. Lactated Ringer's would have to suffice until he got the man admitted to the ICU. After securing the IV, he poured in the fluids as fast as they would go.

He wheeled over some portable monitors, hooked up his new patient, and took a blood sample for lab values. Chandler's blood pressure was 64/30. No wonder he had passed out. Several minutes later, the ISTAT machine beeped. Chandler's hemoglobin was an absurdly low 3 grams/deciliter. *That's impossible,* thought Mueller. *Must be a machine glitch. No one could walk around with a hemoglobin of three.*

Amazingly, Chandler opened his eyes and looked up at him from the floor. Then he spoke. "I'm not going back to the ICU."

"You don't have much choice," Mueller said. "You've lost an awful lot of blood."

"I know."

Mueller punched the machine for another blood pressure reading.

Chandler made a feeble attempt to sit up. "What are you doing?" Mueller said, putting his hand on Chandler's chest to restrain him. "Lie still. Your neck wounds are severe. And you're still bleeding."

"Fucking dog," Chandler said.

Dog? That would explain the bite marks, Mueller thought. The BP machine beeped with its new reading—85/50. The fluid was helping.

"I feel better," Chandler said, trying to prop himself up on his elbows.

"You're in no shape to go anywhere, my friend. If I hadn't just given you that fluid, you'd probably be dead."

"We need to talk," Chandler said, pushing Mueller's hand away. "I must see your notes."

"You're not getting this," Mueller said. "You practically died—for the second time. Besides, I've got nothing to say to you."

Chandler just stared at him, his flat eyes boring through him, unreadable.

Mueller's curiosity got the best of him. "Why the hell did you kill that girl?"

"I needed to escape."

"You didn't need to kill her."

Now Chandler smiled a bit. "You're right."

"Then why on earth *did* you?"

"Would you believe it if I told you I didn't intend to?"

"What?" Mueller stammered.

"I didn't think so. My arm was much stronger than I realized," Chandler said matter-of-factly.

Horror gripped Mueller.

"It doesn't matter," Chandler said.

"That's *insane*," Mueller replied. "Of course it does."

"Anything that stands in my way is fair game," Chandler said, locking eyes with him.

Mueller tried again to read Chandler's expressionless eyes and only then began to sense that he was in the presence of something unique. *Evil, perhaps?*

"But what *is* evil?" Chandler said, his tone mocking.

Icy tendrils of fear ran down Mueller's spine and he could only stare wide-eyed at Chandler.

"I prefer to think of myself as unencumbered," Chandler continued. "I have true free will."

"Rubbish," Mueller answered weakly, his mind still reeling.

"Perhaps, *you* are the one who is evil, Dr. Mueller. After all, this lab is yours." He swept his hand around the expansive lab. "And you created me."

His BP was now 120/75. His neck had stopped bleeding.

"I didn't *create* you. I saved your life," Mueller retorted.

Chandler ripped the cuff off his arm and pushed to his feet. He looked over at the woman on the litter across the room. "Who is she?"

"None of your damn business."

"My business is anything I want it to be," Chandler said, looking back at him. "Now, tell me."

"I will not."

Chandler walked over to the supply cabinet. "I need more fluid." He opened another bag of Ringer's and spiked it on his IV.

"You need blood," Mueller countered. "You need that wound closed properly. You need antibiotics. You need to be admitted."

Chandler ignored him and walked over to the woman on the stretcher—the woman tethered to the machine that hummed with power. Suddenly Chandler drew in his breath. "It's her!"

"Do you *know* her?"

"Yes and no," Chandler said cryptically, and touched her arm. "So cold, though."

"So were you," Mueller said. "Don't you remember?"

Chandler stared off into space, apparently lost in thought. Then he turned and locked eyes with Mueller again. "She's not far enough."

"What do you mean?" Mueller asked.

"She's not dead enough."

"Of course she's not. I'm trying to keep her alive, you fool."

Chandler studied the monitor with its EKG and multiple pressure tracings from the Swan Ganz catheter in her heart. He looked at what drips she was on and then bent down to examine her Foley catheter with her urine. His eyes came to rest for a moment on the surgical tray at her bedside. Several hemostats, scalpels, needle drivers, and suture material were arranged neatly there.

"You must bleed her some more first," Chandler said with his back to him.

"You're mad."

"Am I? How do you think I survived *my* illness?"

"I have no idea."

Chandler turned and sneered at him. "You smart people are all alike—and you make me sick. You have no fuckin' clue."

"Why don't you enlighten me?"

"The brain is very powerful—more powerful than I think you can imagine. You scientists are just beginning to scratch the surface of it." Chandler stopped as if listening to something. "But I see you have considered this possibility. I see your concern over a certain EEG pattern of mine."

Mueller recoiled in shock. "How could you possibly know this? Have you read my files?" Adrenaline surged through him and his fear notched up into panic. *What the hell is going on?*

"Not yet. But I can see into your thoughts, Dr. Mueller."

"That's impossible." But Mueller's analytical mind was beginning to wonder about impossibilities. How could this man before him even be standing, with a hemoglobin of three? How had he survived complete multi-organ system failure? And that wound on his neck looked as if it had come close to removing his head.

"Is it?" Chandler glanced over at the large, squat heart-lung machine. He concentrated for a moment, staring at the woman on the litter. "Her name is Laura Landry. She was in a terrible biking accident and suffered a tension pneumothorax. While in the OR, she had a massive fat embolus from her crushed femur that came close to killing her. You are trying valiantly to revive her." Chandler whirled to face him. "And her husband is here now, helping you. And will be back soon." Chandler glanced about the room. "And you think she is beautiful, too."

"Amazing," Mueller said, the breath escaping from his mouth in a whistle.

"Do you believe me now?"

Dr. Mueller's amazement was cut short as the scalpel blade ripped across his throat. Chandler was somehow standing beside him now, carving up his neck. Mueller barely had time to register surprise before the blackness came.

CHAPTER 40

Sunday, 8:30 a.m.

Kristin walked into her old bedroom and sat down on the bed. She ran her hands over the silky surface of the white quilted bedspread and tried to get a grip on her emotions. It had been tough going back down in the basement—really tough—even with Chip leading the way. She wasn't sure she would ever go back there again. All she could think of was Smokey and the fact that he wasn't coming home. She wondered if she would ever be happy again. She wondered if the crying would ever stop. She wrapped her arms around herself, rocked on the bed, and fought back the tears.

After a time, her thoughts turned to Chip. She felt bad for giving him a hard time about flunking out of med school. That had been uncalled for, downright cruel. What had she been thinking? He had been a real trooper to come over and listen to her and put up with her grief; he *was* a good friend. And she couldn't deny that it had been a long time since someone had held her like that—and that it had felt good.

She glanced around the room and saw that Dad had left it untouched—everything was just the way she remembered it from when she had moved out two years ago. Even her old pictures were there, framed and neatly arranged on her bookcase.

There was one from the Homecoming dance, senior year at Halifax High School. Although she hadn't made the Homecoming Court, Kristin never missed a dance. Her date that night had been "Shorty" Eddie Wachinsky. At six foot six he towered over her, and had looked especially goofy in his formal wear; his long arms stuck out from sleeves that were way too short. Even though Shorty had been the star center on the b-ball team, he was clumsy as an oaf on the dance floor. Nevertheless, the two had a blast that night, and she smiled at the memory.

Her eyes traveled to the field hockey team shot. She'd played center halfback. The team went undefeated her senior year, but lost in the first round at districts. Her best friend, Karen, who would go with her to radiology school after graduation, was standing right next to her.

Then there was a shot climbing Mount Washington in New Hampshire on a family summer vacation—she was sixteen and hadn't adopted her braid back then; her hair was wild and wind-swept on the summit. Her younger brother, taller than her, stood on one side and her mother on the other—her dad had taken the picture. Her mom had her arm wrapped around Kristin and a big smile on her face. That, of course, had been before the car wreck.

Finally, there was a more recent one of her and her boyfriend at the time, Andrew. They were kneeling on the wooden porch of a farmhouse with a puppy between them—a black Labrador retriever pup. She didn't stand a chance against this one. Tears quickly came to her eyes. She recalled that day two years ago when she and Karen had first met little Smokey.

* * *

"He's adorable!" Kristin exclaimed, already on her knees and stroking the pup's velvety ears. "What's his name?"

"I named him Smokey," Andrew said, "because he's mostly coal black, but has streaks of lighter gray running through his fur."

"I like it," Kristin said as Smokey sniffed and licked her ears with abandon.

"It looks like he likes you, too," Andrew said, and smiled his perfect smile at her. "Watch out for his little teeth—he'll nip you." Andrew knelt down beside her and started petting the little furball.

"Oh, that's so cute," Karen said. "Hang on for a second and I'll take your picture."

Karen fussed with her camera and then clicked away. "Is he yours?" Karen asked Andrew.

"Well, sort of," Andrew explained. "He came with the farmhouse I'm renting. I'm minding him for the owner while he's away."

"How cool," Karen said.

"Let me show you ladies around," Andrew said, rising to his feet. "I sure hope you like the place."

"How could we not?" Karen said, giggling, eyes fixed on Andrew.

After the tour, while Karen lounged on the back deck taking in some afternoon sun, Andrew took Kristin in his arms and hugged her tightly. He was much taller than her and it felt good to sink into his strong body and breathe in the nice clean smell of him. Kristin remembered thinking she was in heaven when she was in his arms.

"So," Andrew said, "you really think your father will go for you moving in here?"

"We *have* been seeing each other for six months," Kristin said, smiling up at his dark eyes and storybook handsome face. "It doesn't even matter—I'm twenty-one and can do as I please.

No, really—he likes you. Besides, if you can't trust a doctor, who can you trust?" Kristin quipped.

"Well, technically, I'm still a med student—"

"Relax. He'll be okay with it. And if Karen agrees to move in too, it'll make things more—I dunno—acceptable. We'll be splitting the place to save on rent and food while Karen and I get through x-ray tech school. Dad likes that sort of thinking."

"So do I," Andrew said and kissed her.

Kristin kissed him back and luxuriated in his embrace for a few moments longer. "Besides, once my dad sees your dog, he'll be sold. He's a softie for dogs—especially cute little puppies."

"Okay then, it's settled," he said. "Now we just have to convince Karen to sign the lease."

"Look at her," Kristin said, nodding toward the back deck. "She's in love with the place already."

Three months later, after the new roomies were comfortably settled into the farmhouse, things took a turn for the worse. One day, Kristin found herself late for class because she had spent too much time playing with little Smokey—scratch that—obedience training the dog. Karen and Andrew had already left. "You're going to be my downfall," she scolded the pup as she put him back in his crate. He looked up at her with such puppy sad eyes that her irritation evaporated in an instant and all she could do was smile.

Ten minutes later, Kristin was speeding recklessly down the winding back road, halfway to the med center, when she realized she had forgotten her MRI workbook. "Damn it!" she said and swung her car onto the shoulder, skidding dangerously on the loose gravel. When the coast was clear, she hung a U-turn and raced back toward the farmhouse. She'd definitely be late for class now.

As she slammed her car to a stop in the driveway, it didn't register with her that Andrew's car was also there. She left her engine running and car door open, and barged in through the front door. Smokey sat up in the crate, tail going a mile a minute, panting to beat the band. She trotted back to her bedroom, passing right by Karen's open bedroom door.

Staring wide-eyed at her from the bed, in various stages of undress, were Karen and Andrew. She would never forget the expressions of guilt and embarrassment that played across their faces. Kristin's shock quickly gave way to anger and she ran head-long out of the farmhouse, almost falling down the front porch steps. She ignored Smokey's distressed barking and forgot all about the MRI notebook. Consumed by feelings of betrayal and hurt, she roared out of the driveway.

* * *

Her bedroom door opened and her father walked in. "Are you okay? I thought I heard something."

She wiped her eyes and sniffled a bit. "I'm okay, Daddy." She pointed to the bookcase and said, "It's just that picture of Smokey as a puppy . . ." Her voice trailed off as her throat closed up and more tears came.

"There, there now, pumpkin," he said, opening his arms to her.

She welcomed the warmth of his embrace and let her tears break loose, her head bobbing up and down on her father's flannel shirt. He wrapped one strong arm around her and patted her head with a big hand.

After ten minutes or so, when she had cried herself out, she gazed up at him. "I miss him so much, Daddy. He saved my life."

"I know, pumpkin." He handed her some Kleenex. "That dog was one in a million."

"It hurts badly." Kristin sat back down on the bed and dabbed at her eyes and wiped her nose. "Will it ever get better?" She looked up into her father's kind blue eyes and watched his brow crease as he collected his thoughts.

"Yes and no," he said slowly. "They say time heals all wounds and that memories fade, but I don't know about that." Her father stared across the room, a pained expression crossing his face. "There's not a day that goes by that I don't think of your mother."

"I miss her, too."

"It's been five years since the accident," he said, "but I remember her like it was yesterday."

"Really?"

"I can still hear her voice and feel her touch," he said, his voice thickening with emotion. "She's with me wherever I go." He tapped his chest over his heart. Kristin felt her tears threatening to return. "I've come to accept it," her dad continued. "She's in a better place, I'm sure of it." He looked at her. "I think God called her home early because he missed her, too."

Kristin returned her dad's bittersweet smile and noticed the moistness in his eyes.

"And," he said, "I know she wouldn't have meant for me to live a life full of grief."

She reached out and squeezed his hand. "Thanks, Dad."

"Sure," he said. He shook his head slightly and tried to put on a happier face. "Things will get better, honey."

She smiled weakly and looked at the floor

"Where did you go this morning?" he asked. "When I woke up, you were gone."

"I went back to the apartment."

He looked surprised. "Did you forget something?"

"No. I met Chip there to show him something."

"Chip?"

"I work with him at the med center. He was there the night Heather got—" She stopped.

"Promise me you won't go back there again until this creep is caught."

"I promise."

"Is Chip a med student?" her father asked, his voice wary.

"Not anymore." Her dad raised his eyebrows at this. "Don't worry, Dad—I'm not getting involved."

"Honey, it's okay if you do."

"I'm not ready."

"That's fine. No one's pressuring you. You've got the rest of your life. You'll meet the right guy."

"Yeah, but how do you *know* when he's the right guy? Andrew seemed like the right guy." She teared up again. "People shouldn't be allowed to lie, Dad."

"You're right."

"Smokey never lied to me—ever."

"Dogs are good like that."

"It's scary, not knowing if you can ever trust anyone again."

"Right, again. It *is* scary—and risky, too." He smiled tenderly and patted her head. "Love is all those things, pumpkin. But it's more than that. Only by putting yourself out there, becoming vulnerable, giving of yourself without considering what you'll get in return, can you truly understand love. It's a mystery and a puzzle for sure, but no question, it's the best thing going. You'll see some day."

"Thanks again, Dad." She hugged the big man. "You're the best and I love you."

"I love you, too."

From the security of her father's arms, without looking up at him, Kristin asked, "Do you think people can actually read minds?"

CHAPTER 41

Sunday, 8:30 a.m.

Juggling his load of egg sandwiches, orange juice, toast, and glazed donuts, Doug opened the door and entered the PML. The door closed behind him and he was immediately immersed in darkness. He quickly set the breakfast tray on the floor and tried to make sense of things. The only thing he could see was the glowing bank of monitors above Laura's bed, which bathed the room in an eerie phosphorescent green glow. *Why the hell are the lights out?* "Dr. Mueller, I'm back," he called out.

Silence. Only the whirring of the heart-lung machine that was keeping his wife alive.

Doug fumbled along the wall by the door and eventually found the light switch. He flipped on the lights and walked over to the bedside and gazed into the unseeing face of his wife. She looked ghastly. Her pale face was swollen, and she had an endotracheal tube coming out of her mouth and a Swan Ganz catheter in her neck. But the worst part was that her head was encased in ice— her nasal temp read 25 degrees Celsius.

Laura's EKG was flatline. This was just as it should be; she was on full cardiopulmonary bypass to rest her heart. The heart-lung machine was doing the work now and was responsible for maintaining an adequate perfusion pressure to her brain and vital organs. But Laura's MAP—her mean arterial pressure—was only 30 mmHg and falling. Something was wrong; this was *way* too low.

"Dr. Mueller?" Doug called out again, the first real stab of fear running through him.

Still no response.

It was then that he noticed a large bore, antecubital IV in Laura's right arm. He wasn't positive, but he could've sworn that it wasn't there earlier; he was intimately familiar with all her lines. The tubing was filled with blood. Perhaps last night while he'd slept, Mueller had seen fit to start another IV to give her a transfusion—not that unusual in a critically ill patient. Except he realized there was no unit of blood or fluid hanging on the IV pole. The tubing ran out of sight off the other side of the bed. *Strange. Very strange.*

Doug leaned over to follow the tubing and in a moment of shock and horror, saw a man lying on the floor. He appeared to be unconscious. The tubing was going right into his arm. Blood flows downhill. This could only mean one thing. Laura's blood was flowing out of her and into this man. *What the hell?* Doug felt queasy. Something was badly amiss here. *And where is Mueller?*

Laura's MAP was now 20 mmHg. Doug knew she wouldn't last long like this; she was already very fragile, with all that she had been through. He quickly removed the IV from her arm and applied pressure to stop the bleeding.

The man on the floor spoke. "Perhaps I can answer your questions."

Doug almost jumped out of his skin. "W-what? Who the hell are you?"

"Nick Chandler." Chandler sat up and swiped a gray wig off his head. "I'm with environmental services." He ripped the IV out of his own arm.

Doug felt as if he had entered the twilight zone; none of this was making any sense. He could only stare at the man and shake his head, hoping he would wake up out of this nightmare—and that the apparition would be gone. "What the hell are you doing here?"

Chandler didn't answer, but appeared to be studying him.

Doug turned his attention back to Laura. She looked so pale—unquestionably, she needed blood right away. "I don't have time for this," Doug muttered. "This woman is my wife and she's dying."

"I know."

Doug ignored the strange man and searched around the area for drugs. Specifically, he needed some Neo or ephedrine or epi—anything to bring her pressure up. And he needed it now.

"You don't know me, Dr. Landry. But I know you and Laura." Chandler smiled condescendingly. "I was a patient of Dr. Mueller's, too—his first real success story."

Doug did his best to block this guy out. What the man was doing here, hooked up to Laura, he couldn't begin to guess. But time was running out. Laura's MAP was now 15 mmHg and her pulse ox no longer registered—she would be dead soon. Doug found an anesthesia cart off to the side containing the drugs he was looking for. "I have to give her some medicine now," Doug mumbled. "Her pressure's way too low."

"I can't let you do that."

"What?" The twilight zone had now expanded grotesquely, pushing aside reality, engulfing him in its insanity. *This can't be real—could it?*

"I *said*, I can't let you do that," Chandler repeated.

Only one thing mattered. Doug ignored him and prepared to inject Laura's IV with some epinephrine, but suddenly, Chandler was in front of him, wielding a bloody scalpel blade. Chandler slashed at him. A gash appeared in Doug's arm. Blood immediately welled up and ran onto the floor, and he dropped the epinephrine syringe. Then he felt the burning pain and winced. *What the hell!*

But the pain served to jolt him back to reality. Doug grabbed for the metal instrument tray at Laura's bedside—something he could use as a shield, or perhaps as a weapon to beat this guy's brains in.

Before he could reach it, Chandler already had it in his hands. He flung it aside.

Exploding with frustration and rage, Doug leapt straight at Chandler, oblivious to the scalpel blade. Chandler sliced at him, but only managed to tear another gash in his arm. Doug hit him squarely in the chest and drove him to the floor. The scalpel blade flew out of Chandler's hand. Doug wrapped his hands around his neck and squeezed. An image of throttling Raskin years ago flashed across his mind.

Chandler howled in pain, but Doug didn't let up. Doug realized Chandler's neck was a mess—all slimy and bloody. Soon blood started flowing again from the open wounds there. How the heck had Chandler survived these neck wounds? Some creature had been gnawing on his neck. A lion, perhaps? Blood was now flowing freely onto the floor. Chandler appeared to pass out.

And Laura's alarm sang out in the background.

Doug glanced up in time to see her pressure line bottom out. *Shit!* She would be dead in roughly two minutes. Letting go of Chandler, Doug rushed to Laura's side. He punched the Code Blue button at the bedside and then gave the entire syringe of epinephrine. Out of the corner of his eye, he saw movement from Chandler.

Doug frantically flung open the drawers of the anesthesia cart, searching for more epinephrine.

Chandler began dragging himself with one arm toward the door. With his other arm, he clutched at his neck, where blood seeped out between his fingers to run onto the floor; he left a broad trail of smeared blood behind him.

CHAPTER 42

Sunday, 10:00 a.m.

Chandler closed the door, threw the dead bolt, then slid down to the floor, his breaths coming in ragged gasps. *Shit! That was close,* he thought. Very close. Landry had almost killed him! He had almost died at the hands of that fucker, Doug Landry. He started to shake his head in disbelief but quickly aborted this; his neck throbbed so miserably that he felt light-headed. Perhaps Mueller had been right—he should be back in the ICU receiving proper medical treatment. But he knew what he really needed was more blood.

Blood. He could feel Laura Landry's blood running through his veins, mingling with his blood, pumped by his heart to the farthest reaches of his body. He savored the knowledge; it felt good. He pictured her beautiful face. If only Landry hadn't come in when he did. In another fifteen or twenty minutes, the transfusion would have been complete and Laura would have tasted death—just as he had. He pounded the floor and howled with rage and frustration.

Slowly, his rage gave way to clearer thinking as his self-preservation instincts kicked in. If he wanted to win, he had to stick to a plan. He needed a strategy. Mostly, he needed some time to heal. All his powers were for naught, if he couldn't stand up.

Chandler crawled to the kitchen, leaving a streak of blood along the hardwood floor. He grabbed the countertop and pulled himself up to stand. The room swam momentarily as he swayed with vertigo. After retrieving what items he needed from the cabinet, he slumped down on the floor, leaning against the refrigerator door for support. When he had caught his breath, he struggled to pop the top of an Ensure can. *Shit!* He was ridiculously weak. After several tries he finally succeeded in opening it; he washed down a load of iron pills and vitamins, to help with the synthesis of hemoglobin and generalized healing.

From his position, sprawled on the kitchen floor, he directed his bone marrow to rev production of red blood cells up to the max. He constricted the blood vessels in his neck to staunch the blood flow from the gashes. *Fucking dog!* He also directed an avalanche of white blood cells, killer t-cells and lymphocytes and phagocytes, to his neck region to help ward off infection. He also recruited fibroblasts, stimulating them to lay down scar tissue and promote healing and skin growth.

Perhaps it had been a mistake to visit Mueller in the first place, to return to the med center so soon, with his wounds so fresh. But the urge to see Mueller had been overwhelming—he wanted to learn what had happened to him, and why. Mueller had proven very useful in this regard and Chandler now figured he had a much better understanding of his transformation. Killing Mueller had not been part of his original plan, but it had felt right at the time.

Besides, his sixth sense had proven a godsend. How else would he have crossed paths with Laura Landry? Clearly fate had been responsible for bringing them back together after he had first laid eyes on her at the CVS. Just as fate had chosen him for the transformation, it had chosen her to be by his side.

He finished off the can of Ensure and made his way on all fours to the bathroom. Using the sink as leverage, he hauled himself upright again. He regarded his neck wounds in the vanity mirror. It was not a sight for the faint-hearted. His neck musculature had been ripped aside, exposing the vital structures beneath. He could see the outline of his trachea with its regularly spaced cartilaginous rings, glistening in the bathroom light. His carotid artery—miraculously still intact—pulsed defiantly with every beat of his heart. There wasn't much left of his shredded internal jugular vein; the remnant still seeped blood. If he turned his neck far enough, ignoring the exquisite pain, he could even make out his vertebral column way in the back, which housed his delicate spinal cord, the main neural pathway to and from the brain.

Chandler realized he was lucky to be alive. He swabbed some iodine on his wounds and immersed himself in the stinging pain. He was actually learning how to modulate the nociceptors responsible for the transmission of pain impulses. With practice, he believed he would be able to abolish the sensation completely.

Using some sterile gauzes and cotton balls and tape, he redressed his wounds as best he could, then staggered into the master bedroom and crawled between the flannel sheets of the Kopenhavers' king-size bed, oblivious to the bloodstains he left everywhere. He laid his head on the soft down pillow and tried to relax, but couldn't. Sadness and despair pushed aside any chance for peace he might have had. The more he took note of them, the greater they seemed to become. He felt so alone—him against the world. Why was it so hard? Why had they hurt him so? He thought back to earlier, happier times with Toby and tears came to his eyes; he missed his good friend.

Chandler cried for several minutes more, mostly for himself—until his mind recoiled. Until he remembered that they had almost killed him twice in the past two days. He had been through so much, and gained so much, that it would be a tragic waste to give it all up now. This self-pity was a weakness; he had no use for it.

Chandler cut the parasympathetic nerve output to his lacrimal ducts, thereby effectively cutting off any more tears. He ordered his mind to bury the memory of Toby down deep. He tried to override his limbic system, the seat of his emotions, and blunt the sad, lonely feelings, but he was less successful there. These pathways were not at all logical, but rather horribly tangled and convoluted.

Chandler yawned deeply. Now, on top of his physical exhaustion, he was mentally drained, and the urge to sleep became overwhelming. But he knew he needed to think things through a bit longer—to make a plan—so he quickly dialed up his brain's reticular activating system to peak levels to ward off sleep.

He reviewed his potential enemies—those who were privy to his secrets. Mueller was no longer a threat. He searched his mind for some shred of remorse, but could find none. Curiosity flickered briefly that he felt nothing for the man who had given him his rebirth, but he quickly let it go.

Also in the "no longer a threat" category was the fucking dog. The dog's teeth had somehow missed his carotid artery by the narrowest of margins, otherwise, he *would* be dead. Then there was Kristin, the dog's sorry ass owner. He dismissed her. After all, she had fled away from him in terror the first chance she got, and left her beloved dog to die at his hand.

The Allison boy came next to mind. Chandler smiled; he didn't represent much of a threat, either—he was almost completely hamstrung by his own problems, alcohol not the least of them. Strange, though; the boy's mind was not entirely open to him. Perhaps due to the alcohol?

And that left Douglas fucking Landry. Landry had almost killed him. Although his mind stubbornly refused to accept this, Chandler forced himself to embrace this fact, internalize it, study it from every angle. Desperately, he needed to learn from this experience, so he wouldn't make the same mistake again. He couldn't get too overconfident. He had real limitations. In spite of all his gifts—his strength, his speed, his healing ability, his mind-reading prowess—he wasn't immortal. And he could be beaten—he could be killed—if he was weakened sufficiently. He must properly rest and heal and stick with the plan.

His mind also kept returning to the woman in the bed in the lab. The woman whose blood now flowed in his veins. The wife of Dr. Landry. He refused to put her in the foe category. He knew he should forget about her. He should concentrate on healing his body, lying low until he regained some respectable measure of strength. But he also knew he was drawn to her in some powerful, inexplicable way that he seemed powerless to resist. He had to see her again—to find out the truth. He shut his eyes and allowed sleep to come, and against his better instincts, dreamt of the lovely dark-haired woman.

CHAPTER 43

Sunday, 2:00 p.m.

Chip ascended the three flights of stairs to his apartment with ease, whistling as he went. His legs were sore from his time on the treadmill, but it was a good kind of sore. Ever since he had joined the cross-country team in high school, running had been a part of his life; it had always been his stress-buster. During his senior year, he had lowered his mile time to a respectable 5:30, and he still was friends with two buddies from the team. He had run all through college—on the indoor track when necessary.

This past year, though, his running had become more and more sporadic, until he had finally given up on it entirely. Excuses were never in short supply. He was always too busy either going to class, studying, or partying. Somewhere along the line, he had just plain lost the fire.

But today, he thought with a smile, he had dragged his sorry butt to the fitness center and huffed and puffed his way through a mile and a half, pounding noisily on the Precor treadmill. The sweat had poured off him and his heart had hammered at an alarming pace. And the time—well, the time was downright embarrassing. But, when all was said and done, he had felt much better than he had in a long time.

He keyed the lock of his apartment and entered the foyer, tossing his gym bag on the floor. For perhaps the hundredth time that day, he wondered if his good mood had anything to do with Kristin. He couldn't deny that he had been thinking about her all day. But his thoughts didn't just center around the strange conversation they'd had this morning about Chandler. More importantly, he was genuinely touched that Kristin had wanted to share her moment of intense grief with *him*, and that she had opened up to *him* so candidly. Maybe the whole boyfriend thing wasn't rock solid?

Second, he was also surprised at how easy it was to talk with her; his usual tongue-tied nervousness just hadn't been an issue. True, she wasn't a glamour girl like Heather or Michelle—Victor had been right about that—but that seemed irrelevant. In fact, it seemed like a plus. When, in God's name, had he ever had such a deep conversation with a girl? Or hugged someone for real—to help them deal with the loss of a loved one? Never.

He slowed as he approached the kitchen, as his mood shifted. He knew what lay ahead. What had seemed like such a good idea while flying along on the treadmill now seemed a bit foolish. Or at least unnecessary. What was the point of burning all your bridges, anyway; removing all your safety nets? *Isn't that what being prepared means?*

His pace slowed to a crawl. This whole thing had a decidedly drastic feel to it. If he was so serious about severing the relationship, why couldn't he just avoid them? No need to dump them. Besides, wouldn't that be a waste of money? Waste not, want not. Maybe he should just pour *some* of them out, like a peace offering or maybe to serve as a deterrent in some way.

No, he thought, shaking his head vehemently. He meant to go through with this, and he had to hurry, before he lost his nerve.

He recognized that his life was spiraling down the drain, and for the first time in a long time, he was determined to take back some measure of control. Getting hammered all the time was not the path to a good career, or getting back into school, or really, for anything worthwhile. *What girl's gonna want to go out with a drunken loser?*

Besides, he always told himself, he could stop anytime. Just like that. *Isn't that what they all say? Time to prove it. Time to put my money where my mouth is. Where the rubber meets the road, and all that happy horseshit.*

He opened the kitchen cabinet under the sink where his friends hung out. Time to put up or shut up. They stared up at him uneasily. The tequila bottle, who usually took the lead, spoke up: *Careful now, pal. You wanna think this through. Sure, you might feel strong now, but who knows what shit's coming down the pike. You're a bad luck magnet, you know that. Calamity is just waiting for you around the next corner. And then who's gonna have your back? Your weasely med school buds? Your new girl pal who already has a boyfriend? Your dad? Right, I didn't think so.*

Chip steeled his nerve and then poured the contents of each bottle, one after the other, down the sink. They gurgled loudly, protesting as they went, until all six were empty, and the voices fell silent. He chucked the empties into the recycling bin.

CHAPTER 44

Sunday, 8:00 p.m.

Chip checked the rhythm again for 237. No question about it—she was in flutter with the distinctive sawtooth pattern; when he started his shift she had been in Afib. He rubbed his eyes, thankful that his head didn't hurt with a nasty hangover. He was proud of himself for emptying his stash. He might even be able to concentrate on his work, for a change—except for the fact that he was preoccupied with a certain girl with a long braid, and the strange and gruesome tale she had told him that morning.

Part of her story didn't make sense. There was a piece that didn't fit, and it bothered him. *Why* had Chandler attacked Kristin in the first place? How did he even know where she lived? Surely it had nothing to do with her photographs, as *she* thought. Chip gave Kristin a pass on this. After all, she was in a highly emotional state because of the death of Smokey, and undoubtedly wasn't thinking straight.

He glanced back at the screen. Now 237's rhythm looked like a three-to-one block—wait, no, it was four-to-one. Seemed pretty unstable, although that was predictable—the patient was another Mueller special. How weird was that? They'd been having a run of them lately. The difference was that Chip knew this lady. Well, sort of.

Footsteps approached, interrupting Chip's thoughts. He looked up in time to see Dr. Landry, who looked as if he hadn't slept in days. "Hi, Dr. Landry," he said.

Landry stopped and eyed Chip, his brow knotted in confusion. "Do I know you?"

"No, not really," Chip said. Up close, Landry looked agitated on top of being exhausted. "I listened to your airway lecture the other day," Chip added.

"Oh." Landry sounded wholly disinterested.

"I'm Chip Allison, the evening shift monitor watcher." Chip held out his hand.

"I see." Doug transferred his coffee cup to his left hand and shook Chip's hand. "Keep a close eye on 237. That's my wife in there, and she's been through hell."

"I know. She's at the top of my list, sir."

"Call me Doug."

"Okay. She's in A-flutter, now." Chip brushed back a lock of his stubborn hair. "Seems very stable."

Landry smiled wryly. "Let's see . . . twelve hours ago, she was on full cardiopulmonary bypass in some basement lab with her body packed in ice. And a blood pressure of zero. She's been pretty close to death now—several times. So, if you want to call that stable, well . . ."

Chip cleared his throat, not sure what to say. "I guess she did okay in there—in Mueller's lab. I mean, she came out."

Landry eyed him curiously for several moments.

"Some don't," Chip added sheepishly.

"Right." Landry wore a pained expression. "Listen Chip, I've had a really bizarre day and I'm still trying to make sense of it all. I should go check on my wife." Landry turned to leave.

"Is it true, what they're saying about Mueller?" Chip blurted.

Landry stopped and turned his head. "Why, what have you heard?"

"That he's dead."

Landry grimaced. "Word travels around here fast."

Chip shrugged.

"Yeah, he's dead all right," Landry said.

"They say he died in a lab accident," Chip continued. "Sounds a bit bogus, but hey, you know—stuff happens."

"Lab accident? Huh. I guess you could call it that."

"Something else?" Chip prodded.

Landry looked around, then lowered his voice. "I'm not sure I should be talking to you about this. Can I trust you?"

"Absolutely."

"You remind me of a med student I knew once, several years ago. Seems like another lifetime." Landry took a sip of his coffee. "But I guess all this will hit the papers soon enough."

"So true."

"Well," Landry said, "I spent the better part of the day trying to convince the Hershey PD that *I* didn't kill him." Landry paused and Chip sensed a reluctance to reveal too much.

"Why on earth would they suspect *you*?" Chip asked. "Mueller's trying to save your wife's life."

"I don't know—maybe since *I* found Mueller's body."

"Yikes. Where?"

"Stuffed in a storage locker in the PML. The police detective kept questioning me over and over about the details of how his body got into the locker—of which I had no idea."

"Hmmm . . ." Chip recalled his own ordeal with the Hershey PD. "So, what happened to Mueller, if you don't mind me asking?" he said, half afraid to hear the answer.

"His throat had been sliced open."

"Yuck." Chip recoiled at the image. "He was *murdered*?"

"Yes."

"Did you see it?"

"No. But I showed the detective the smeared blood trail left by the killer, leading out of the lab. He wasn't very impressed."

"Do they have any leads on the murderer?"

"Well, maybe." Landry shot glances around the room. "I described the guy to, uh . . . Marky or Markel—whatever his name was—"

"Wait—you *saw* the guy?" Chip asked, stunned.

"Yeah. And finally the detective started taking me seriously."

"Why?"

"He said the description fit the guy who killed the ICU nurse last week."

"*What?*" A suffocating dread began to envelop Chip, making it hard to breathe.

"Some guy named Nick Chandler. Apparently, a former patient of Dr. Mueller. Why?" Landry was now staring at him.

Chip felt as if he had been sucker punched. He couldn't respond; all he could do was struggle for air.

"Are you all right?" Landry asked.

"Yeah," Chip spluttered, finally finding his voice. *How could this be, Chandler not dead, but still on the loose, killing people?.* Waves of nausea and dizziness coursed through him.

"Do you *know* this guy?" Landry asked.

"I was here the night he attacked Heather," Chip said softly.

"You were?"

"Heather was in the same room as your wife," Chip added.

Landry digested this. "I read the account of her death in the *Patriot News*," he said, "but they were awful scant on details." An intense look came into his eyes. "So *you* saw Chandler up close?"

"Yeah," Chip said, struggling to regain his composure. "Real close. He tossed me aside like I was a scarecrow."

Landry raised his eyebrows. "That's bizarre, all right, Chip."

Chip hesitated; it was now his turn to be reluctant. "That's not the half of it, Dr. Landry."

Landry was alert now, all traces of fatigue gone as he focused on Chip.

Chip cleared his throat again. "I was over at a friend's house this morning. She works here as a x-ray tech."

"Yeah . . ." Landry coaxed.

"Chandler attacked her at her apartment."

"What! Are you kidding?" Landry looked incredulous. "Why would he attack your girlfriend?"

"She's not my girlfriend. She's a friend who's a girl."

"Okay—but why?"

"I don't know. She was here the night he killed Heather, too." Chip decided to leave the talk of Kirlian photography and auras out of his rendition.

"When did this happen?"

"Just yesterday. Afternoon."

"Jesus—that's amazing. What happened?"

"Well, he attacked her in her basement—"

"Do the police know about this?" Landry began to pace back and forth, running his fingers through his hair.

"Yes, they were at her apartment investigating—Markel was in on this, as well."

"Is your friend okay?"

"Yeah, she's fine. But only because her dog fought him off."

Landry froze in his tracks. "Did you say *dog*?" he said, his voice urgent.

"Yes."

Landry reached out and gripped Chip's shoulder. "Chip, by chance, did she mention where her dog bit him?"

"Yeah. According to Kristin, he bit him real good in the neck. But Chandler got away. She thinks he climbed out the basement window, but I'm not sure that's possible." Chip paused as Landry's words sank in. "How did you know about the dog?"

Landry didn't answer, instead staring off into space.

"Her dog died in the fight," Chip continued.

"That's incredible." Landry ran his hand through his thoroughly mussed up hair and resumed pacing. Finally, he took Chip by the elbow and led him around the corner, out of earshot of the nurse's station. In a voice barely above a whisper, he said, "Chip, I have to tell you what else happened in the PML this morning. You're not going to believe it."

Chip listened with horrid fascination as Landry recounted his fight with Chandler. He spilled it all out in rapid fashion and Chip didn't interrupt him; he could see the fierce emotion playing across Landry's face as he relived the encounter. Finally, Landry came to the end of his tale, and took several deep breaths.

"That's crazy, all right," Chip said. "What do you think Chandler was doing at the med center in the first place? He knows the police are hunting him. And why go to the PML?"

"I've been asking myself the same thing," Landry said. "He must've gone to see Mueller. Perhaps to question him. He couldn't possibly have known that Laura or I would be there."

"Why would he kill Mueller, the man who saved his life?"

"I don't know. Same reason, I guess, that he killed that nurse, and was trying to kill your friend. They got in his way, or were witnesses. Lucky she had a dog to fight him off."

"The way Kristin talked, her dog practically took his head off."

"She wasn't exaggerating, Chip. I saw his neck wound up close—it *was* severe. I'm afraid I didn't help matters, either." Landry's hands clenched and unclenched spasmodically as he said this. "He probably crawled off somewhere to die. Good riddance."

"That's what we thought, too. Yesterday." Chip recalled Kristin's creepy feeling about Chandler. "But I'm thinking this guy doesn't die so easily," he added.

CHAPTER 45

Monday, 8:00 a.m.

Chip made his way out of the med center and stepped into a thick fog that blanketed the landscape, clinging to everything. Visibility was reduced to about ten feet or less. The pale ghostly disc of the sun appeared oddly disjointed, suspended low in the eastern sky. The only other thing he could make out were the tall xenon lights struggling to illuminate the parking lot, about a hundred yards distant. Even though he figured the fog would burn off soon, it was downright spooky-looking right now, and it wasn't even Halloween yet. Of course, everything seemed spookier with that monster Chandler roaming around.

Chip quickened his pace, anxious to get to the relative safety of his car. His legs protested slightly; they were still sore from his treadmill workout yesterday. His mind, however, was going a mile a minute; the conversation with Dr. Landry had been a real shocker. Especially on top of Kristin's horrifying tale. Something Landry had said kept replaying in his mind: "Chandler sliced Mueller's throat open with a scalpel blade." *Could any of this*

*Chandler stuff be real? Where is that bastard now? Has he bled
to death somewhere?*

He heard heavy footsteps approaching him on the walkway,
echoing strangely in the dense air. He slowed almost to a stop
and strained to see, but couldn't make out anything through the
impenetrable mist. The footsteps got louder. Involuntarily, he
tensed; his heart started to pound. Finally the white coat of a med
student materialized out of the fog, not five feet in front of him.
The student passed by and quickly faded into oblivion behind
him. Chip resumed breathing.

Eventually he found his car through the fog—the Camry's
faded, dull gray paint made it all the more difficult to see. He
hopped into the beat-up '98 Toyota and pulled the door shut with
more force than usual. After punching the automatic lock switch,
he fired up the reliable four-cylinder and gripped the steering
wheel hard, trying to collect his thoughts.

*Let's see—Chandler has now killed two people and a dog,
and tried to kill two more. He's still on the loose. How is that possible? Why can't the police catch this guy?* Chip pictured Markel
and Hershey's finest and figured he had answered his own question. He approached the med center main entrance. At the last
minute, he swung the Camry out of the left turn lane and went
straight, in the opposite direction from his apartment.

Chip executed a slow drive-by, rolling down the window, trying to see through the blasted fog. Kristin's apartment building
looked deserted—no lights on, no cars out front. He parked in
front of a neighbor's house and sat there for a few minutes, trying
to come up with a better plan than "investigate further."

Yellow crime scene tape was strung all over the relatively
narrow space, twenty feet at most, between the two buildings.
Briefly debating his course of action, he exited his car and quickly
ducked under the tape. He scrambled over to the side of her apartment building and crouched down to catch his breath. Still no sign
of anyone around.

Sparse forsythia shrubs lined the wall every four feet or so. He wasn't really sure what he was looking for or what he hoped to accomplish here, but then he caught sight of the basement transom window behind one of the bushes. He crawled over to his left, toward the window, and promptly cut the palm of his hand on a piece of broken glass. *Damn!*

Chip pulled his hand back and carefully brushed away several glass fragments. The little window was shattered, all right, and slivers of glass were strewn all over the place, indicating it had been broken from the inside, just as Kristin had said. There was blood, too. And not just a little bit. There were gobs of congealed blood, coating the dirt and nearby grass. *Holy shit!* Someone— make that Chandler—had bled profusely here. It looked like a fatal amount. Kristin had been right—again.

What else had she said that he had dismissed as crazy talk? "It was like he saw my intentions."

Chip followed the blood trail; it looked like it led out to the street. There was something strange about the trail, though. The gobs weren't spaced at regular intervals; they were spreading out as he neared the street. That meant that either Chandler's blood flow was decreasing as he went, or he was picking up speed— probably running.

At the street, the blood trail disappeared altogether. Did this mean Chandler had a car?

A police cruiser pulled up to the curb, startling Chip. *Double shit!* He quickly ran back and ducked behind one of the forsythia plants. The little shrub didn't provide much cover, but hopefully the fog would do the rest. He held his breath.

The car door opened and out stepped a familiar figure. Chip recognized the beer gut instantly—Detective Markel. Markel ambled onto the porch, out of Chip's line of sight.

Chip considered making a run for it. He could probably make it, concealed by the fog. He stood up, but before he could run, another car pulled up. Two people, a guy and a girl, got out and walked up onto the front porch. Chip didn't think he recognized either of them, but it was hard to tell for sure through the fog. Flattened against the wall behind the forsythia, he inched his way to the front corner of the building and peeked around, trying to get a better look.

"Thanks for meeting us here," the guy said. He was tall and muscular—looked like a college football player or something.

"I'm Detective Markel. Hershey PD." Markel shook the guy's hand, then launched into a gruff warning. "Get your stuff out of the apartment. Don't touch anything else in the place—remember, this is a crime scene. Hi-tech forensics—CSI stuff going on here. Got that?"

"Yes, sir," the guy said. "Again, we appreciate your time, officer."

"Sure," Markel said. "To protect and serve the community."

Slowly it dawned on Chip—the guy must be Kristin's roommate, Chris. A polite fucker, to boot. He still had no idea who the girl was.

Markel whipped out his notebook, pulled out a form, and addressed the girl. "Miss, if you don't mind, I need a little more info for my report."

"Okay," she said. She pulled out some keys and turned to the guy. "I just need the hanging stuff out of my closet in the bedroom. Do you mind?"

"No problem," the guy said, taking the keys. He walked to the far edge of the porch and unlocked the door to the second floor apartment. Soon his boots could be heard clunking up the wooden stairs to the second floor.

"Now, Miss O'Neil," Markel said, licking the tip of his pen. "How do you spell your first name? With a C or a K?"

"C. C-H-R-I-S," she spelled.

Chip was dumbfounded. *What the hell!* he mouthed to himself.

"Do you live alone?" Markel asked, staring at her.

"Yes," she said.

"And your male friend?" Markel nodded toward the second floor stairs.

"That's Josh—Josh Cole. He's my boyfriend. He visits from time to time."

"I see," Markel said, scribbling some notes. "Now, what about the occupants of this domicile?" He tapped on the frame of the screened-in front door with his pen.

"Kristin lives there, by herself," Chris said. "With her dog," she added, undoubtedly trying to be helpful.

"Yes, I know that," Markel said, sounding irritated. "Do you know if she got her possessions out?"

"Oh—yes. Her dad came by Saturday night and moved her out."

"Good," Markel grunted and snapped his notebook closed.

"Is it true, officer?" Chris said, suddenly sounding very distraught. "Was that man—the man who broke in—the one who killed that nurse? And did he really kill Kristin's dog?"

"Sorry, ma'am," Markel answered quickly. "I'm not at liberty to say—it's an ongoing investigation. Besides, there's privacy concerns at issue here."

Just then, Chip's phone buzzed on his hip. Thank God he had silenced it. *Who the hell would be texting me now?*

CHAPTER 46

Monday, 8:00 a.m.

Kristin yawned again and forced her eyes open even wider. After Chip's late night phone call in which he detailed his conversation with Dr. Landry, she hadn't been able to go back to sleep. Ever since she had looked at those prints in the darkroom—ever since she'd had her run-in with Chandler—her mind had been churning with thoughts of strange creatures from storybooks and nightmares. Learning of Mueller's death and hearing of Dr. Landry's encounter with Chandler only amped up her fearful imagination. *What the hell is going on?*

She jammed her foot down on the accelerator and her Honda Fit sped across the Walnut Street Bridge, heading straight toward the capitol building, its dome of newly refurbished green tiles barely discernable in the fog. She was playing another hunch.

At the end of the bridge, she passed by the twin towers guarding the entrance to the city. Atop the towers were winged creatures—gargoyles or something. She had never paid them much attention, but now, with her mind on the fantastical already, she craned her neck to get a better view; they looked especially eerie in the swirling mist.

She found a parking space, fed the meter, and walked up to the marble façade of the State Library building. With two hands, she heaved open the heavy door and strode inside. She felt as if she had been transported back in time fifty years; the architecture and library decor were definitely from a bygone era.

Undeterred, Kristin navigated the labyrinth of narrow corridors deeper and deeper into the library. The marble floors in this section were worn by years of heavy use to a smooth concavity. Hopefully, she thought, she could find what she was looking for in the historical books section.

After an hour spent poring over old and musty volumes in a forgotten alcove, Kristin flipped the page and her breath caught in her throat. There it was in front of her—an old daguerreotype from the late 1800s, showing two men standing in an old world study of sorts. To the left of the men was a huge world globe mounted in an ornate wooden floor stand with brass fixtures. In the background, by the fireplace, stood a suit of armor, its armored fist clutching an upright lance. Both men held tumblers of liquor, and one of them was puffing on a cigar. But what caught her attention was the halo rimming one man's thinning hair. An aura. The other, taller man didn't have one.

She couldn't really make out the features on the taller man's face because the photo was cracked and damaged there. Perhaps water damage was responsible for her not seeing an aura? She studied the photo more closely. No, just his face was obscured; his thick black hair was clearly visible. She read the caption under the photo: *Early photograph of two men from Corvinesti Castle, Central Romania, circa 1890. NB: The picture was developed using the Tesla methodology of electrophotography, a direct precursor of Kirlian photography.*

She scanned the text, trying in vain to slow her breathing. Her heart was pounding in her chest like a runaway train. The taller man was Baron Adrian Dobrogeanu. Her excitement turned to dread and she shuddered as she read the next line. It said he was long rumored to be a vampire!

But then the rational part of her mind kicked in. *Whoa, Kristin, hold on! Vampires aren't real. They're the stuff of movies and folktales.* Chandler hadn't tried to suck her blood, he had tried to kill her. But she couldn't deny that the man in the photo didn't have an aura—and he looked every bit alive. Maybe the photo had been altered? She checked the copyright on the book. It was printed in 1940. They didn't have Photoshop back then.

Kristin got up and checked her surroundings—no one in sight. She knew she wasn't allowed to check the book out or even copy it—it was an old reference book. She whipped out her cell phone, quickly looked around once more, and clicked several pictures. Replacing the book on its shelf, she ran out of the library, her mind spinning with possibilities and goosebumps peppering her skin.

CHAPTER 47

Monday, 10:00 a.m.

"Thanks for meeting me," Kristin said.

"Sure," Chip said flatly, surveying the small coffee shop. Starbucks was doing its usual brisk business; the line was about ten people deep. "I got your text. What's up?"

"You okay?" Kristin asked, studying him.

"Yeah, long night, that's all." Chip sat down across the small table from her.

"I got you a coffee," she said, pushing a cup toward him. "I didn't know how you take it, so I didn't put anything it."

"Black's fine."

"Boy, do I have something to show you," she said excitedly as she rummaged around in her purse.

"What?"

"It's a picture," Kristin said. "After you called last night, I got to thinking."

"Hmmm," Chip said, taking a small sip of the coffee; it was still way too hot and he burned the tip of his tongue.

She had retrieved her cell phone and was fiddling with it. "I went to the State Library in Harrisburg. Ever been there?"

"No."

"It's by the capitol."

"Oh."

"Are you *sure* you're okay?"

"Yeah. What's the picture of?"

She handed him her phone. "What do you make of *that*?"

"What, two old guys in a study somewhere drinking whiskey? Not that exciting." He tried to hand the phone back to her but she wouldn't take it.

"Look closely at it," she said.

"Okay." Chip studied the image again. "One guy's taller. When is this picture from? Looks old."

"Very good, Sherlock," she said sarcastically. "Eighteen-nineties."

"All right, I give up. What're you getting at?" Chip set her phone down on the table. He definitely wasn't in the mood for twenty questions.

"It's a *Kirlian* photograph—one of the first of its kind."

"So . . ."

"God, no wonder you flunked out," she said, but quickly flashed him a smile.

Chip put up both hands. "Hey, I don't need this—"

"I was just *kidding*. What's gotten into you this morning?"

"Nothing."

"Look, I'll forgive you this time because you've probably never seen one—"

"You're right about that," Chip said, trying hard to rein in his emotions.

"The guy on the left has an aura and the other guy doesn't," she continued.

"Seriously? I thought those were just watermarks or smudges in an old photograph. Here, let me see." Chip took a third look at the image. "You can't even see the one guy's face."

"I know, I know—the photo's not perfect. But clearly, the one man *has* an aura." She reached across the table and pointed to the screen. "And the other *doesn't.*"

"All right, I guess I'll buy it, if you say so." He handed the phone back to her.

Kristin let out a big sigh and settled back in her seat. "Okay, hang on, now, here comes the zinger." She smiled and paused for effect. "The caption said the man without the aura was suspected of being a vampire."

"*Vampire?*" Chip blurted, almost spilling his coffee.

"Yes. Keep your voice down." Several people at a neighboring table were now staring at them. "That's what it said."

"That's crazy talk," Chip said, shaking his head.

Her smile faded and she looked hurt. "I thought you'd be interested," she said.

"I don't think I'm even buying all this Kirlian aura crap."

Kristin didn't respond to that, but a frown darkened her face.

"I stopped by your apartment this morning," Chip said.

Kristin raised her eyebrows. "Why?"

"To check on something. It doesn't matter."

"And?"

"I saw Chris."

The color drained from her face. "Oh."

"That's it? That's all you have to say?"

"What would you like me to say?" she said quietly, inspecting her fingernails.

"The truth, for one thing," Chip said, his voice rising further. People were definitely staring now. "Why on earth did you tell me Chris was a *guy*? Your *roommate*? Your *boyfriend*? One-year anniversary and all that bullshit."

"I don't know," she said, still refusing to meet his gaze.

"I thought we were friends. That's what *you* said, anyway."

"Look, Chip, it's complicated. Let's not get into it here." She nodded in the direction of their nosy neighbors. "It has nothing to do with you."

"You lied to me. *That* has to do with me," Chip said, loud enough now for everyone in the coffee shop to hear.

"Okay, you're right. I was going to tell you."

"Right," Chip said in disgust. He stood. "I don't like people playing games with me. I already went down that road once." He shoved his chair back under the table and stalked out.

CHAPTER 48

Monday, 11:30 a.m.

Back in his apartment, Chip flopped down on the sofa and loosened the metal screw cap. What a hassle, he thought. *What a fucking hassle!* Everyone treated him like he was a criminal or something. He wasn't breaking any laws; he knew his rights. The checkout lady at the State Store had eyed him with such unvarnished disdain and disapproval that he had been tempted to call her on it. *Mind your own fucking beeswax.* Then, she had taken her sweet time inspecting his license, alternating long looks between his photo ID and his face. Shaking her head the whole time, she had finally rung up the sale and stuffed his new acquisition in a narrow brown paper bag. *Nosy bitch.*

For a while, he stared at the fifth of vodka gripped in his hands—cheapest stuff money could buy. Should he? Where was all his righteous resolve bullshit from yesterday?

The bottle didn't waste any time speaking up: *Look, champ, you can still keep all those promises you made to yourself. You can still get your life back. Don't sweat it. This is just temporary.*

Doesn't mean a damn thing. You just need a little smidge to help you through this rough spot. Then it'll be right back on track. Stick to the plan, Stan.

There's still plenty of time before work. Besides, just think, it's not even your fault. Why did she have to lie to you, anyway? Did you make her lie? I didn't think so. She's just like Michelle—only not as good-looking. You'll forget about her soon enough.

Besides, look on the bright side—you only bought one bottle. That took guts right there. So, it'll be all right. Plus—and you can take this one to the fuckin' bank—you dumped the shit out once, you proved you could do it. It only gets easier—everyone knows that. Better hurry, though—time's running out. And don't forget, vodka usually doesn't give you those nasty headaches like that tequila shit.

Chip clutched his head for several minutes. Finally, with trembling hands, he quickly screwed the cap back on and tried to set the bottle on the side table. The bottle came down crooked, on top of a stray ballpoint pen, and almost tipped over onto the floor. He caught it and repositioned the bottle, safe and secure on the tabletop. *Shit, that was close.* He flipped on the TV, hoping to distract himself.

CHAPTER 49

Monday, 7:00 p.m.

"Late, as usual, Allison," Victor said, shaking his head in exasperation.

"Sorry, Victor," Chip replied, trying not to slur his words. He set his backpack down and took another large slug of his coffee.

"I got a life, too, you know." Victor slid out of the monitor watcher's chair and picked up his computer bag from the floor. "All right, here's the deal. They're all pretty much the same. Except 237 is now in sinus rhythm." He pointed to the trace. "Seems much more stable than yesterday."

"Go figure."

Victor shouldered his bag and turned to leave. "Oh, and one more thing. This cleaning lady has been spending a lot of time in 237. Are you listening to me?"

"Yeah, I got it," Chip said. He set his coffee on the countertop and prepared to sit, but he had to stop and steady himself on the wooden railing as he swayed on his feet.

"You okay?" Victor asked, his voice rising in alarm.

"Yeah, don't worry about me." Chip made hushing gestures with his hands. "I'm fine."

"Jesus Christ!" Victor exclaimed. "I knew it." He dropped his voice down to a harsh whisper. "You're drunk again. I thought you said you had it under control. That you were done with all that shit." Victor shot glances all around. "You're going to get us both fired. And me kicked out of school. Like you."

"Chill out, man. I got coffee here. I'll be fine. Just go."

"I'm done with you, Allison. I'm going to have to report this, you know. It's not my fault."

"Whatever," Chip muttered.

Victor stomped off, leaving him alone to stew in his own thoughts. Chip kicked his backpack out of the way and rolled his chair into a better position. He was pissed at the world. He was also mad at himself for coming to work drunk—almost as mad as he was at Kristin.

Several hours into the shift, Chip needed to hit the bathroom. All that damn coffee had to go somewhere. Although he had finally calmed down and sobered up, his head hurt in spite of the four Advils he had dry swallowed an hour ago. Would Victor really turn him in? He didn't know the answer to that. What he did know was that he couldn't afford to get fired from this job, especially for drinking. His dad would kill him.

"Jenny," Chip called over to the charge nurse sitting at a nearby desk. "Can you cover me for a minute? Gotta use the B-R."

"Sure, Chip." She rose and walked over to his telemetry station. "Night's slow. Take a break. I'll watch things for you."

"Thanks. You're a lifesaver."

Fifteen minutes later, as Chip made his way back to his station, he noticed a cleaning cart parked outside Room 237. He would've sworn that wasn't there when he'd gone on break. The door to the room was now closed. And the shades were drawn. Strange. Perhaps they were doing a procedure on Mrs. Landry?

Didn't explain the cleaning cart, though. What was it Victor had said about the cleaning lady?

Chip bent down and peeked through a crack in the blinds. What he saw filled him with fear and dread.

He quickly retreated several steps, pulled out his cell phone, and dialed.

"Hello," came a sleepy voice.

"Dr. Landry," Chip said, breathing fast. "You better get in here. I think Chandler's in the room with your wife."

"What! Are you sure?"

"No. I went out for a break. When I came back, he was in the room. He's dressed like a cleaning lady. With gray hair. But I'm pretty sure it's him."

"Did he see you?"

"I don't think so."

"Listen, I'm on my way. I'll be there in fifteen minutes. Get him out of there. No, wait—call security. Maybe they can catch him."

"Will do," Chip said, and hustled back to his station.

Chip peered over the bank of monitors into room 237 as he dialed security. He waited while the phone rang. *Pick up, damn it, pick up!*

The door to 237 opened.

"Security. How can I help you?"

"Come to the ICU, right away," Chip whispered, his heart hammering in his chest.

The cleaning lady stepped out into the hallway, paused at her cart, and looked around.

"What seems to be the problem?" security asked. "I can barely hear you."

"Just come," Chip hissed into the phone as loud as he dared. "Intruder alert. Bring a gun if you have one."

The cleaning lady suddenly bolted across the ICU, passing right by Chip's station. She locked eyes with him briefly, her upper lip curled up in a sneer. Chip's hair stood up on the back of his neck as he gazed into Chandler's flat gray eyes. He tensed, ready for a fight, but Chandler headed straight for the exit door, opened it, and disappeared.

Chip resumed breathing and ran into Room 237, afraid of what he might see. Thank God—Mrs. Landry seemed fine. Still unconscious, but her vital signs were all stable. Through the window, he caught sight of a man running across the north parking lot. The man jumped into a parked vehicle—an older model Chevy Impala or Caprice, maybe, and some shade of silver or light gray; it was hard to tell the exact color in the lot's arc lighting. The Chevy lurched back out of the space, then sped forward. As the car roared by, close to the building, he got a good look at the driver. Although the wig was gone, there was no mistaking it—the man driving the car was Chandler. Chip couldn't make out the license plate.

"Hold it right there, young man!" growled a stern voice behind him.

Chip jumped, then spun around to find himself face to face with a large security guard. The guard's feet were planted, and he gripped a revolver in shaking hands. The gun was pointed directly at Chip's chest.

CHAPTER 50

Tuesday, 8:00 a.m.

"Here, let me buy you breakfast," Dr. Landry said, stifling a yawn. "As a thank you." After spending half the night on the fold-out sofa in his wife's room, Landry definitely looked worse for wear. Prominent bags sagged under his eyes and he had a serious case of bed-head, which was only to be outdone by the rumpled nature of his clothes. Clearly he hadn't gotten much sleep.

"You don't have to do that," Chip said, although he had to admit he *was* really hungry.

"No, I really appreciate you looking out for my wife. And chasing Chandler away." Landry shook his head. "To think that scumbag is still lurking around. Gives me the creeps."

"Yeah, me too," Chip said. "I didn't really chase him, though. He just scooted, right after I called you."

"Well, thanks for calling me, anyway. I can't tell you how relieved I feel to have the police involved." He gestured to the uniformed officer standing guard outside Mrs. Landry's room. "Makes me feel a lot safer." Another yawn surfaced and Landry fought to suppress it, but he was only partially successful. "Where do you want to go?" he asked. "The cafeteria?"

Chip hesitated, but only for a second. "There's a new coffee shop—Au Bon Pain—that just opened on the med school side. They have really good bagel egg sandwiches."

"All right, sounds good," Landry said, returning Chip's smile. "Lead the way. I could use some coffee, too."

Traveling along one of the long corridors that connected the hospital side of the med center to the medical school side, Landry and Chip passed by one of the main entrances just as Kristin entered, walking briskly, head down.

"Hey, Kristin," Chip said.

She stopped and looked up, her smile fading. "Oh. Hi Chip," she said coolly.

"You're here early," Chip remarked.

"I have some paperwork to catch up on," she said matter-of-factly.

"No problem. We won't hold you up. Oh—this is Dr. Landry. This is my friend, Kristin, who works in radiology."

"Pleased to meet you," Landry said, extending his hand to her.

"Nice to meet you, sir. I listened to your lecture—"

"Call me Doug."

"Okay," she said.

"We were just heading for breakfast," Landry said. "Why don't you join us?"

Chip groaned inwardly and Kristin looked uncomfortable. "Well," she said, "I really should get started on—"

Landry held up his hands and interjected, "I insist. It's my treat."

"Well, okay," she said with a tight smile. She glanced at her watch. "I guess I could—but just a quickie."

"Great." They resumed walking. "Chip here," Landry patted Chip's shoulder, "saved my wife from Chandler last night."

"*What?*" Kristin gaped from Landry to Chip.

"I understand you've had your share of run-ins with Chandler as well," Landry said.

"Yes." She turned to Chip. "What happened?"

"Chandler was back here at the med center," Chip said. "In Mrs. Landry's room."

Kristin's eyes widened.

"I'll fill you in over breakfast. I'm starved," he added, ushering the two of them into the crowded coffee shop. "If you guys would order, I'll grab a table. Can you get me a bagel egg sandwich with bacon and a large coffee and some OJ?"

Ten minutes later, Kristin took a small bite of her avocado bagel sandwich and washed it down with some organic apple juice before asking Chip, "So, was it really him?"

"It was him, all right," Chip said.

"What'd you do?"

"Right after I hung up with Dr. Landry, I called security."

"Did they catch him?" she asked excitedly.

"No," Chip said. "He left just before they got there."

"Dang it," Kristin said, balling one hand into a fist.

"And I saw Chandler leave in an old model silver or gray Chevy sedan," Chip said. "I even called the tip line at the Hershey PD and told them about the car."

"Is Mrs. Landry okay?" Kristin asked Dr. Landry.

"Yes," Doug said. "Laura's fine. He didn't touch her. In fact, I don't even think she knew he was there."

"Do you think Chandler read your mind?" Kristin asked Chip.

Chip almost choked on his sandwich and Landry raised his eyebrows.

"When you called security?" she added.

"I dunno," Chip said quietly.

Kristin turned to Landry. "We suspect Chandler can read minds."

Here we go, Chip thought, and was glad Kristin couldn't read his mind.

Without waiting for a response from Landry, she continued. "At least *I* do. Chip's never been alone with Chandler, fighting for his life."

"Chip told me about that," Landry said.

"My dog saved me," she said, her voice tight. "Chandler killed him."

"I'm sorry about your dog," Landry said.

"Thank you," Kristin said, her eyes beginning to mist over. "You fought with Chandler, right, Dr. Landry?" she asked.

"Yes."

"So what do you think? Did he read *your* mind?" she asked, quickly dabbing her eyes with a napkin.

"It's possible; I can't say. But what I do know is that your dog may have saved *my* life, too."

"How so?" Kristin asked, looking intently at Landry.

"Chandler was extremely weak from blood loss," Landry said, "and his neck wounds were severe—they looked fatal to me. Somehow, he still managed to put up one helluva fight. I'm not sure I'd ever want to tangle with him when he's healthy."

"Banjo was quite an extraordinary dog," Chip said.

Kristin did a double take at Chip, her ponytail swinging. "My dog's—"

Chip quickly interrupted her. "Smartest dog I've ever seen," he said, and silenced her with a hard stare.

Landry eyed the two of them curiously. "How Chandler's walking about now, I don't have a clue," Landry said. "He's one tough bastard."

"Agreed," Chip said.

"What did you think of my Kirlian photograph?" she asked.

"Huh?" Landry said, looking blank.

Her head whipped toward Chip. "You *did* tell him, didn't you?" she demanded.

"Well, not yet," Chip managed. "I was getting around to it."

"Right," Kristin said with a huff. "I know *you* don't believe in them. But I thought maybe someone with a broader background, more experience, might have a different take on it. Dr. Landry, surely *you've* heard of Kirlian photography?"

Landry's brow creased, struggling with this one. "You mean the pictures with the halos?"

"Yes." Kristin beamed at him. "The auras."

Relief washed over Landry's face.

"See?" She glared at Chip before turning back to Landry. "Well, I took one of Chandler the other day," she said, "and his photo showed no aura."

"That's amazing," Landry said evenly.

"Exactly. I told you he'd understand." She threw Chip another sour look.

"What does it mean?" Landry asked, his tone tentative.

"Well, we don't know, exactly," she admitted.

"You might as well tell him about the picture from the library," Chip said, unable to hold back a sigh.

"All right, I will," Kristin said indignantly. "I found an old picture of a man without an aura in the State Library."

"I see," Landry said.

Kristin leaned forward. *Here it comes,* Chip thought, and played with his sandwich. In a hushed voice, she said, "It said he was suspected of being a vampire."

"Oh," Landry said. An awkward silence followed and everyone sipped their drinks. Finally Landry said to her, "So you think Chandler's a vampire?"

"I didn't say that," she said, her tone defensive. "It's just that there's stuff we can't explain about him. Like how he heals so fast, and is resistant to dying."

"You've got a point there," Landry said. Another uncomfortable silence followed.

"Look," Kristin said, rising abruptly. "I can tell you guys think I've lost my marbles. I really *do* have to get to work." She left her bagel sandwich—hardly touched—on her plate and made a quick exit.

CHAPTER 51

Tuesday, 8:30 a.m.

They both watched Kristin leave, her boots clomping loudly on the tile floor. Chip polished off his bagel sandwich while Landry played with the cardboard sleeve around his coffee cup. When she was no longer in sight, Chip cleared his throat. "She just told me the vampire stuff yesterday," he said in a low voice. "If you ask me, I think it's kind of crazy."

"It *is* pretty far out there," Landry admitted.

"She's usually very level-headed," Chip said.

"I'm sure she is," Landry replied.

"I think this whole Chandler thing—and losing her dog—have thrown her for a loop."

"Undoubtedly." Landry looked like he wanted to say more, but didn't.

"Dr. Landry, you said his wounds looked fatal. You're a doctor. How do you think Chandler survived that?"

"I don't know. I've been asking myself the same thing. But I don't think he's a vampire," Landry added with a smile.

"Me either." Chip returned the smile. "She has quite the imagination."

"I wasn't going to say this," Landry said slowly, "but I thought you said you guys were friends. Seemed a bit frosty to me."

"We had a slight disagreement—well, an argument—yesterday."

"About the vampire picture?"

"No, not exactly," Chip said, wincing. "She lied to me about having a boyfriend. I mean, I can put up with a lot of things—I'm really pretty easygoing. But lying is not one of them. In my book, it's pretty serious."

"How long has she been going out with the guy?" Landry asked.

"That's just it—she's not."

"What do you mean?"

"She made the guy up. She said she was going out with this guy, but she's not; he doesn't exist."

"That *is* different," Landry conceded. "Why would she do that?"

"I have no idea. She said it's complicated."

"It always is," Landry said, his smile returning. "Look, Chip, I'm no expert at these things—far from it—but I think she likes you."

"*Why* do you say that? I thought you just said *frosty*."

"I did," Landry said. "But frosty implies some kind of emotional attachment. I think she cares about what you think. Besides, look on the bright side—she doesn't have a boyfriend."

"Well, whatever—I'm not going there. Lying is lying."

Landry paused and drank some coffee. He continued in a more thoughtful tone. "So when she said Chandler could read minds and you didn't disagree—even though I know you do—were you lying?"

"That's different," Chip answered quickly. "I was just trying to protect her feelings. She's been through a lot."

"I see."

"So how was Mrs. Landry doing this morning?" Chip asked, ready for a change of subject.

"Great. Laura seems to be making giant strides."

"That *is* good news," Chip said. "Her rhythm has certainly stabilized."

Landry's eyes lit up, erasing his earlier fatigued look. "This morning, early, around six a.m., she opened her eyes for the first time since coming out of the PML. And she squeezed my hand."

"Does she seem . . . uh, okay?" Chip asked.

"Yes. I spent an hour or so filling her in on things."

"Do you think she understands?"

"Absolutely. Her mind seems completely intact. She would nod and shake her head appropriately—she can't talk, of course, because of the breathing tube."

"Right."

"She even wrote me a couple of notes."

"That *is* impressive," Chip said, and meant it.

"I told her about you—how you helped protect her."

Chip drained his coffee.

Landry reached into his pocket and produced several scraps of paper. "Here, look a this." He handed Chip one.

The note, neatly printed, read: *I would like to meet Chip and thank him myself.*

"Nice," Chip said and handed the note back. "You guys have a special relationship, don't you?" Chip asked, meeting Landry's eyes.

"Yes, we do."

"After all those years—" Chip stopped himself and he felt his face redden. "Sorry about that. You know what I mean. What I'm trying to say is, was it always that way for you?"

"Yes," Landry said, looking off into space and showing no sign of being offended. "It was love at first sight."

"Seriously? I always thought that was make-believe—you know, fake."

"Nope, it's for real," Landry said, refocusing on Chip.

Chip thought for a few moments, then said, "So, which is more out there, I wonder? Love at first sight? Or vampires?"

Landry chuckled at this.

"Or love at first bite?" Chip added.

Landry's grin sagged a bit. "I can't wait to take her home."

"I'm sure you can't," Chip said, even as he thought Landry was rushing things a bit. Two days ago, Mrs. Landry had been close to death in the PML.

Landry paused for several moments, a contemplative look settling on his face. "Her progress is truly remarkable."

"Yeah, remarkable," Chip said, looking away.

CHAPTER 52

Tuesday, 11:30 p.m.

Chip banged on the door again, louder. As he stood waiting on the cement stoop, gusts of wind whipped his short hair into a mess.

Finally, the door opened halfway and Kristin stood there in her nightgown. "What are you doing here?" she asked, rubbing her eyes. She looked as if she'd just awakened. She also didn't look too happy to see him.

"You said your dad lives in Halifax—I looked up his address. Besides, I saw your car parked outside." He knew he should've called, but there was that small issue of his missing phone.

"Is your dad home?" Chip asked, looking around.

"Yes. He went to bed already." She brushed her long hair out of her face—no ponytail this evening. "So did I." She was still regarding him with suspicion.

"Look, I'm sorry about the surprise visit. I can explain. But I need to talk to you," Chip insisted. "*Please.*"

She hesitated, then opened the door wider. "All right, since you drove all the way up here—c'mon in."

"Thanks," Chip said as he entered.

"Have a seat while I put some clothes on." She gestured to the living room.

"All right." He made himself comfortable on the upholstered sofa.

"What's so urgent, Allison?" she said as she moved away.

"I saw his car again."

That stopped her in her tracks. "Whose car?"

"Chandler's."

Kristin came back into the living room and sat on the edge of a chair across from him. "Really?"

"Yes. I was just leaving the med center after my shift and I saw it in the parking lot."

"Are you sure?" she asked, staring at him intently.

"Yes. I got a good look at it this time, complete with license plate number. It's a '69 silver Impala, by the way. Do you have your computer around?"

"Yes. Why?"

"Get it. I'll show you."

She slid out of the chair and padded in her bare feet across the living room throw rug. He couldn't help but notice how short her nightgown was and that her underwear showed through the white gauzy fabric. She retrieved a computer bag from a cabinet under the bookcase. "Don't you think we should call the police?" she said as she fished her laptop out. The Mac chimed as she opened the lid and turned it on.

"I already did. They took down the plate number and said they'll send some officers to check it out soon."

"Good," she said, and handed him the computer.

Chip rapidly called up a Google map and pointed at the little red marker in the center of the screen. "Here it is."

Kristin leaned over to look at the screen. "It looks like the med center. What's the red dot?" She sat down on the sofa beside him.

"My phone. I threw it onto the backseat of his car." He looked over at her, trying to gauge her reaction.

"*What?*" she asked incredulously, meeting his eyes.

"The back window was open a crack, so I slipped it in."

"Why would you do that?"

"So I can track his car."

Kristin frowned.

"With this app I have on the phone," he said, "I can track its whereabouts—locate it."

She smiled as understanding dawned. "Nice," she said, but her smile soon gave way to a worried look. "Do you think he knows it's there? Did he see you or get near you?"

"I don't think so. I didn't see him around anywhere."

"So, Chandler's back at the med center," she said, her eyes narrowing. "What do you think he's up to?"

"I don't know," Chip said. "But I *am* wondering how Mrs. Landry fits in."

"What could *she* possibly have to do with any of this?" she asked.

"I don't know," Chip said. "But Chandler's obviously interested in her. He was in her room the other night. And there was that whole blood transfusion story in the PML I told you about."

"Right."

"Listen, I need to ask you a favor."

"What?" she said, although he thought he could detect some of her initial wariness returning.

"Can you develop some film for me?"

"What are you talking about?" she asked.

"I took some pictures. Remember I told you I have an old Minolta X-700 that uses 35 millimeter film?"

"Uh-huh. You use it to take pictures with your telescope."

"Exactly," Chip said, surprised she remembered.

"Well, all my stuff's back at my apartment," she said. "In the basement."

"I'll drive you there." Chip stood.

"You mean *tonight*?" she asked. "What's gotten into you?"

"It's really important. I think you'll want to see these pictures."

"Well, I'd like to help you out, but my enlarger's busted," she said, sounding genuinely disappointed. "Just take them to Rite Aid."

"I was hoping *you'd* develop them. Using the *Kirlian* technique. I don't think Rite Aid offers that service."

"No, they don't." She half smiled and eyed him curiously. "I guess I could. But what would be the point? I mean, who believes in Kirlian photography, anyway?"

"I'd like to give it a—"

"It's a bunch of crap, right?"

"I'm sorry I said—"

"That's crazy talk, right?"

Chip groaned and held up his hands. "I know, I know. You got me."

"And you made a fool of me in front of Dr. Landry this morning."

Chip sighed and looked away. After a moment he said quietly, "I'm sorry about all that. I guess I was upset by the whole Chris thing."

Now it was her turn to be silent.

"Look," Chip said, "I know Kirlian photography is your baby. Even though I'm not sold on it, I'm trying to keep an open mind."

"You didn't really give me a chance to explain, you know," she said.

"What? About Kirlian photography?"

"No—the whole Chris thing, as you put it."

"I guess I didn't," Chip said.

"Will you let me now?" The edge had disappeared from her voice.

"Sure." Chip sat back down.

She met his eyes. "First off, I promise I wasn't playing games with you." He thought this sounded sincere. She continued. "I've had some bad experiences with guys—real bad. Lied to, cheated on, you name it. Guys can be real douchebags. I'm taking a break from the dating scene for a while. This little stunt—the Chris thing—proved the most effective way of keeping guys away." She brushed her hair out of her face again. "I'm kinda in the habit of telling my little story, so when we first met, it just came out. I didn't mean anything by it, honest."

"I guess that's plausible."

"It's the truth," Kristin said. "And I'm sorry for deceiving you. No more stories, I promise."

"All right, thanks," Chip said, trying hard not to stare at her nightgown, the way she filled it out and the way the low-cut neckline offered glimpses of what lay beneath. "And I promise not to doubt you."

"Deal," she said and smiled broadly, her face lighting up. When she smiled, he thought, she was downright pretty. "Let me put some clothes on and I'll go with you."

"Sure," Chip said, although he was sorry that the nightgown would be going away.

She hopped off the sofa and scampered out of the room.

"What are your pictures of, anyway?" she called out from the bedroom. "The moon or the stars? Planets?"

"You'll see."

CHAPTER 53

Tuesday, 11:30 p.m.

Doug stood tensely against the wall in Laura's ICU room, trying to stay out of the way. A crowd of solemn-looking doctors, residents, and med students were gathered around her bedside.

One of the intensivists, Dr. Bagdonavich, spoke up first. He was darkly complected and although his heavy beard was neatly trimmed, it only made his face look darker. "We have been on weaning protocol all evening," he said in his deep and heavily accented voice. Doug figured he was of Middle Eastern descent. "This morning all parameters look good. Tidal volumes are up to five hundred ccs and NIF is minus forty-five centimeters of water. She's down to forty percent O2 with sats. ranging above ninety-five percent. Patient is also regaining consciousness. All in all, I believe she is extubatable."

Dr. Leffler, the cardiologist in charge of Laura's care, glanced over at Doug and gave him a thumbs-up along with a warm smile.

Bagdonavich nodded to Novacinski. Novacinski suctioned Laura's mouth out with a Yankauer plastic suction cannula, making her gag violently. He then roughly pulled the tape holding the endotracheal tube from her face and yanked the tube from her mouth in one swift motion. Laura coughed, gagged some more, and sputtered for breath. Novacinski plunked a plastic oxygen mask on her face and cinched the elastic band tightly around her head.

Breathe, Laura, Doug thought. *Breathe.*

The room fell deathly quiet, the only sound coming from Laura's ragged efforts to breathe and the pulse oximeter, which chimed out its findings. The pulse ox tone began to fall as her saturation level dropped through the 80s. Laura coughed and took several stuttering deep breaths. Her pulse oximeter continued to fall and her lips began to shade into duskiness.

Doug started toward the bedside in alarm—no one seemed to be moving. He felt sure they would need to assist her breathing with the Ambu bag. Finally, Laura took several deeper breaths and the pulse ox began to climb. Her sat eventually hit 98% and held steady. Doug took several breaths of his own and willed himself to calm down.

Novacinski glanced over at him with a condescending look, one that said "Relax, old man, we got this." The crowd, all smiles now, passed congratulatory murmurs around and then quickly dispersed.

Doug approached the bedside and took Laura's hand. "Feel better?"

Laura nodded and mustered a faint smile.

"Breathe, okay?"

She nodded again.

He squeezed her hand and she squeezed back.

"You're doing so well," Doug assured her. "You're getting better by leaps and bounds."

She looked up at him, smiling wider.

"You should be able to talk now," he said.

"Be careful what you wish for," she croaked, her voice very hoarse from the endotracheal tube.

Doug chuckled.

"I'm so tired, though," she said, eyelids drooping.

"That's normal, honey. You've been through a lot."

"I love you," she said, her voice barely a whisper now.

"I love you, too," Doug said, hearing his voice tighten with emotion. He patted her arm and watched her drift off to sleep.

Doug eased himself into the chair in the corner of Laura's room and felt his own fatigue taking hold. He had spent so much time in this chair over the past week that it seemed the foam rubber underneath the vinyl covering had begun to mold itself to his body. He was utterly exhausted, but had refused to give in to it, remaining vigilant for Laura's sake. Now, with her recovery finally taking shape, he could begin to relax. He settled back, willing his aching muscles to rest. But Doug's mind would not unwind so easily.

He gazed over at Laura. She was sleeping peacefully. Laura was definitely on the mend and thank God, her mind also appeared to be intact, something never to be taken for granted after resuscitations and the deep coma used in Mueller's PML. She would probably spend many hours sleeping, courtesy of the pain meds. Doug knew they had dodged a bullet—no, many bullets. He flashed back to the A-10 Warthog they had seen while on the fateful bike ride and its Vulcan machine gunfire. Weird image, he thought, and dismissed it. It seemed the nightmare was coming to an end.

Still restless, Doug pulled a notebook from his backpack. This was the first chance he'd had to take a serious look at it. A simple two- by three-inch white label on the front of the notebook bore a handwritten title: *PML#5*. Large blood smears also adorned the cover.

He had discovered Mueller's private lab notebook in the same storage cabinet where Chandler had unceremoniously stuffed the researcher's body. Doug reasoned there must be four other manuals locked somewhere in Mueller's lab, which was now a crime scene. There was no doubt that Doug had stumbled upon this one because Mueller had been murdered before he had a chance to put it away. Uncharacteristically, Doug had lied to the police on this point and kept the notebook's existence a secret. He couldn't say why, exactly, but he had a feeling that this notebook might shed some light on Laura's condition. Besides, he felt he had paid a steep price for admission to this weird carnival and was therefore entitled to some special treatment. He would turn the notebook over to the authorities after he had examined it.

Doug flipped through the pages, trying to extract some meaning, some gestalt from Mueller's tight scrawl. The entries began one year ago. Doug had no trouble envisioning the bespectacled researcher hunched over his desk, painstakingly keeping his notes. He couldn't help feeling a certain degree of sympathy for the man. Pathologists, in general, often occupied the bottom rung of the clinical ladder and Mueller, in particular, had been shunned by the medical community, thanks to his morbid research interests.

But Mueller's dogged persistence over the years had finally paid off; he had tapped into some unseen potential and his work truly represented a quantum leap forward in resuscitation science. Not to mention, his groundbreaking research was directly responsible for Laura being alive. Doug owed Dr. Mueller a lot. It was a cruel twist of fate that he had been murdered by a patient who had been saved by his research. The whole Chandler story was most unnerving. Was it just an unhappy coincidence that he was a product of Mueller's lab?

And what about the accounts from Chip and Kristin—could they be believed? Doug had seen Chandler's wounds with his own eyes, had wrapped his own fingers around the raw meat that was Chandler's neck. Surely Kristin was telling the truth about her dog saving her life. But she believed Chandler could read minds. *Can he? Is that even possible?* Of course, she also toyed with the idea that Chandler was a vampire. Doug drew the line here—her imagination was getting the best of her.

But he had to admit, Chandler *did* seem to be highly intuitive. And god-awful strong. And there was no denying that those neck wounds should have been fatal. There must be some other explanation.

This brought him full circle to the elephant in the room. What in God's name was the connection between Chandler and his wife? Another coincidence? As many times as he had glossed over this and tried to rationalize it or ignore it, it wouldn't go away. The question seemed crucial to his understanding of this whole bizarre circumstance. Sadly, he didn't seem any closer to an answer.

Doug turned back to the notebook, hopeful that he could glean some insight into Mueller's research. Perhaps it would even hold the key to his question. He flipped through page after page of tables and graphs, tables full of every conceivable variable with corresponding graphs and figures to further illustrate the data. He viewed electron micrographs of mitochondria and lysosomes and nuclei and other structures he didn't recognize or had never heard of. What quickly became evident was that Mueller was exceedingly thorough in his documentation of everything, to the point of overkill. No data was deemed too trivial.

Doug sighed and ran his fingers across his stubbly chin. It would take days to pore through this notebook and he probably would never understand half of it. His initial hopes began to fade.

Toward the back of the notebook, Doug found EEG tracings from nine subjects. Several of them showed a segment of the EEG in the high frequency range that was flatline. That seemed peculiar. In fact, Mueller had circled these regions with red highlighter and written several question marks on the traces. The text below didn't shed any light on the tracings; it just said *More clinical correlation required.* Doug thought this was uncharacteristically vague for Mueller. None of the subjects were identified by name. Subject number nine was coded 35MNC. But there was also a tenth subject, 40FLL, that had no EEG trace attached.

The final pages of the notebook were devoted to MRI images of the brain. There were photocopies of MRI scans, again with subject codes. Only four scans were present. On each scan, one particular region of the mid-brain was circled with red highlighter; there was a strange shadow here that stood out from the normal brain tissue. Then Doug noticed that the page numbers jumped from 121 to 125, and he realized that several pages must've been torn out. This would explain why there were only four subjects.

At the bottom of page 121 was an obscure handwritten note, scribbled diagonally in tiny letters. It appeared to be Mueller's script, but sloppily rendered, probably in haste—not his usual, meticulous writing. It read *MRI scans /BM 10/12/ NB: amygdala/ cingular gyrus shadow??* and had a big red X through it.

Laura began to stir, and Doug closed the notebook, noticing as he did that there was a pocket inside the back cover. In the pocket was a folded piece of paper.

Laura opened her eyes, her expression confused and fearful. Her gaze darted about the room, undoubtedly trying to find something familiar with which to orient herself, get her bearings. Finally she locked onto his face and visibly relaxed.

"I'm here, Laura," Doug said, smiling at her as he fished out the paper. "Everything's okay." He unfolded the paper and saw that it was another EEG scan. Like some of the others, it showed the peculiar absence of signal in the higher energy spectrum. The region was again circled in red.

"Sorry. I forgot where I was," Laura said in a weak voice. She attempted to clear her throat. "I've been having the most vivid dreams."

Doug stood, the scan still grasped in one hand, and reached out with his other hand to stroke her forearm. "You're safe now."

"What's that?" she asked, gazing at the paper he held.

"Just work stuff. You just concentrate on getting better, honey. We need to get you home in time for your birthday." Laura's forty-first birthday was coming up in two weeks. He opened the notebook to put the tracing back into the pocket, then paused. On the back of the tracing, scrawled in Mueller's unmistakable tight script, was *40FLL*. A chill went through Doug as the meaning of the code hit him.

CHAPTER 54

Tuesday, 11:55 p.m.

Kristin opened the door to the basement and stepped onto the wooden staircase; the crime scene tape had been removed.

"You okay to go down there?" Chip asked, right behind her.

"Yeah, I'll be all right," she said and he saw her jaw tighten.

"Good," Chip said, following Kristin onto the creaky stairs. Several steps down, he added, "I didn't flunk out, just so you know."

"Oh," she said.

"I got asked to leave for cheating."

She stopped halfway down, grasped the handrail and turned to study him.

"I wasn't even cheating for myself," he said. "I gave someone a copy of a pharm test."

"Someone?"

"Yeah—a nursing student."

"Why would you do that?"

"I felt sorry for her and—" Chip stopped himself and cleared his throat. "That's not quite right. She came on to me and I folded. I know it's horrible."

Kristin didn't say anything.

"Don't look at me like that—my dad looks at me like that."

"It's just—it just doesn't seem like you," she said. "You seem like a good guy—you know, honest."

"I didn't lie. When they called me in, I didn't try to deny it. I knew it was wrong. I didn't even turn the girl in."

They walked down the remainder of the staircase in silence and she led him into the darkroom. Involuntarily he cringed as he imagined meeting Chandler down here in this little room and fighting for his life.

Several minutes later, Chip gave up on waiting for any further reaction from her. "So what do you think?" he asked. His eyes still hadn't adjusted to the strange red light; apparently this was as bright as it would get. He wasn't prone to claustrophobia, but the darkroom in Kristin's basement felt very confining and the dim light wasn't helping matters.

"Huh?" She was busy rooting through her cabinets, looking for something.

"Of what I just told you?"

"I dunno. I guess we all make mistakes." She didn't sound overly concerned.

"First," she said, back to business, "we have to mix a new batch of chemicals and let them come to room temperature." She tore open some chemical packets one by one and poured the powdery contents into three separate plastic trays. Next, she turned on the faucet and added water to a Pyrex measuring cup, which she then meted out into the trays.

"Here, make yourself useful," she said, and handed him a large plastic spatula. "Stir these trays while I look for my thermometer."

Chip stirred the contents with the spatula, being careful not to spill any. He weighed his words for a moment before continuing. "So you really think our friend, Chandler, is a vampire?"

"Will you guys get off it?" she shot back, turning to face him. "I never *said* he's a vampire."

He couldn't read her expression in the dim light, but he was pretty sure she was scowling. "Just checking," he said, lifting his empty hand in a defensive gesture.

"But you have to agree," she said, toning it down, "something weird is going on with him."

"I agree there's a lot of stuff we can't explain."

"Like him being so strong. And healing so fast."

"Right," Chip said.

"And don't forget the mind-reading part," she said.

"I'm still not convinced about that."

"Remember, this morning you talked about keeping an open mind." She opened one of the drawers. "Besides, you said Dr. Landry wondered about this, too."

"What he *said* was that Chandler seemed to anticipate his moves."

"Ah, here it is." She plucked a thermometer out of the drawer and placed it in one of the trays. "Oh, and another thing. Why the *hell* did you tell Dr. Landry that my dog's name was Banjo?"

Chip couldn't help smiling. "I got it from a World War Two spy novel."

"Huh?" She bent down to get a look at the thermometer.

"I'll explain later," he said.

"Well, anyway, Chandler anticipated my moves, too."

"Right," Chip said. "But that doesn't necessarily imply mind-reading. And just because we can't think of rational explanations for these things doesn't mean there aren't any. I'm just not ready to invoke supernatural creatures, like vampires or werewolves, to explain stuff. That's too much."

She paused in thought. "I don't really believe in vampires either."

She sounded sincere. "Thank God," he said.

"But what about the lack of aura in Chandler?" she said. "And in that picture from the library?"

"A coincidence?" he offered.

"I doubt it. I've been giving this a lot of thought."

"Uh-huh." Chip had no trouble believing this part.

"I want to deal only in the facts, though," she said. "Let's try to square the facts with what happened."

"Now you're talking," Chip said.

"We know Chandler was extremely sick when he came in," she said. "His heart and organ systems were trashed."

"Right."

"Then essentially, he coded one too many times and died."

"Well, I don't know if you can say he died," Chip said. "He was near death."

"Okay, near death. Near enough to death that he earned a trip to Mueller's PML."

"Correct," he said.

"And you remember what Mueller said about his EEG—an absence of signal . . ." Kristin stared off into space. Chip had begun to associate these looks with her intuition kicking in. "What if . . ."

"What?" Chip was afraid to hear what she might come up with now.

"What if he doesn't have a soul?"

"What?"

"What if his soul departed?" she said.

"*What?* I thought we left the fairytales and make believe things behind?"

"I'm serious, Chip. Hear me out. I'm not talking fantasyland here. Many people think that the aura shown in Kirlian photos is physical evidence of the human soul."

Chip knew he wasn't one of those people, open mind or not.

"And," she continued, on a roll, "what if his not having an aura fits with the absence of a high frequency signal on his EEG that Mueller had never seen before?"

"Okay," Chip said, "for the sake of argument, let's say you're right. But you said dead people don't have auras. I'll buy that their soul is gone. But Chandler's obviously not dead."

"Yeah, but for a time, he *was*—for all intents and purposes, he *was* dead. Maybe his soul left him—I mean, think about it: when does the soul leave? You heard Mueller. The body dies in parts—different organs die at different times, not all exactly at once. So, does the soul leave when the heart dies? The brain? The kidneys or liver? Who knows?"

Chip didn't know what to say to this.

"Maybe," she continued, "his soul left him—was triggered to leave as death came upon him—in a normal, end of life scenario. But then in a freak of science, Mueller pulls him back from the edge and resuscitates his body. Except his soul has *already* left."

"I doubt that's possible," Chip said.

"A couple of days ago, we didn't think people could read minds, either. Now we're considering it." Kristin checked the thermometer again. "They didn't think people could land on the moon, either."

"So you're saying he's alive, but has no soul?" Chip ran his hand through his hair. "Great—so we're done with vampires, but have moved on to zombies?"

"Chandler's no zombie, Chip. Besides, what does anyone really know about a soulless being, anyway?"

"Nothing," Chip said. "That's the point—they don't exist."

She was staring away again. "Maybe the soul exerts a limiting influence on the human brain."

Chip didn't respond, but watched her closely. Even though he didn't agree with her, he admired her creative thinking.

"Maybe the brain is capable of so much more," she continued, speaking rapidly now. "What if the soul acts like a governor of sorts? Remove it, and the brain is free to rev up, hit new levels. Maybe this would explain the healing, the strength, the mind-reading. Nothing really contradicts the laws of physics here."

Chip whistled. "You've got one heck of an imagination there, Earthgirl."

"I'll take that as a compliment."

"Hey, do you have your phone with you?" Chip asked.

"Yeah. Why?"

"I want to check to see if Chandler's car has moved yet." She handed him the phone. "How long will it take to develop the film?" he asked.

"A half-hour or so, I'm afraid. That is, if my equipment still works. Of course, my enlarger is trashed."

"Oh shit!" Chip said, looking at the phone.

"I'll try to go faster—"

"No. His car isn't at the med center anymore."

"What?" she asked. "Where is it?"

"Seems to have stopped at—wait, let me blow this up." Chip manipulated the phone screen. "Looks like Caracas Avenue in Hershey. Listen Kristin, I've gotta go to the police and show them this. Maybe they can pick him up."

"Are you sure?"

"Yes," Chip said, heading for the door. "Why don't you finish developing these and call me when you're done. Wait—I don't have a phone. Never mind, don't call."

"That was a smart move, putting your phone in his car, by the way," she said.

"Thanks."

"Brave, too."

Chip felt himself blush and was glad she probably couldn't see it in the dim light. "I'll call you from the police station in half an hour."

"All right, sounds good," she said.

"Will you be okay here? Alone?"

"Yeah, I'll be fine," she said. "I'll go as fast as I can and then scoot. I need twenty minutes to apply the electrical current to the film before I develop it."

"All right—be careful," he said.

"I will. You too."

CHAPTER 55

Tuesday, midnight

Chip stepped up to the counter. A rotund policeman, mid-fifties, a sergeant by his stripes, was seated off to one side, typing at a computer. He could have been Detective Markel's brother except he had more hair; it was slicked back in an old-fashioned Brylcreem style.

Chip coughed.

"I'll be right with you," said the policeman without glancing up from his screen.

Chip looked around for help; there was no one. Finally the man spun his chair around and looked in his direction. "I'm Officer Maloney. What can I do for you, son?"

"I *need* to speak to a detective."

"Hang on. Let me get the proper form." Maloney leaned forward and rummaged around underneath the counter. After several grunts, he came back up with a sheet of paper. Slightly out of breath, his face red, he nodded at Chip. "Okay, go ahead."

"My name is Chip Allison and I—"

"Is Chip a nickname?"

"Yes." Chip leaned in through the little window. "Listen, this is urgent."

Maloney ignored this. "Real name?"

"Charles."

"Last name?"

"Allison."

"One or two Ls?"

"Two." Chip took a big breath, trying to remain calm. "Listen, this really is *urgent.*"

"Just a couple more questions, Mr. Allison. Are you a Derry Township resident?"

"Yes."

"And what is the nature of your concern?"

Finally. "I have information about the man who killed that nurse."

"*What?* Why didn't you say so?" Maloney regarded him seriously for the first time.

"I think I know where Nick Chandler is—now."

Maloney's eyes narrowed. "How do you know his name?"

"Look, I work at the med center," Chip said, speaking rapidly. "I was there the night Chandler killed her. I *know* him. I called in a tip last night about the late model sedan he's driving. I saw the car again tonight at the med center and called you guys an hour ago with the make, model, and license number. They said they'd be sending officers."

Maloney eyed him suspiciously, then hoisted himself out of his swivel chair with a groan. "Wait here, I'll be right back."

Chip ran his hand through his hair and paced around on the worn linoleum floor.

Maloney came back after several minutes with a manila file folder in hand. "Okay, Mr. Allison. I have your folder." He smacked the folder on the countertop. "My officers just reported in. They found no '69 Chevy Impala at the med center."

"I'm trying to tell you—his car isn't there anymore."

"Where is it?" Maloney asked, impatience clipping his words.

"Fifty-nine Caracas Avenue in Hershey."

"How could you *possibly* know that?" Maloney said, his voice rising. "We've been searching for him all-out for days now."

"I tracked my phone."

"What? What are you talking about?"

"I put my phone in his car, and tracked it to that address."

"Is this a joke? If this is a joke, son, we don't take these things lightly. You'll be—"

"It's no joke. My phone has an app on it that allows you to locate it. You've got to believe me." Again Chip looked around for help.

Maloney's eyebrows knotted together and his lips compressed in a pained expression. "Son, if I wake up the captain at home for some bullshit story—"

"It's the truth," Chip insisted.

Maloney shook his head, then picked up the phone on his desk and dialed. After a pause, the policeman said into the phone, "It's me, Maloney. Sorry to bother you at home, sir, but—" Maloney's face reddened again and Chip could hear yelling coming from the other end. "Just past midnight," Maloney said sheepishly.

More loud chatter from the other end. Maloney took a deep breath before replying. "Some kid here—" he glanced down at the form "—Charles Allison. He says he knows where Chandler is holed up."

Maloney gave Chip a penetrating look while holding the receiver tightly to his ear. After several moments, Maloney said, "Fifty-nine Caracas." Maloney paused again to listen, tapping his beefy fingers on the desk, then answered, "Markel and Yancy— out on patrol." Maloney's eyes widened briefly and then he said, "Yes, sir. Right away."

He hung up the phone and turned back to Chip. "Okay," he said with a shrug, "the captain's trusting you." Evidently Maloney didn't share that trust.

Maloney swiveled his chair around to the police radio behind him and snapped a couple of toggle switches. Mounted on the front panel and tethered to it with a thick black coiled cord was a microphone. Maloney grabbed it, thumbed the transmit button on the side of the mic, and barked out several terse orders.

Maloney turned back to Chip and looked him square in the eye. "Do not go anywhere near Caracas Avenue," he said sternly. "We're sending officers to apprehend the suspect. I repeat, do not go anywhere near there."

"Are you sending a SWAT team?" Chip asked.

"What?" Maloney asked, irritation now obvious in his voice.

"You really should send a SWAT team," Chip said.

"No time for that, son," Maloney replied. "This is known in the business as actionable intelligence. We have to act now, before he slips through our fingers. Don't worry—we'll get him."

"Listen, you need to warn the officers."

"Do you have reason to believe he's armed?"

"No," Chip said. "I mean, I don't know. But he's dangerous. You must warn them."

"We appreciate your concern." Maloney lapsed into talking-to-a-moron speak. "We know he's dangerous. He's a murder sus-pect. We'll be careful."

Chip ran his fingers through his hair again. This was proving much more difficult than he had anticipated. How could he make him understand? "Look—he's also very strong—super strong. He tossed me aside with one arm and I weigh close to two hundred pounds."

"I read your statement." Maloney pushed his chair back from the desk.

"No, wait—you don't understand. There's more. He's also extremely smart."

Silence, followed by a cough.

"Look," Chip said, "I don't know how to say this, so I'll just say it. He's so smart, it's like he knows what you're going to do."

"Come again?" Maloney asked.

"He seems to know what you're going to do before you do it."

"All right, Mr. Allison," Maloney said, and stood. Apparently he had heard enough. "Thanks again for the tip. I'll be sure and pass it on to our detectives. Have a good night."

CHAPTER 56

Tuesday, midnight

The unmarked patrol car fishtailed dramatically on the dry pavement, complete with squealing tires, as it roared out of the medical center parking lot.

"Take it easy, Paul," Detective Markel said from the passenger seat. The force of the turn had him pressed against the door. The driver, Paul Yancy, who couldn't be more than twenty-two, hair high and tight, was sitting bolt upright behind the wheel, gripping it tightly with both hands. Markel still wasn't so sure taking a rookie along was such a great idea. Yancy was plenty amped up for this—probably too amped—but his experience was basically nil. "No need to alert the perp we're coming."

"Sorry," Yancy replied and eased up on the gas. A traffic light on Route 422 by the Friendly's stopped them. Yancy checked the rearview mirror for the hundredth time. "So, you think he'll go easily?"

"I dunno," Markel replied. "You heard the briefing the other day. He's a nut job—you know, looney-tunes. All bets are off with these guys."

"He killed that pretty nurse in cold blood."

"I know," Markel said.

"Maybe we should shoot first, ask questions later?" Yancy shot him a look. He was smiling, but Markel could tell he was plenty worried.

"Yeah, good idea."

"What'd you make of that message from Maloney?" Yancy asked.

"Well, we'll know soon enough whether this is another effing goose chase or not."

"No, I mean the stuff he said about Chandler."

"You mean telling us the perp's dangerous?" Markel forced a laugh. "Ya think?"

"Yeah. Duh!" Yancy eased his grip on the steering wheel a bit. "And like, he's super smart."

"Whatever. I brought some extra firepower along." Markel patted the shotgun in the rack behind them. "A little insurance."

"Good thinking."

Markel tapped his forehead. "Makes *us* smarter." This time, his laugh was genuine.

Soon they turned onto Caracas Avenue. Yancy swung the patrol car to the curb and jammed on the brakes. Markel was thrown forward in his seat hard; the shoulder restraint belt locked and held him. *Jesus, Yancy.* The kid was amped up, all right.

Yancy was already opening his door. Markel quickly reached over and put his hand on his shoulder. "You wait here. I'll go to the door. You back me up from the car."

"How come you go to the door? I thought I would—"

"Trust me," Markel said, "it's better this way. You man the radio."

Yancy looked crestfallen, but to his credit didn't say anything.

"Don't worry, kid. Your time will come." Markel unfastened his seatbelt and checked his weapon, a Glock 23 that he carried concealed underneath his Kevlar vest in a shoulder holster.

"All set?" Yancy asked, trying to sound upbeat.

"Yep." Markel put the gun back in its holster. He opened his door and suffered a moment of indecision. He recalled the mayhem at Swatara Regional several years back. He would never forget the bloodbath he had found that night—the night Senator Pierce almost died. It didn't pay to underestimate the criminal element. "Mister Remington's going with me, too." Markel retrieved the shotgun from the rack.

"You know that's against protocol."

"Jesus, Yancy!" Markel said, shaking his head. "Fuck protocol. Protocol ain't going to the door—I am." He grabbed some cartridges and fed them into the shotgun's breech.

"Yeah, sorry. Fuck protocol."

Markel stepped out of the car onto the sidewalk.

"I got your back, Frank," Yancy called after him.

Markel surveyed Caracas Avenue; it was well lit by streetlights. Other than the wind whistling through the trees lining the street, it was a very quiet residential neighborhood. Everyone had long since turned in. A full moon was also shining brightly overhead and he felt conspicuous with the shotgun at his side. This was Hershey, after all, Chocolate Town, USA, not freaking downtown Chicago. Nonetheless, he felt strangely on edge—this guy *was* a murderer. Best not to forget that.

He walked down the sidewalk a couple of houses until he came to the right address; the number *59* was stenciled on the top riser of a small cement staircase. He climbed several steps onto a wooden porch. A painted sign near the door read *The Kopenhavers: All Friends Welcome!* He knocked on the front door and tried to ignore his heart pounding in his chest.

No answer.

He peered in the window, but the shades were drawn. He saw an enclosed staircase on the side of the building and made note that the upper floor was a separate apartment. *Good. One less floor to worry about.*

He looked back at Yancy and had to smile. He was crouched behind the patrol car, gun drawn, as if he were ready to shoot it out with Bonnie and Clyde. Yancy was a good kid; not the brightest, maybe, but willing to work and learn. Markel gave him a thumbs-up and turned back to the door.

He knocked again, louder. "Mr. Nick Chandler. This is the Derry Township Police. We have a warrant for your arrest. Open the door."

Again, no answer. Markel tried the door and to his surprise, found it was unlocked. He swung it open, trying to be quiet about it, but the hinges squeaked loudly. Markel entered the foyer, the hardwood floor creaking under his feet. The interior was poorly lit; a solitary lamp shone feebly from the living room, off to the left. A terrible stench hung in the air. He paused to let his eyes adjust to the light. No one in sight. The living room appeared empty. He listened and didn't hear anything other than his own heavy breathing.

Markel walked forward into what appeared to be the dining room. Same creaky hardwood floor. No one here, either. *Was that dried blood on the floor?* He could make out hallways leading to a kitchen and presumably a bedroom area. The shades were drawn here as well and the gloom pressed in on him. He called out to the emptiness in front of him, "Nick Chandler. This is the police. We have a warrant for your arrest."

Suddenly, footsteps. A man came into view from the kitchen.

Markel flinched and his heart lurched painfully in his chest. He ignored the jolt of adrenaline and locked eyes with the man. "Nick Chandler?"

"Yes," Chandler said calmly. "What can I do for you, officer?"

"Nick Chandler, you're under arrest for the murder of Heather Lindstrom. Put your hands up where I can see them."

Chandler took a few steps toward Markel.

"Don't come any closer," Markel said. Chandler stopped. He was about five feet away. This guy was a fuckin' fruitcake, all right. He didn't seem to show any outward sign of fear.

Markel figured it was time to bring Mr. Remington front and center, just in case Chandler hadn't noticed it yet. He hefted the shotgun to a firing position and cocked it menacingly. A warning shot from Mr. Remington in this confined space, and this punk would be crying for his mama.

Chandler put his hands up. "No problem, officer. I'll come peaceably."

There, that was better. The double barrel of a 12-gauge in your face never failed to command respect. Cold steel diplomacy, he liked to call it. Markel began to read Chandler his rights, keeping a close eye on the perp.

Suddenly, with amazing speed, Chandler reached behind his back. *Shit.*

Markel was ready for this, though. He quickly discharged the Remington above Chandler's head. The big gun roared and the blast tore a ragged hole in the ceiling. Plaster rained down on Chandler like falling snow. Markel's ears hurt, but it was a satisfying hurt, nonetheless. "You don't want to fuck with me, boy. Now, put your fucking hands out—"

Before he could finish his sentence, Chandler leapt toward him, seeming to fly through the air. Markel managed to recock the Remington, but somehow it wasn't fast enough. Chandler had erased the distance between them and was already on him, knocking him backward to the floor. Markel fired the shotgun again as he went down, but he had no real chance of hitting Chandler, who was now right on top of him.

Markel dropped the shotgun, useless in these tight quarters, and reached for his revolver. He'd make this bastard pay yet.

A knife flashed in Chandler's hand. Markel frantically groped under his vest for his gun, but found only an empty holster. *Shit!* Before he could bring his hand back to defend himself, he felt the cold steel at his throat. Chandler grunted, and the blade went deep—real deep. Markel didn't feel much else, other than a dull ripping sensation; everything was happening so fast. Then he saw and felt the blood—his blood—shooting out of his neck. He reflexively reached up and covered the wound with one hand, only to feel the blood spurt out between his fingers. He tried to call out to Yancy, but produced only a gurgle. He groped around the hardwood floor, now becoming slippery with his blood, for the shotgun. Gone. So was Chandler. He caught sight of his Glock, far away, on the floor across the room.

Markel scrabbled to all fours, intent on crawling to the Glock, but his vision started to swirl viciously around him. He could barely breathe; blood choked him and flowed freely out of his mouth onto the floor.

He could hear Yancy screaming over the police radio, "Officer down! Officer down! Need backup! Need backup, *now!*"

Next, he heard Yancy's service revolver firing rapidly.

Then he heard the loud boom of Mr. Remington. Once. Twice.

Finally, as his vision dimmed to gray and he collapsed onto the bloody floor, the Glock still maddeningly out of reach, he realized Yancy's gun had gone silent.

CHAPTER 57

Wednesday, 12:20 a.m.

Kristin definitely had a case of the creeps, being back in the basement . . . alone.

Although she had assured Chip she'd be fine, the actual experience was proving more difficult. A faint nauseating odor hung in the stagnant air, even though she had thoroughly cleansed all the blood—Smokey's and Chandler's—from the floor and walls with Clorox. The red light in the little room didn't help, either; everything looked as if it was drenched in blood, and the darkness was suffocating. *Maybe this wasn't such a great idea.*

"Stop it!" she scolded herself, shaking her head to throw off the negative thoughts. She needed to buck up, see this through. She focused on her dead dog in an effort to gain strength. With grim determination, she carefully wound the film onto the plastic developing spool.

A loud noise—a creaking or banging—upstairs somewhere.

Kristin's breath caught in her throat and she froze, straining to listen. *Déjà vu, here we go, all over again.* Silence. *Was it just the shifting of the old apartment? Or the wind? Or just my shot nerves?*

No new sounds followed and she returned to the film. With trembling hands, she put the spool in the developer tank and poured in the developer solution, spilling a little on the countertop. *Careful.* She didn't want to screw this up—Chip was counting on her.

Her thoughts turned to Chip; his easygoing nature and his boyish good looks obviously didn't tell the whole story. Cheating on an exam was serious business, no matter how you sliced it. And that wasn't the extent of his dark side—she knew about his drinking, as well. But, she was touched that he had come to her to try a Kirlian photograph. Maybe he didn't think she was a total loon after all.

She checked the temperature and noted it was close enough. She hooked up the wires to the brass electrodes on the outside of the developing tank. She flipped on the power transformer designed to deliver the correct Kirlian electric current across the film. The apparatus hummed softly and she activated the timer, knowing the next twenty minutes would pass like an eternity. She washed her hands, all the while wondering what she would do without her enlarger. The mangled remnants of it were visible in the trashcan and served as a stark reminder of what had happened just a few short days ago.

Another creak came from upstairs, louder this time. She didn't dare open the darkroom door or the light would ruin the film. "Chip, is that you?" she called out, her voice sounding way too high and squeaky.

No answer. Her heart hammered in her chest, making it hard to hear. "Is anyone up there?" she shouted. Silence—only the rushing of blood in her ears.

Suddenly, her phone beeped a text message. She about jumped out of her skin. The message was from Chip.

<Don't worry Kristin. Police have Chandler in custody.>

Kristin breathed a long sigh of relief. *Thank God.* She typed back: <Pictures done soon.>

CHAPTER 58

Wednesday, 12:20 a.m.

Chip stood and began pacing across the linoleum tiles, sometimes sliding his sneakers, leaving imprints on the dusty floor. The small waiting room of the Derry Township Police Department was no longer empty. An elderly lady was seated across the room in one of the plastic chairs, her hands neatly folded across her lap. *What is she doing here at this time of night?*

Chip checked his watch again. Too much time was passing and he had no idea what was happening. *Should I go back to Kristin's? Or call her?* He was hoping to get word of Chandler's arrest. He walked up to the window. Maloney was nowhere to be seen.

Next to the service window was a closed door that led to the interior of the police station. On the door was a placard stating *Authorized Personnel Only Beyond This Point* in bold letters. Chip approached the door and knocked. No response. The place seemed deserted except for the old lady, who was now eyeing him with disapproval. Chip hesitated, then tried the door handle; it was unlocked.

Suddenly, loud screams came in over the police radio, startling Chip.

"Officer down! Officer down! Need backup! Need backup, *now!*"

This was followed by the crack-crack-crack of rapid gunfire, then two loud booms that sounded like shotgun blasts.

Chip's blood ran cold as he listened to the anguished cries for help.

Outside, a patrol car screeched out of the parking lot with sirens blaring.

What the hell is going on? Chip opened the door and quickly sat down in Maloney's chair. He clacked away on the noisy keyboard of the police computer. A minute later he had his answer. *Shit!* His phone was on the move again. Chip watched with growing horror as the red beacon moved away from Caracas Avenue, down the streets of Hershey—right toward Kristin's apartment.

Chip snatched up the phone receiver and started punching buttons before he realized the phone was dead. There was no dial tone. Chip scanned the elaborate phone console, looking for a way to select a different line out. He pushed several buttons labeled with different extensions but nothing worked. Then he noticed a lock off to one side—minus the key. Maloney must've taken the key when he left. "Damn!"

Chip ran out to the waiting room, frightening the old lady. "Can I use your phone?" he asked.

"Excuse me?" she asked, flustered.

"Do you have a cell phone?" Chip asked, out of breath.

"No." She was wringing her hands.

"It's an emergency."

"I don't own one, young man," she said, crossing her arms and looking away.

Chip sprinted toward the parking lot, figuring she wouldn't have given it to him even if she had one.

CHAPTER 59

Wednesday, 12:35 a.m.

After twenty minutes of agitating the film roll in the developing tank, Kristin turned off the power supply and disconnected the wires. Extracting the film roll, all curly and wet, she glanced at the film and saw she had images. *Thank God.* She dunked the film into the stop bath and gently shook it with her tongs.

She held the film spool up to the safelight. The stop bath dripped all over the table, but she ignored it. These were no moon shots. She recognized the ICU. There was a patient lying in a bed. She bent down closer and tried to make out details. *Is that Laura Landry?* The 35 millimeter negative was too small to make out anything; the size of a person's head was only a couple of millimeters wide. If only her enlarger wasn't in pieces in the trash.

Her thoughts were interrupted by more creaking from upstairs. Kristin felt her fear return with a vengeance; panic swelled inside her and her heart resumed its painful banging in her chest. Her mouth went dry, her palms sweaty. She wanted to run—*needed* to run. But the only way out was up the basement stairs.

Kristin gripped the countertop hard with trembling hands, anchoring herself. She squelched a nascent scream that was trying to break loose. With tremendous effort, she slowed her breathing and forced herself not to bolt. She needed to finish this somehow—for Chip. For Smokey.

She pulled the enlarger body out of the trash and examined it. There was one lens that wasn't totally smashed; about a third of it remained intact. She tried to extricate the lens from its metal holder, but it was stuck fast. She yanked harder. She felt the lens pop free, but she also felt a burning pain in her fingers as the rough edge of the broken glass gouged her.

She held the crescent moon-shaped lens up to the film, ignoring her bloody finger. She held them both up to the light. Just as she had hoped, the lens worked to magnify the images. The first few frames of the roll were pictures of Chip, posing foolishly in his apartment. She looked closer. She could clearly make out an aura around Chip's head, proving the Kirlian technique was indeed working.

Then she moved on to the pictures of the bed in the ICU. She could make out facial features now—a pretty nose and mouth and long black hair that flowed down around a woman's face. There was no mistaking it—it *was* Laura Landry.

She moved the film closer to the light. She angled the broken lens every way possible and positioned it at varying distances from the film. Her movements were slow and deliberate at first, but became more and more frantic as she squinted at the film, searching. "Holy Mother of God," escaped from her lips as a tortured yelp.

CHAPTER 60

Wednesday, 12:35 a.m.

Victor Cohen settled in for a long, boring night shift. The ICU census was way down and the only three patients he had to keep tabs on tonight seemed pretty stable. He had his trusty thermos filled with coffee and some pathology notes to keep him company. He couldn't afford to fall asleep like his loser buddy, Allison.

Of course, what was really on Victor's mind was the student nurse mixer this Friday. A new crop of nurselets had just arrived from State College and Victor had his eye on a certain Sharon Enfield. She wasn't the prettiest—okay, her nose was way too big—but she had these boobs that went on forever. And she seemed fairly naïve, which suited Victor just fine. To Victor, dumb was an asset.

A loud commotion from across the hall spoiled his daydream of Sharon and her boobs. Dr. Landry emerged from Room 237, waving his arms and shouting, "Call the MRI suite. Tell them I'm bringing down an emergency case and to clear the machine. We'll be there in ten minutes."

Jenny, the head ICU nurse, looked exasperated as she picked up the phone. After a brief conversation, she held the receiver to her chest and shouted back at Landry, "They need a diagnosis."

Landry hesitated. "Okay. Tell them acute cerebral hemorrhage. Need to rule out a ruptured aneurysm."

"Ordering physician?"

"Me. STAT, okay?"

Jenny completed her conversation and hung up the phone. "They're finishing up a scan now and should be ready by the time you get there."

"Great," Landry said.

"I don't have a spare nurse at the moment," Jenny said. "Becky should be back from break soon."

"We can't wait." Doug turned to the policeman standing guard outside Laura's room. "Help me push the bed—we're going to the MRI. She needs a scan."

Officer Dodson grunted as he hauled himself out of his chair; he was a large man—not overweight, just big-framed, and standing at least six-four. His eyes were half open slits; he had no doubt been dozing. Several magazines and two empty vending machine coffee cups sat on the floor by his feet.

"Is something wrong, Dr. Landry?" Victor said, now on his feet, unable to contain his curiosity.

"No," Landry replied. "Just precautionary."

That sure sounded bogus, and Landry definitely looked worried, but Victor knew better than to challenge attending physicians. "Her rhythm's rock stable now," Victor added.

"Yes, I know. Thanks for your concern, but we gotta move."

He was getting the brush-off, that much was clear.

After Landry and the big cop rolled the heavy ICU bed with Mrs. Landry in it down the hall, Victor whipped out his cell phone. After several rings, Chip's voice mail message announced, "You've reached Chip's phone. Obviously I'm busy. Leave a message, if you feel like it."

"Chip, it's me, Victor." Victor paused a moment to look around before continuing in a hushed voice, "You said to let you know if anything weird was happening with Mrs. Landry. Well, I'm not sure what to make of it, but Dr. Landry just whisked her away to the MRI for an emergency brain scan. Get this—to rule out a cerebral aneurysm. She seemed fine to me, but hey, what do *I* know? Anyway, I promised I'd call."

CHAPTER 61

Wednesday, 12:35 a.m.

Chip hopped in the Camry, fired it up, and jammed his foot down on the accelerator. The old four-cylinder coughed twice, threatening to stall, but finally revved up to speed. Although lacking the horsepower or torque to peel out like the police cruisers, the Toyota flew across the parking lot nonetheless. Chip ignored the stop sign at the lot exit and barreled right out onto Hockersville Road. The light up ahead at the intersection with Chocolate Avenue quickly came into view—it was red. Traffic was virtually nonexistent, so Chip rolled through the light, going about thirty, tires squealing in protest as he made a right turn.

Five seconds later, a car sped right by him in the passing lane, startling him. It was an older model silver Impala headed in the direction of Kristin's apartment.

Chip floored it and gave chase. The Impala was several hundred yards ahead, passing the Giant now. The Camry's speedometer nudged up past sixty. Chip's hands were white-knuckled on the steering wheel. He was gaining on the Chevy.

All of a sudden, less than a hundred yards in front of him, the silver car made a screeching U-turn, right in front of the Rite Aid. *What the hell!*

CHAPTER 62

Wednesday, 12:35 a.m.

Doug and Officer Dodson cleared the ICU automatic doors and proceeded out into the main hallway. The heavy bed bumped as it rolled onto the carpeted hallway; Laura's oxygen cylinder rattled against the headboard and her eyelids fluttered but then closed again.

"We need to take the main elevator down to the basement and then head to the MRI suite," Doug said to the policeman. The bed was much harder to push, here on the carpet.

"Whatever you say, doc," Dodson said, more alert now. "You're in charge."

"Okay, great," Doug murmured. He was actually glad to have Dodson along. First, he seemed more personable than some of the other members of the Hershey PD. And, of course, Doug wouldn't deny that he also found the service revolver on his belt reassuring.

"Do you think she'll be all right?" Dodson asked, nodding toward Laura.

"I sure hope so," Doug said.

"She seems pretty out of it," Dodson said, looking worried.

"I gave her some sedation for the scan," Doug said, surprised by the big man's perceptiveness. "She gets claustrophobic."

"My youngest daughter, Alicia, gets that too—she hates to climb through the plastic tunnel tubes on the playground." Dodson smiled at the thought, then asked, "Do you guys have kids?"

"Yes," Doug said, and smiled tightly. "We have three boys. What about you, Officer Dodson?"

"Call me Bob," the big man said, a twinkle coming into his brown eyes. "Yeah, my wife and I have two little girls, five and eight. Hellions, I call 'em," he added with a toothy smile. "But I wouldn't trade 'em for the world."

"I know what you mean," Doug said sincerely. It was funny, Doug thought, to see this big, burly man with the square jaw and menacing gun strapped to his waist reduced to sentimental giggling by the mere mention of his two daughters. But Doug understood the emotion all too well.

Dodson reined in his mirth and paused in thought; his smile faded. "I heard you say aneurysm back there," he said, his voice now edged with concern. "My wife's brother died from one in his belly."

"Sorry to hear that," Doug replied, matching his somber tone.

"They said it burst like a bad inner tube."

Doug didn't answer.

"I hope . . ." Dodson started, then trailed off.

The two men continued down the long, empty hallway in silence, the only noise the squeaking wheels of the bed as it lumbered forward on the carpeted floor. When they reached the elevator, Doug's phone rang; he pulled it out and saw Kristin's number. "Hello," he said.

"Dr. Landry, thank God I got through to you," Kristin blurted, breathless.

"What is it, Kristin?" Doug said impatiently. He pushed the Down button for the elevator.

"Is Chip with you?"

"No."

"Hmmm. I have . . . uh, some information. I just developed some pictures."

"That's nice." The elevator dinged and the door opened.

"Of your wife."

"What?" Doug exclaimed as he and Dodson maneuvered the bed onto the elevator. "What are you talking about?"

"Where are you?" she asked. "You sound funny."

"Getting in the elevator—heading to the MRI suite. Listen, Kristin, I might lose you here." The elevator door closed and the signal cut out.

When the elevator jerked to a stop in the basement, the two men muscled the bed out and down the hallway. Doug navigated the radiology complex, following signs on the wall bearing a picture of a large magnet with an arrow pointing straight ahead. Doug's phone rang again as they approached double doors marked *MRI Suite*. Another sign on the wall read, *DANGER: HIGH INTENSITY MAGNETIC FIELD*.

"Hello."

"Dr. Landry," Kristin said, her voice now shrill.

"Kristin, I'm not sure I have time for this right now."

"No wait, you gotta listen to me. I just devel . . . Laur . . . tures."

"Kristin you're breaking up again. The magnetic field must be screwing with the signal."

"Laur . . . pic . . ."

"What?"

" . . . aura. I repeat, no . . ."

"What?"

" . . . pictures . . ."

"Sorry Kristin, you'll have to tell me later," Doug said and broke the connection.

CHAPTER 63

Wednesday, 12:40 a.m.

With Doug pulling the heavy bed from up front and Dodson pushing from behind, they maneuvered Laura's ICU bed into the tight quarters of the MRI control room.

A thin female radiology tech in her early twenties was seated at a console that looked as if it would be more at home on a starship. The tech had long, feathered blonde hair with highlights, and wore high black boots that disappeared under her white lab coat. She didn't appear overjoyed to see them. "Can I help you?" she said, sounding anything but helpful. She eyed the policeman with frank suspicion.

"Yes," Doug said. "This is the patient who needs the emergency scan."

The tech drew in a long breath, as if to compose herself. "Name?"

"Laura Landry." Doug wondered how many emergency MRI scans there could be at this time of night.

She scribbled something down in her logbook and muttered, "When it rains, it pours."

"Look, we're trying to rule out a hemorrhagic cerebral aneurysm," Doug added, his patience running thin.

"Yeah, I got that in the report. We'll need to transfer her to the MRI litter. Can you help? We're a little short-handed." She threw a glance around the empty room to make her point.

Doug nodded and the three transferred Laura to the plastic and aluminum litter designed to go safely into the magnet room.

"You need to leave all metallic items outside the room," the tech said, handing Doug a plastic tray. "Do you have any internal metal objects? Pacemaker? Surgical clips?"

"No," Doug said. He knew the drill and emptied his pockets of keys and change, then also removed his watch, belt, and cell phone.

"He'll have to wait outside," she said, gesturing at Officer Dodson. "Especially on account of *that*." She pointed at Dodson's gun.

Dodson raised his eyebrows at this and looked over at Doug. Doug gave him a nod and the big man took a seat, mild relief washing across his face.

"What about her oxygen?" Doug asked, pointing to the green oxygen E-cylinder lying on Laura's ICU bed. It was still hooked up to her nasal prongs.

"Just disconnect it," the tech said, her tone imperious. "We have oxygen inside." She swiped her badge through the unlocking mechanism, then swung the heavy door open into the scan room. Bright yellow and black diagonal stripes on the threshold indicated the presence of the high intensity magnetic field.

Doug disconnected the oxygen tank and helped the tech wheel Laura into the scan room—a confining affair not much bigger than twelve by twelve feet. They transferred Laura from her litter over to the MRI table. Dodson watched intently from his perch outside the room.

"You'll have to leave now, sir," she said to Doug, the corners of her mouth turning up slightly in a small but unmistakable smile.

"I'd prefer to stay with her."

"It's against protocol," she said without missing a beat.

"I'm not leaving her side," Doug said firmly, returning her stare.

The smile vanished and the tech looked as if she were about to put up a major fuss. Then her beeper went off. "Shit," she mouthed as she regarded the beeper.

"Look," Doug added, "I sedated her and need to be here as her anesthesiologist."

The tech weighed this for a moment. "Okay, fine. *I* need to go to the ER to take care of *another* emergency patient." She rolled her eyes. "I'll program her scan, then leave—you can stay with her. I'll be back as soon as I can."

"Thanks for your help," Doug said, not bothering to blunt his sarcasm.

She gave him a sour smile and stood there for a moment, not saying anything, perhaps trying to come up with a snappy reply. "Use the intercom if you have any problems," she finally huffed, pointing to a panel by the door and then to Dodson. "I'll give him my swipe card to unlock the door, in case of any emergency." With that, she whirled and left, closing the door behind her. The automatic lock engaged with a loud metallic clunk.

Doug turned to Laura and patted her arm. "This won't take long, Laura. Just try to lie as still as you can."

Laura surprised him by responding; he had thought she was still out of it. "I'll try, Doug," she said, looking up at him.

"I gave you a little sedation to make it easier," Doug said. "It's a bit tight in there."

"What's hap'nen to me?"

"You're having a scan. It's just a precaution." Doug didn't know what else to say. "It won't hurt."

"Okay," she said and closed her eyes.

The MRI scanner began to hum and soon the gantry lurched into motion, drawing Laura into the magnet's hollow core. He squeezed her hand and she squeezed back. Once her head and upper torso disappeared into the core, loud bumping and grinding noises emanated from deep within the machine. Doug patted her toes, then started pacing in the little room. After a few minutes, he sat down in an uncomfortable molded plastic chair in the corner. His thoughts inevitably turned to what the scan might reveal.

Fifteen minutes later, the scanner fell silent. Doug waited for several minutes before going over to the intercom, wondering if the tech was back yet. "Are you getting good slices? Is the scan finished? Is she holding still enough?"

No answer.

Doug looked around. There was no window to the control room. He tried the door and it was locked. He spied a lit-up keypad next to the door that undoubtedly controlled the locking mechanism, but he didn't know the code. He saw a video camera high up on the wall, facing the magnet, but Doug realized this was just for one-way video monitoring.

He tried the intercom again. "Officer Dodson—Bob—are you there?"

Again, no answer.

Damn it! He eyed the intercom, wondering if the dang thing even worked. *Or maybe Dodson is dozing again.* Doug started to pace again in the little room. Finally the MRI scanner came to life and the bumping and grinding noises started up again. *Thank God.* There was nothing else to do but wait until the end of the scan.

CHAPTER 64

Wednesday, 12:50 a.m.

Doug's nerves were fraying badly and his patience had long since deserted him. He stood still for a moment and gripped his head in his hands and squeezed his temples tightly, trying to tamp down the growing ache inside his skull. *What the hell is going on?* He had never felt so helpless, locked in this small room with no contact. He reached for his cell phone before he remembered he had left it outside. It would be useless in here anyway—no way there'd be a signal. *What had Kristin been trying to tell me before she got cut off?*

He forced himself to draw some deep breaths. He headed toward the plastic chair, but never made it.

An incredibly strong arm wrapped around Doug's neck and a pointy object dug into his back. "Don't move or I'll kill you," Chandler said, his face inches from Doug's ear.

Doug stiffened. "What do you want?" he said, his voice tight with fear. He knew Chandler wouldn't hesitate to make good on his threat. The sight of Mueller's dead body with his neck sliced ear to ear flooded his mind.

"Pull her out of the machine," Chandler ordered.

"Why?" Doug said, struggling to think, desperately trying to push back the panic. He glanced up at the video camera.

"Just do it."

He felt the sharp object poke more insistently at his back, undoubtedly drawing blood. "I don't know how it works," Doug said, stalling and arching his back away from the sharp object.

"Figure it out or I'll kill *her*," Chandler hissed.

"Okay. Let me go."

Chandler released him and Doug went over and inspected the controls on the MRI housing. He stole several glances at Chandler and the video camera. Chandler was standing close to the wall underneath the camera. He held a foot-long spike that resembled a tent stake in his right hand. Even though the spike was thin and probably made of lightweight aluminum, it still looked plenty dangerous. The video camera was aimed at the patient. Depending on what type of lens the camera employed—wide angle or not— Chandler might not even be in the field of view.

"Hurry up," said Chandler, becoming agitated.

"It's complicated," Doug barked back, hoping to mask his burgeoning fear; the panic was reasserting itself. "Give me a second." Doug glared at Chandler. Last time he had seen him, Chandler's neck had been a gruesome mess. Now his wounds, although still plainly visible, were healed to an extent Doug would have thought impossible. The sight of fresh scar tissue this soon was particularly shocking. Chandler bore little resemblance to the frail creature weakened from blood loss that Doug had fought with before. Now, Chandler stood crouched in a boxer's stance, coiled for action.

Doug pressed the Cancel Scan button and the bumping and grinding noises coming from the machine ceased. He also located the gantry eject button, but pushed one of the others instead; it turned up the volume of the piped-in music playing for the patient.

"Hurry up," Chandler said.

"What do you want with her?" Doug asked. "Can't you just leave her out of this?"

"I'm afraid not," Chandler said. "We need to talk, Dr. Landry—the three of us." Chandler stared at him for a moment with his dull gray eyes. Frustration flickered across his face before he continued. "I know you'd like to kill me, but that will have to wait."

That much was true—Doug wanted nothing more than to kill this slimy bastard once and for all. *Did Chandler just read my mind? Or are my intentions that obvious?* Doug recalled the way Chandler seemed to anticipate his moves when they had fought in the PML. And how Kristin had sworn Chandler could read her mind. *Can he really do that?*

Doug looked up at the camera again. *Where is Dodson?* A sickening thought followed—*Did Chandler already kill him?*

Chandler followed his gaze. "That skinny blond bitch can't help you. If she comes in, I'll cut her." Chandler waved the spike in the air across his own throat. He then approached the gantry, apparently not worried about the camera anymore, and gestured toward Laura's body. "Now, get her the fuck out of this damn machine."

Doug hit the Eject button. With a loud mechanical whine, the gantry began to move. As the scanner slowly ejected Laura from within the magnet core, Doug thought furiously. *Why didn't Chandler mention the policeman? Surely, if he had killed him, he wouldn't miss an opportunity to gloat. Maybe Dodson is alive? But if Chandler can read my mind; he would know that Dodson is right outside. So, either he can't read minds after all—or maybe the magnetic field is playing havoc with his abilities, just as it interfered with the cell phone signal. Perhaps he's vulnerable!*

Doug jumped as the latch to the scan room door clicked loudly. He and Chandler turned toward the heavy door as it swung inward. Officer Dodson stood at the entrance, his feet straddling the diagonal yellow and black lines. "What's going on in here?" he boomed.

Everything happened very fast.

At first Chandler froze, genuinely surprised to see the cop there. But then, with amazing speed, Chandler darted behind the magnet assembly, out of view—probably where he had been hiding in the first place.

"Come out with your hands up, now! Or I'll shoot!" Dodson yelled, simultaneously drawing his gun.

Doug shouted, "*No-o-o-o!*"

But Dodson wasn't listening. As the officer swung his gun up to a firing position, his hand crossed into the room, well beyond the striped warning line on the floor.

The magnetic field ripped the gun from his hand, almost taking his trigger finger off with it. The gun discharged, the deafening report ringing through the small room. Doug reflexively put his hands to his ears—too late. The gun flew across the room and struck the magnet housing, slamming into the front panel with a loud metallic clang. It stuck fast to the magnet, suspended three feet off the ground. The bullet lodged in the scanner machinery, off to the right side. Dodson cursed loudly as he vigorously rubbed his bloodied trigger finger.

Before the policeman could even look up, Chandler was across the room and upon him. Dodson managed to get one arm up to defend himself, but it was too late. Chandler stabbed him repeatedly in the upper chest and neck with the spike. Dodson let out several howls before crumpling to the floor, blood rapidly saturating his blue uniform.

Doug snapped out of his own paralysis. He ran at Chandler and leapt, hitting him squarely in the torso with his full weight. Knocked off his feet, Chandler hit the floor hard. The spike clattered across the floor.

Doug quickly knelt by Dodson's body and checked for a carotid pulse. The policeman was already dead. Time slowed further as Doug's mind raced. He had to—

Doug sprang toward the magnet as Chandler climbed to his feet.

Doug frantically tried to pry the gun from the magnet. No matter how hard he tried—ripping the skin from his fingertips—he couldn't get the thing loose; the gun might as well have been welded in place.

Chandler bent and retrieved the spike.

A distinct hissing drew Doug's attention. A cloud of white vapor boiled from the bullet hole in the magnet assembly. *Liquid helium boiling out. Not good.*

Chandler was slowly approaching now, bloody spike in hand.

Doug hesitated for a second more, then bolted for the door, almost tripping over Dodson's body. Chandler's voice followed after him as he ran out of the magnet room, burning him with his words: "Thought you had more balls than that, Landry. Go ahead and run! Doesn't matter—I'm interested in your wife anyway."

CHAPTER 65

Wednesday, 12:55 a.m.

Doug muscled the ICU bed toward the open door to the magnet room. He could see the large bed would never fit through the small scan door, but he pushed anyway. Inside the room, Chandler was leaning over Laura. Talking to her?

Three more feet to go. *Perfect position.* Chandler looked up, vaguely surprised to see Doug and the approaching bed. But he didn't move or react.

Two feet. Chandler continued his conversation. Apparently, he had no clue what was coming.

One foot.

Breathing hard now, Doug gave one last shove forward. As the ICU bed hit the doorframe and jarred to a stop, the green oxygen E-cylinder lying on the bed began to tremble, then roll. It rolled across the bed, picking up speed, until it smacked against the headboard with a dull clang and stopped. Chandler looked up again at the noise.

The cylinder began to shake violently against the headboard, caught in the grip of the ultra-intense magnetic field. The cylinder bobbed up and continued to roll, this time straight up, six inches to the top of the headboard.

The E-cylinder cleared the top of the headboard and flew through the air toward the magnet, accelerating in flight, attaining a top speed of over ninety miles an hour. The flying fifty-pound steel missile scored a glancing blow to Chandler's temple, then smacked hard into the scanner with a deafening clang. It came to rest four feet off the ground, stuck fast to the magnet housing.

Chandler dropped like a rock, unconscious or dead.

Doug ran back into the scan room and leaned over Laura. "Laura, are you okay?"

"Yes," she said, her eyelids fluttering open. "I heard a loud bang. Is everything all right?"

"Everything's fine now, hon." Doug slipped his arms under her and began to lift her off the gantry. "Let's get you out of here."

As Doug hoisted Laura off the gantry, he saw tremendous clouds of vapor billowing out of the bullet hole in the magnet. The hissing noise was growing louder, the temperature in the room dropping rapidly. With Laura in his arms, Doug took two steps toward the door. He felt immense pressure building in his ears and a bolt of pain shot through his skull. Before he could carry Laura out of the room, the large door swung closed and he heard the latch engage.

"God damn it!" Doug yelled in exasperation. He set Laura back down on the litter. How long could they survive in a room filling up with cold, pressurized helium? Five minutes? Ten at the most. They would either freeze to death or asphyxiate.

Doug searched the room for anything useful. Behind the scanner he found a service door, but it was locked. Further searching yielded nothing. With no other options, Doug pounded on the main door, even though he was pretty sure it was hopeless; he doubted anyone could hear him through the thick, metal-shielded door.

"Anyone out there! Help us! Open the door!"

After several minutes, hands stinging, Doug sat back down beside Laura, resigned and discouraged. His ears popped, relieving some of the intense pressure inside his head. But the temperature continued to drop and the air already felt much thinner. *So this is how it ends,* he thought. He cradled his aching head in his hands and gazed at his wife. She still appeared deeply sedated and he was thankful for small favors. Doug stroked her arm, then leaned down and kissed her on the cheek. "I love you," he said. Laura gave no response.

Doug glanced at Chandler's body. His chest rose and fell with shallow breathing, so he wasn't dead. The only good thing that would come from their deaths, Doug thought, would be that Chandler would die, too.

Abruptly, the wall intercom came to life. "Dr. Landry! It's me, Chip. Can you hear me?"

"Chip!" Doug sprang to his feet. "Open the door! Get us out of here."

There was a brief pause, then Chip's voice came through the tinny intercom. "I can't—the door's locked. I don't know the code."

"Try your swipe badge."

"Already did—no dice."

"The tech's around somewhere—she went to the ER," Doug said. "Find her. Call someone."

"Okay," Chip said. "I followed Chandler to the med center. The ICU nurses said you were down here. What happened?"

"No time to explain," Doug said. "The helium's boiling. Oxygen level's dropping fast. Get us out of here!"

"Okay," Chip said. "I'm on it."

"Hurry!" Doug said through chattering teeth.

Doug wrapped Laura's shivering body in her blanket and tried to ignore the cold seeping into his own body. He crawled under the blanket beside her in an effort to conserve their body heat. From this position, he looked directly up at the green oxygen cylinder stuck to the magnet housing above them. It reminded him of a circumstance several years ago at Mercy Hospital, when an oxygen cylinder had saved his life.

With a flash of intuition, he reached up and screwed the pressure valve on the tank all the way open. At first he thought the valve had been damaged on impact; he didn't hear any air flowing. But then he felt the fresh gas wash over his face and realized the loud hiss of the leaking helium was masking the sound. Precious oxygen was flowing out of the cylinder toward Laura and him, creating a halo of enriched air for them.

CHAPTER 66

Wednesday, 1:05 a.m.

"Kristin gave me the code!" Chip shouted toward the intercom, hoping he wasn't too late. "Couldn't find the tech." On the video monitor, he saw Landry slowly getting to his feet.

"Great," Landry said, sounding weaker than he had several minutes ago.

"Punching it in now," Chip said.

The door latch clicked loudly. Chip grasped the handle and pushed hard on the heavy door. "It's stuck!" Chip said, horrified. "It's unlocked, but I can't open the door."

"Damn it!" Landry cried out. "Must be the pressure in the room, with all the helium. Let's try together."

For several minutes, the two men tried to force the door, to no avail.

"Shit, it won't budge," Chip said breathlessly. He stood bent over, hands on his thighs. "Kristin's on her way. She'll know how to get it open. Can you hold out?"

"We'll have to," Landry said, dropping to his knees, breathing hard. He didn't sound too hopeful.

Chip looked back up at the video monitor. "Is that Chandler on the floor? Is he dead?"

"Unconscious."

"How'd you do that?"

"Oxygen tank. I'll explain later."

"How's Mrs. Landry holding up?"

"She's okay."

"Is she awake?"

"I dunno—I sedated her for the scan."

"Kristin told me about the pictures of Mrs. Landry. She said she told you."

"I don't care about Kristin's pictures," Landry said.

Chip was silent for a minute, contemplating the unthinkable.

"Chip, are you still there?" Landry asked.

"Yes," Chip said. "Dr. Landry, listen—you must kill Chandler before he revives."

"What! Are you kidding? He's out cold."

"Good," Chip said.

"I'm not sure I can kill a defenseless man."

"You're not getting this, Dr. Landry," Chip said, growing frustrated. "This may be our only chance."

"Call the police," Landry said. "We'll turn him over to them."

"The police are all dead."

"What're you talking about?"

"He killed them."

"What?" Landry asked, sounding shocked.

"He must've killed them all, otherwise they'd be here by now. He butchered them when they tried to arrest him—I heard the screams on the police radio."

Now Landry was silent, staring across the room.

"Where's Dodson?" Chip asked.

"He's dead, too," Landry said slowly. "He's by the door, so you probably can't see him. Chandler killed him."

"Kill him now," Chip said. "Before someone comes."

"Maybe you're right," Landry said.

"You can use Dodson's gun. We can say Dodson shot him."

"The gun's no good—I already tried. It's stuck to the fricking magnet."

"Oh," Chip said, deflated.

"How long till Kristin gets here?" Landry asked. "Air's getting thin and it's getting colder—we're running out of time."

"Not long, five minutes, maybe." Chip studied the gauges on the console. *Oh shit!* "Dr. Landry, the magnetic field strength is collapsing. Maybe you can get the gun now." Chip also noticed that the temperature of the magnet was approaching redline. Once the magnet warmed above that temp, all superconductivity would be lost and the magnet would heat up rapidly—possibly explosively.

CHAPTER 67

Wednesday, 1:10 a.m.

With considerable effort, Doug pried the gun off the wall. "I got it."

Laura suddenly sat bolt upright on the litter, startling Doug. "Why is it so cold in here?" she asked. She seemed more awake and lucid than he would've thought possible. Then with alarm she said, "Doug, what are you doing?"

"Lie down, honey. You're too weak for this." Although, she didn't look particularly weak. "I'll explain later." He walked over to Chandler.

"Are you going to *kill* him?" she said.

Doug hesitated. "Lie down, Laura. I'll handle this."

"You *are* going to kill him," she said, her voice becoming shrill.

"He's evil, Laura. He's an evil creature. He has to be destroyed."

"Think about what you're doing," she said, her words coming quick and low with alarm.

"It's like putting down a rabid animal."

"No, Doug. It would be like *murder*."

"I have to do this, Laura. Chip's right." Doug walked over to Chandler's limp body, gun in his right hand, and inspected the nasty gash on Chandler's forehead where the oxygen tank had struck him. "He's probably gonna die from this head wound anyway," he assured her, although Doug had his doubts about that.

"No, Doug," Laura implored him. "Please don't."

"Laura, it's okay. I need to do this. He tried to hurt you."

"Do it!" Chip yelled through the intercom.

"Doug, you don't understand," she said.

"I think I do," Doug said.

"He's not evil," she said.

"You don't know what you're talking about—you've been unconscious."

"I've talked to him."

Doug felt as if he had been punched in the gut. "What?" he got out weakly.

"He came to me tonight in the ICU and spoke with me."

"What're you saying, Laura?"

"That he's not an evil creature."

"She's lying!" Chip screamed through the intercom. Chip was pounding on the door. "The camera's getting frosted over—I can barely see."

Doug ignored Chip. "Laura, why are you defending him? What's gotten into you? I can't believe I'm hearing this."

"Doug!" Chip shouted. "Remember, he gutted Kristin's dog like a butcher."

Laura hesitated a moment. "Chandler explained to me about the dog," Laura said. "He was just defending himself."

"What?" Doug struggled to make sense of this. His head was pounding so painfully he could barely think; the cold and lack of oxygen were taking their toll. The hissing was growing louder. It also seemed harder to breathe. God, he wanted to believe her. He wanted to get her out of here. Away from Chandler. Out of this room.

Laura looked into his eyes for a moment—tenderly, lovingly, like the Laura before the accident. Doug felt his suspicions begin to melt in her gaze. She continued in a sweet, sincere tone, tinged with just the right amount of regret; he wanted desperately to believe her.

"He didn't mean to kill the dog," Laura said, touching his arm. "He said he even felt sorry for Banjo."

"Dr. Landry," Chip said, his voice steady, intense. "Listen to me very closely."

"What?" Doug snapped, not taking his eyes off Laura.

"Did you tell Laura the dog's name?" Chip asked.

"What are you talking about?" Doug snapped again, his irritation growing.

"Have you ever had a conversation with Laura about Kristin's dog?"

"No, of course not," Doug said.

"Exactly," Chip said. "Think. How did she know the dog's name?"

"I don't know—who cares?" But Doug noticed Laura's sweet smile had evaporated.

"Shut up, Chip!" Laura said coldly. "Leave us alone. Go get help."

"Ask her how she knew," Chip insisted.

The pain shooting through Doug's head was now exquisite. In a voice barely above a whisper, he asked, "How, Laura?"

Laura glanced over at Chandler. She brushed her long hair out of her face. "Chandler told me," she said finally. "I told you, he explained to me about the dog."

That seemed plausible. Doug wanted to believe her, so badly.

Chip was screaming now. "Banjo's not the dog's name!"

"What are you talking about?" Doug asked.

"Dr. Landry, I lied to you," Chip said. "I gave you a fake name."

"Why would you do that?" Doug said, confused.

"She read your mind just now. How else do you think she came up with the name? She can do it, just like *he* can."

"That's crazy," Doug said. He stood there staring at Laura, studying the face he knew so well, looking for a sign—anything that would indicate she was in league with that devil. "Laura, did you read my mind?" he asked. "Can you?"

"Of course not, Doug. I love you. Sometimes we think alike. You know this. You've even said it."

Doug groaned in anguish—it sounded like bullshit. *What the hell is happening?* He was being ripped apart and his head felt as if it was going to explode. If he could just complete the MRI scan, he could put all these wild theories to rest and take his wife home. But there was no time.

"Laura, I'm going to kill him now," Doug said, his voice strained. "If you can read my mind, you'll see I'm not bluffing. It's the right thing to do. I have to do it."

"He's moving!" Chip screamed through the intercom.

Chandler was indeed starting to stir. Doug put the gun up to the man's injured temple, now purple and grotesquely swollen. Chandler moaned.

"Doug, wait!" Laura screamed, and swung her feet to the floor to stand.

"Hurry, Doug," Chip said. "Do it!"

Chandler opened his eyes and said with amazing clarity, "The fucking dog's name was Smokey!"

Doug pulled the trigger.

CHAPTER 68

Wednesday, 1:15 a.m.

The frost now completely coated the camera lens, rendering the video monitor useless. The audio was still functional, however, and Chip could make out some low moaning. The ominous hissing noise was also getting louder.

"Doug, wait!" Laura Landry screamed.

The next thing he heard made his blood run cold—the unmistakable sound of Chandler's voice: "The fucking dog's name was Smokey!"

Then the loud report of a single gunshot.

"Did you shoot him?" Chip called out.

He heard sounds of a scuffle.

"Is he dead?" Chip said, louder.

But all he could hear was the hissing noise, which now sounded like the full-throated roar of a jet engine, obliterating all other sounds.

Chip paced frantically about the control room, dread rapidly consuming him. He heaved his shoulder several times against the heavy door—it remained unyielding. People were no doubt dying in there, and he was stuck outside. *Where is Kristin? She should be here by now.*

Chip stood still for a moment and strained to hear anything over the intercom. Nothing but the god-awful hissing noise. He stared at the magnet temp gauge, willing it downward. The needle crept inexorably up to the red line, then passed it. The helium would be boiling uncontrollably now, and the magnet might blow apart any second. Strangely, this didn't seem to matter that much anymore; they would all be dead shortly, from lack of oxygen or frozen to death. And he was powerless to help them.

And then it hit him.

He reached up and slammed the red button on the wall.

Alarms sounded and he heard the whoosh of several large pumps and fans spin up to speed. The helium would be vented to the atmosphere, thereby relieving the pressure in the room. He couldn't remember exactly, but he also thought the quench switch would ramp down the magnet, siphoning out the electricity circulating in the core, preventing a meltdown.

He hoped to God he wasn't too late.

A minute later, he heard a loud noise coming from the door; it sounded like an air lock being opened and pressures equalizing.

CHAPTER 69

Wednesday, 1:15 a.m.

Just as Doug pulled the trigger, Laura crashed into his arm. The bullet went wide, missing Chandler's head by an inch.

Before Doug could re-aim and fire, Chandler grabbed Doug's arm and slammed it against the magnet housing with tremendous force. Doug's knuckles screamed in pain as the back of his gun hand absorbed the brunt of the blow. The revolver flew from his hand and went sliding across the floor.

Doug threw several punches at Chandler, ignoring the pain in his hand. Chandler blocked the punches easily, seeming to sense where each one was coming from. Doug reached out to strangle Chandler, but again Chandler was one step ahead and easily parried his efforts. Then Chandler landed a solid blow to the side of Doug's head, sending spikes of pain lancing through his skull.

Doug staggered back, struggling to remain standing. He gasped for air—all the exertion on top of the depleted oxygen level was proving too much for him. The room began to spin. Doug's vision blurred.

So cold . . .

Unbearable pressure crushed his eardrums.

Doug fought to remain conscious—it was his only hope of staying alive and saving Laura—but his legs buckled and he dropped to his knees. He glanced over at Laura. She lay motionless on the floor where she'd fallen after slamming into him. *Why on earth did she do that?*

Chandler was on the move. Doug watched in helpless horror as he walked over to the door. Somehow the lack of oxygen was not slowing him down.

Alarms suddenly screeched. Somewhere overhead, large fans and pumps activated, quickly coming up to speed. In less than ten seconds, the billowing cloud of boiling helium began to slow, then stopped altogether.

Chandler picked up the gun.

Doug felt the pressure in his head ease. He heard a loud whoosh of air, and the door began to open inward. "Chip," he shouted, but his voice was ridiculously weak. "Don't come in."

Chip bounded into the room, his face steeled with determination. Chandler immediately slammed the door behind Chip and leveled the gun at him. Chip froze, bewilderment twisting his face.

"Over there," Chandler ordered, motioning with the gun for him to stand next to Doug.

Chip walked slowly over to Doug. "I thought you *shot* him," he murmured to Doug.

"He tried," Chandler said.

Chip's look of confusion turned to one of betrayal.

"Mrs. Landry had a different idea," Chandler said.

Laura began to move on the floor, groaning. Doug found he could breathe easier. The frigid cold was easing, as well.

Chandler studied Chip for a moment. "I do believe you saved our lives just now, Mr. Allison. The quench switch was brilliant."

Laura sat up on the floor and looked around, taking in the situation.

"Laura, why?" Doug asked her.

She didn't respond; she was staring at Chandler.

"I told you we needed to talk," Chandler said to Doug.

"I've got nothing to say to you," Doug said. "Just leave us alone. We won't come after you."

"You know too much, Dr. Landry. But I have something to say to you. And more importantly, so does your wife."

Doug watched in stunned horror and disbelief as Laura got up and walked over to Chandler. Chandler handed her the gun.

"Laura, shoot him!" Doug shouted.

Laura still didn't say anything. She gently shook her head. She was beginning to tear up.

"You *must*," Doug pleaded.

"She won't," Chip said. "I've been trying to tell you—she's become like him."

Doug refused to believe this.

"Go ahead, Laura," Chandler said.

Laura raised the gun and took aim at Doug's chest.

"Laura, *what* are you doing?" Doug said, horrified, even as understanding finally sank in.

Her arm began to tremble.

"Think, Laura—you don't have to do this," Doug said, but his plea was only half-hearted. He felt as if he deserved his fate; he had failed to protect Laura from this monster.

"Do it now," Chandler ordered.

Laura's arm now shook and tears rolled down her face.

"Remember what we have become," Chandler said to her. "I have chosen you."

"Think of the boys, Laura," Doug said, trying to lock eyes with her.

"I have given you the gift," Chandler said, worry suddenly glittering in his usually flat, dull eyes.

"I didn't ask for the gift," she said, her face twisted in anguish. Finally her gun arm sagged and she said, "I can't. I love him."

Without warning, Laura quickly put the gun to her own temple. Before Chandler could stop her, she pulled the trigger.

Doug screamed.

CHAPTER 70

Wednesday, 1:20 a.m.

Kristin could hear the wailing of the magnet alarm through the small service door. She stood there for a moment, pressed up against the door, gathering her courage. Chip had warned her that Chandler was at the med center—not captured—and she felt certain that the bastard was here.

She keyed in the code and heard the lock click open. She took a deep breath and with her heart in her throat, entered the room. The piercing alarm was much louder inside, disorienting her. The room was also bitterly cold, though she found the air breathable. A blinking red light on the magnet's back control panel indicated that someone had activated the emergency quench switch. *Not good.*

She inched forward, straining to hear . . . anything.

Voices, speaking loudly above the racket of the alarm.

"Remember what we have become."

Chandler! Kristin involuntarily cringed and her knees went weak.

"I have chosen you," Chandler continued.

"Think of the boys, Laura," came Dr. Landry's voice, thick with fear.

"I have given you the gift," Chandler said.

"I didn't ask for the gift," a woman's anguished voice answered—no doubt Laura Landry. "I can't. I love him."

A gunshot made Kristin flinch so hard, she bit her tongue.

A scream. *Dr. Landry.*

Kristin quickly edged up to the front of the magnet and peeked around it, her ears still ringing from the gunshot. There was Laura Landry, lying on the floor not two feet away, with a bullet wound to her head, blood pooling on the floor beneath her. She still grasped the gun in her motionless hand. Chandler was at her side, reaching for the gun. Across the room, Dr. Landry and Chip stood like statues, their faces horror-stricken.

Suddenly Chandler whirled to face her. "I know you're there," he said, looking right at her, his silver-flecked gray eyes flashing with menace.

With Chandler's back turned, Doug and Chip erupted into action, leaping forward toward Chandler, tackling him to the floor. Chandler went down hard, but an instant later, a spike was in his hand. Doug and Chip wrestled frantically with him, trying to subdue him without getting stabbed. Chip was on top, straddling Chandler; Landry was off to the side, keeping Chandler's hand with the spike pinned to the floor. Chip punched Chandler in the face several times, then wrapped his hands around his neck and squeezed.

Kristin pried the gun out of Laura Landry's lifeless fingers and took a step forward. Chandler was only a foot away now. She bent over and took aim. But Chandler was thrashing about so much beneath Chip and Landry that she couldn't get a clean shot.

With a roar of rage, Chandler sat halfway up, throwing Chip off to the side. Landry still had his spike hand pinned to the floor. But with his free hand, Chandler smacked Kristin square across her face, knocking her backward.

Kristin's head hit the magnet housing hard and she crumpled to the floor. The room swam before her eyes; she squeezed them shut against the nauseating vertigo and the pounding in her head. Weakness flowed through her limbs. She felt the blackness beckoning, reaching out for her. It would have felt so good to rest—just a brief rest . . .

She almost surrendered to the blackness.

But then Kristin fought back; with everything she had, she fought to cling to consciousness. She forced her eyes open and ignored the dreadful pain beating a path through her skull. The struggle a few feet away drew her gaze.

Chandler was once again on his back, with Chip's knees planted firmly on his chest. Chip's hands were wrapped around Chandler's neck, and he looked like he was riding a bucking bronco as Chandler repeatedly heaved his body off the floor, trying to throw Chip off. Landry stubbornly kept Chandler's spike hand pinned down, but it seemed to take every ounce of his strength to do this. Chandler swung his free arm wildly about and landed a couple of blows to Chip's face; blood streamed from Chip's nose. It would only be a matter of time before Chandler broke free; he seemed stronger than the two other men combined.

Kristin had to do something—and quickly.

She commanded her mind to function, to shake off the rippling vertigo. *Time to make this bastard pay.* Her hands curled into fists, and she realized she still had the gun in her hand.

Struggling to her hands and knees, still so pathetically weak, she started to crawl toward Chandler. Chandler didn't seem to notice her; he was too focused on freeing his spike hand and shaking off Chip.

Kristin closed the distance.

Suddenly Chandler's eyes widened and his head snapped toward her. He cocked his free arm to knock Kristin away again. Chip quickly rolled off his chest, covering Chandler's arm with his body, saving her. But Chandler, free now of Chip's weight, tried to sit up again, neck muscles bulging as he strained against the two men holding his arms. He brought his body up to a forty-five degree angle. Kristin watched in horror as Chip's entire body was lifted off the floor. She tried to take aim at Chandler's bobbing skull.

Chandler howled again, freeing his spike hand from Landry's grasp.

Chip screamed, "Watch out!"

Before Chandler could bury the spike in Landry's chest, Kristin quickly put the muzzle of the gun up to Chandler's skull. "This is for Smokey!" she shrieked as she pulled the trigger.

The far side of Chandler's head exploded in a mess of blood and brains. His arm with the spike dropped lifelessly to the floor.

"Heal this, you bastard!" Kristin screamed and pulled the trigger repeatedly. She continued firing long after the ammo was exhausted, until the revolver made a series of dull clicking sounds.

Chip gently took the gun from her hand. "He's dead. For real, this time. You can stop."

Tears streamed down her face. Kristin bowed her head and leaned into Chip's shoulder. He wrapped both arms around her and hugged her tightly as she wept.

CHAPTER 71

One week later

There was a knock on the door.

Chip set his backpack down on the floor and jogged across the foyer in his socks. He almost slipped as he came to a stop before the door. "Thanks for coming over," he said as he swung the door open. "C'mon in."

"You walk up those steps everyday?" Kristin asked breathlessly. She had on a light blue stretchy top that matched her eyes, over a pair of tight jeans and sneakers.

"Pretty much," he said. "Unless I just stay in bed."

He ushered her into the small living room. "Here, have a seat." He indicated the worn sofa. Although he had cleaned the place before her arrival, even getting out the rarely used vacuum cleaner, he was still nervous about having a female guest. No dishes or cups strewn about. No beer bottles. To her credit, Kristin didn't even wrinkle her nose at the sofa as she sat down.

"How are you holding up?" he asked.

"Good. The investigation is winding down—with you and Dr. Landry backing me up on everything, they're okay with the self-defense angle. Justifiable homicide is what they're calling it. And no one is pressing charges."

"Good."

"They seem anxious to put an end to all the craziness. And I think they're relieved that Chandler's dead—being a cop-killer and all."

"But are *you* okay?"

"I guess so." She looked down and her chin started to quiver.

"What?" Chip said softly.

"It's just—I never thought I'd shoot anyone." Tears welled up in her eyes.

Chip put his hand on her shoulder. "You did what needed to be done. He would've killed all of us—you know that. You saved at least three lives, probably more."

"Yeah, I guess so." She dabbed her eyes with a tissue and looked up at him. "How're you doing?"

"Fine." Chip tapped the bandaged bridge of his nose lightly with a finger. "My nose still hurts, but other than that, I'm fine."

"The whole thing seems unreal to me," she said wistfully.

"Me too."

"Did it really happen?" She sounded as if she hoped he would tell her it was all a bad dream.

"I'm afraid so," Chip said. "And sadly, no one will ever believe the real story."

"No, I suppose not." She paused to pull the rubber band from her hair and redo her ponytail. "Except Dr. Landry. Have you heard how he's doing?"

"I talked to him a couple of days ago," Chip said. "He's keeping pretty busy with his kids. Sounded kinda numb, though. I don't think it's sunk in, what really happened."

"Probably not." A pained smile appeared on her face. "I can relate to that."

"The funeral's this Wednesday. Are you going?"

"Yes, of course. We need to support him."

"I agree," Chip said. "It's going to be tough for him."

She nodded. "How many kids does he have?"

"Three—all boys."

"Being a single parent is never easy."

"Absolutely," Chip said. "But it's more than that. I think he's going to be lost without her."

"I'm sure most people would say that," she said.

"True, but I believe they were deeply in love with each other. More so than most."

"Why do you say that?" She cocked her head to the side.

Chip sat down on the sofa beside her. "It's just that every time he talked about her, he had this faraway look in his eyes. And his voice would change . . . I dunno—soften. And he was always so concerned about her well-being—he was obsessed with it."

"It must've killed him to see her like that—you know, what happened to her."

"For sure," Chip replied sadly.

"And then taking her own life," she added.

Chip didn't say anything. They stared across the room in silence.

Finally, Chip cleared his throat. "You know, the last couple of days I've been thinking about our whole encounter, ordeal—whatever you want to call it—with Chandler. About your Kirlian photographs, the mind-reading, the healing, the strength. I started to wonder about some things."

"Like what?"

"Remember you talked about a soulless creature? How you thought maybe Chandler had lost his soul and this accounted for his powers? And we even brought vampires into the discussion."

"Well," she said, "some of us did, anyway." Surprisingly, she didn't sound the least bit bitter; in fact, she smiled before continuing. "Usually that was where you would say it's crazy talk, or be polite enough not to say anything."

It was good to see her smile. "Maybe I was wrong," Chip said.

She lifted her eyebrows. "Go on."

"I Googled vampires and did some reading. I came across some amazing coincidences."

"Like what?" She leaned forward and locked her pretty blue eyes with his.

"Well, every kid knows that vampires suck blood from their victims, right?"

"Right."

"This is what got me to thinking. Remember how Dr. Landry told us that Chandler originally tried to bleed Mrs. Landry?"

"Uh-huh."

"Why did he do that? He wouldn't have done it to kill her—he could've done that any number of easier ways."

"True," she said, then shrugged. "I don't know."

"What if he was trying to take her to the edge of death? You know, so her soul would leave. And then revive her, transforming her into a soulless creature."

"Like what happened to him?" she asked.

"Exactly. You said yourself, her picture had no aura, just like his. And she took Chandler's side and seemed to communicate with him."

Kristin nodded. "I'll buy that."

"There's more," Chip said.

Her eyes widened with anticipation.

"I still don't believe in vampires," Chip said, then held up a hand to stop her from interrupting, "but what if, in the past, there existed soulless creatures that were created naturally by some sort of freak of nature?"

"What do you mean?"

"Somehow, someone got injured in some fashion—you know, earthquake, flash flood—so that they were almost dead. Then at the last second they were revived, but their soul had already departed."

"I suppose it could happen," she conceded. "Once in a million, if the timing were perfect."

"Well, think about it. Those beings would possess enormous powers, like Chandler—strength, rapid healing, mind-reading—and would seem almost immortal. Like vampires."

"Right," she said, drawing out the word thoughtfully, obviously warming to his theory.

"The creatures themselves would quickly recognize their abilities, and perhaps try to propagate their kind. One of the easiest ways to do this would be to bleed someone else, thereby taking them close to death. Thus, the whole bloodsucking theme of vampires."

"Makes sense," she said, nodding again.

"And the holly stake through the heart notion just represents the overwhelming type of death necessary to kill such a creature."

"Right."

"So maybe the legend of vampires has its basis in the existence of soulless creatures throughout time."

"I do believe you're onto something," she said, her voice tinged with admiration.

"And of course, the legend gets embellished over time to include such things as bats, coffins, aversion to sunlight."

"You have quite an active imagination there, Chip," she said, smiling and patting his arm.

"Learned from the best," Chip said, returning her smile. He threw a quick look at his backpack.

She paused to look around the room, her ponytail swinging from side to side. A blank look had come into her face, which he recognized as her intuition kicking in.

"What is it?" he said.

"You just made me think of something."

Chip glanced at his backpack.

"This past weekend," she continued, "I was in church—I've been spending a lot of time in church recently—and . . ." She paused, collecting her thoughts.

"Go on," he gently prodded.

"The gospel reading was about casting out demons and unclean spirits from crazed people." She looked at him. "Maybe *those* afflicted people were the soulless creatures of the day, and when Jesus and his followers went about casting out demons, they were actually *restoring* souls to these individuals."

"Wow," he said, "I like it. You really are a creative thinker."

Suddenly, Kristin yelped, jumped up from the sofa, and backed away. "Your backpack," she said, pointing. "It's moving!"

"Oh, that," Chip said nonchalantly. He walked over and knelt by the pack.

"What's in there?" she asked, curious now.

"Let's take a look." Chip unzipped the main compartment. He carefully lifted out a golden retriever puppy that was small enough to hold in one hand. He set the pup down on the carpet and the pup sat still, eyes wide as saucers. He looked overwhelmed.

"Oh my God," Kristin exclaimed. "He's adorable. Ah—he's trembling." She knelt down and began to gently pet the puppy, trying to soothe him. "It's okay, little one. No one's gonna hurt you." She turned to Chip. "When did you get him? What's his name?"

"I just got him two days ago," Chip said. "He's eight weeks old. But I don't know what his name is yet."

She gave him a puzzled look.

"Because he's yours," Chip said.

"Seriously?" Kristin scooped the puppy up, tears coming to her eyes. "He's so soft," she said, her voice breaking. She held the pup up to her face and nuzzled it. The puppy licked her nose.

"Yup. He's a birthday present."

"You're the best, Chip," she said and leaned over and kissed him on the cheek.

Chip felt himself blush. "Happy birthday," he said.

"It's the best birthday present I ever got," she said, tears rolling down her face.

"What do you think you're gonna call him?"

She thought for a moment while stroking the pup's fur. "You'll think I'm crazy, but—"

Chip observed a respectful silence.

"I'm leaning toward Smokey," she said. "It's a funny name for a golden, but somehow it just seems right."

EPILOGUE

Southwestern slope of Denali, Alaska
Present day

Kyle Waters crested the ridgeline and paused, gazing in wonder at the majestic Arctic vista spread out before him. Jagged mountain peaks and snow-blanketed evergreen forests stretched out as far as the eye could see. Ever since yesterday's storm had cleared out, the weather was perfect except for some residual strong winds. Besides the glaring sun, just a few wispy clouds inhabited the dazzling blue sky. Below him, the mighty Kahiltna Glacier, two miles wide and forty miles long, wound its way down from the high mountaintops where it was birthed to the valleys far below. The frozen river of ice sparkled in the waning sunlight, traces of shimmering blue glacial ice catching the light.

Here on the exposed ridge, the wind whipped over him, urging him to seek cover, but Kyle held his ground. Behind him, the lone peak of Denali loomed ridiculously large, blotting out the whole northern horizon. The sun was sinking fast and he knew they needed to hurry.

Beth joined him, out of breath. "Check out the view," Kyle said loudly, to be heard over the wind.

"Amazing," she said.

"You can even make out Fairbanks over there." He pointed.

"I see it."

"And the terminal moraine of the Kahiltna," he added.

She nodded, smiling. "And base camp."

"Right," he said, "base camp." Two words never sounded so good. "No more than five miles." Kyle checked his watch. "It's two-fifteen. We've gotta make some time before the sun sets." He didn't bother to add that he was worried. The thought of spending another night on the mountain rattled him more than he cared to admit. Last night's storm had been horrendous. The unrelenting wind had ripped off their tent's storm-flap; he was thankful the main body of the tent had somehow remained intact until morning. Today had been unusually clear and this meant the night would be brutally cold—probably twenty below. The wind would make it forty below. And they were also running low on food and fuel.

Today's journey had been much more arduous that he would've liked; the last two days had seen four or five feet of fresh snowfall added to the season's record tally, and had created some slow-going and treacherous conditions. He was ready to be done with the mountain, and already imagining a long, hot shower.

"I feel good," Beth said. "Set the pace and I'll follow."

She was special, all right. And to her credit, she didn't sound worried—he knew she trusted him and his advanced mountaineering skills. The two had met in base camp three weeks ago and had hit it off right away. He was drawn to her unusual combination of long black hair and intense blue eyes. She had told him she was of northern Italian descent and that a deep-seated love of the mountains was in her blood. The pair had decided to break off from the main group after summiting four days earlier.

Kyle had also figured that with her athletic body, she'd be good in the ol' mummy bag, and in this, his intuition had proven entirely correct. He gave his head a shake and erased the lingering smile from his face. No time for daydreaming now. His unease returned, becoming palpable, and he set off down the mountain at a brisk clip.

Thirty minutes later, Kyle paused to catch his breath in the thin air. He was once again impressed by Beth's stamina. Most girls—or rather most hikers, male or female—would have had trouble keeping up with him, especially after the grueling slog this morning. But Beth soldiered on without complaint.

Kyle could feel the temperature plummet as the sun dropped toward the horizon. He shivered and kept plodding forward. He knew it was dangerous to push it like this when they were tired, but he felt they didn't have much choice.

A distant sound made Kyle stop and scan the sky, shielding his eyes with one hand. He recognized the distinctive *womp-womp* of an approaching helicopter, its rotors clawing for purchase in the frigid, thin air. Soon he made out the chopper's orange and blue markings. It was from Denali Air, a local tour facility, serving all the cruise ship tourists who had traveled by rail to explore the national park. Hopefully Beth and he wouldn't be spotted. The tourists loved to see animals on the slopes — Dall sheep, caribou, or even bear or moose, if they were lucky. But if the animals weren't obliging, a couple of hikers would do in a pinch.

The chopper flew right by them and headed toward the summit. *Good.*

Suddenly the chopper veered in a tight U-turn and headed back toward them. "Shit," Kyle cursed loudly. "We've been seen."

"So what?" Beth said.

"It's dangerous," he said, and began flailing his arms in an effort to wave them off. She joined him. The helo circled stubbornly above them for several minutes, ignoring their waves, before it finally buzzed off.

The two resumed their downward trek.

Gradually, Kyle became aware of a low frequency vibration in his chest—a building pressure. Soon he could make out a low rumbling sound. Before his brain could process it, the noise level quickly intensified. An inexplicable sense of impending doom engulfed him. A second or two later, he identified the origin of the noise.

An avalanche.

Undoubtedly it had been caused by the helo's rotor wash, high in the unstable peaks, where the new snow lay heavy.

Kyle whipped his head around, trying to make sense out of anything in the sea of white. Then he saw something—a billowing snow wave that was at most several hundred yards away, and coming fast.

"Run!" he screamed to Beth.

They both ran pell-mell down the slope. He knew they couldn't hope to outrun the massive snow wave, which typically traveled at speeds over 100 mph, but perhaps they could get out of its direct path. He led them diagonally off to the right.

Within seconds, the ground around his feet came alive with moving snow, like a fast-moving stream, threatening to trip him. Kyle ran faster, but soon the snow was up to his knees and he went down hard onto his belly. He felt himself being carried down the mountain in a monstrous churning wave that was alive, hugging him and wrapping its tentacles around his body.

Soon the tentacles constricted and the wave became heavier and heavier. As Kyle felt its crushing weight pressing onto his body, he tried frantically to bodysurf and stay near the surface. But his arms quickly became pinned to his side by an unyielding, overwhelming force. Soon his thrashing legs were held motionless as well. The cold snow pushed in on his face and snaked up his nostrils, freezing his brain and making it almost impossible to breathe. He was completely at the mercy of the boiling snow.

Finally, after what seemed like an eternity, the writhing snow mass stopped moving. Dead silence. Kyle couldn't move a muscle;

the snow held him in its viselike grip of cold death. He thought about clearing an airspace around his mouth and nose, but his arms were immobilized at his sides. He was buried alive under a mountain of snow. The cold flowed rapidly into his body.

Kyle knew his only hope was the locating transceiver in his pack. Surely base camp had seen the avalanche and would be sending rescue parties. He just needed to hold on for a little bit. As he exhaled, the snow melted several inches around his mouth and nose. Kyle moved his head for all he was worth, trying to create a little breathing space. He found he was able to breathe in short tiny gasps, using just his diaphragm, as his chest was immobilized by the crushing weight of the snow. But without a fresh air supply, he realized this would just prolong the inevitable for a few minutes.

As the cold rapidly seeped into him and he felt his consciousness flicker, his thoughts turned to Beth. With any luck, she was closer to the surface or the edge of the snow mass than he seemed to be. Sorrow welled up in him; she had placed her trust in him, yet he had not been able to protect her from the unforgiving mountain.

Soon Kyle could no longer ignore his hunger for air; his breaths became more and more rapid as the carbon dioxide built up. With his air supply now exhausted, he succumbed to the blackness.

* * *

The German shepherd started barking insistently and Brad knew she had picked up a scent. His transceiver indicated there were two victims, and that they were both nearby. "Angela's got a scent," he said over his walkie-talkie.

Several hundred yards away, his buddy Joe on the snowmobile answered. "Okay, good. I'm on my way. Don't get your hopes up, Brad. I just found a loose pack over here with a transceiver in it."

Angela was now digging furiously with her front paws. Brad began piercing the snow with his eight-foot-long snow probe, searching for anything solid beneath the snow. He got a hit at roughly six feet. Yanking the shovel from his pack, Brad started digging beside the dog, being careful not to put the shovel blade through a victim's skull.

Five minutes later, the two men hauled a limp body out of the snow. The person looked dark gray and showed no sign of respiration. No pulse, either. Brad started CPR. Joe dashed to the snowmobile and grabbed the emergency pack. They stripped off the victim's parka and applied the defibrillator machine's patches.

The AED went to work analyzing and then announced, "Shockable rhythm." Its mechanical voice sounded eerie on the windswept glacier. Brad figured the vic must be in V-fib from a combination of hypothermia and hypoxia. The machine said, "Clear," and moments later fired its electricity. The vic's body heaved off the snow.

"Get the oxygen and the warming blanket," Brad said, but Joe was already on the move.

The AED repeated, "Shockable rhythm."

Shit, Brad thought, *not good. Been buried too long.*

The AED fired again.

Joe came back with the oxygen tank, Ambu bag, and portable warming blanket. Brad gave the vic two breaths while Joe got the warming blanket going.

The AED discharged a third time.

Seconds later, the vic's eyes flew open, startling the hell out of Brad.

"C-can you hear me?" Brad said. Joe stood there with his mouth hanging open.

"Cold," came the weak reply. "So cold."

Brad quickly checked the settings on the warming blanket. "What's your name?" he asked.

"Beth."

"You're going to be okay, Beth," Brad said, feeling the emotion well up in him. This part—the saving someone's life—made this job the best in the world.

Joe slapped his back. "Way to go, man."

The woman, who had the most intense blue eyes he had ever seen, didn't say anything for several minutes, but stared up at Brad, her face expressionless. Finally she spoke. "Did you find Kyle's body?"

Brad exchanged glances with Joe. "Not yet," Brad said. A vague uneasiness settled on him. Joe was looking over at the snowmobile; the hiker's pack he had found was strapped to the side.

"Thanks for rescuing me," she said.

"Sure," Brad said.

"Will you thank Angela, too?" she asked.

"You can thank her yourself." Brad nodded toward Angela, who was sitting at attention off to the side, panting and waiting patiently for further commands. "She's one hell of a rescue dog. She's got a nose on her that's—that's—off the charts."

Beth turned her head toward the dog and smiled.

Brad's unease now turned to confusion. "Hey," he asked, "how did you know her name?"

Dr. John Benedict, husband and father of three sons, graduated cum laude from Rensselaer Polytechnic Institute and entered post-graduate training at Penn State University College of Medicine. There, he completed medical school, internship, anesthesia residency and a cardiac anesthesia fellowship. He currently works as an anesthesiologist in a busy private practice in Harrisburg, Pennsylvania.

Author website: johnbenedictmd.com
Author email: johnbenedictmd@yahoo.com
(The author welcomes all feedback and correspondence.)

Don't miss *Fatal Complications*, John Benedict's third medical thriller. Coming: December 2014

EXCERPT FROM *FATAL COMPLICATIONS*:

PROLOGUE: 15 years ago

"I got him!" he screamed, as he staggered out of the garage, coughing violently to clear the smoke from his lungs. Flames were now spewing out of the first floor windows, lighting up the summer night sky. Red-hot embers danced and swirled skyward, like millions of drunken fireflies. In his arms, he cradled their trembling chocolate Labrador retriever. He heard the sirens, pretty close now. Marie stood in the driveway, eyes wide with panic. Her mouth worked but nothing came out.

He gently laid Brownie down on the cool asphalt, knelt beside him and smoothed his fur. "I found him cuddled in a ball under the laundry room sink. Poor thing—" He stopped talking and whipped his head around. "Where's David?"

No response. His wife began to shake. He stood up and put his hands on her shoulders. "Marie, where is he?" he screamed, although seeing her up close, he was scared to death he already knew.

"H-he went after you to look for Brownie," she managed to get out between sobs. "He moved too fast—I couldn't stop him." She pointed in the general direction of the garage, her arm swaying wildly.

He ran back into the garage. The metal door leading into the house radiated heat. He touched the surface of the door and pulled his hand away; it was much hotter than it had been five minutes ago. He didn't have time for this safety drill. Ignoring how the knob burnt into the palm of his hand, he opened the door.

Flames burst out of the doorway, growling like some alien beast. The heat and flame bowled him backwards and he lost his footing and went down hard, hitting his back on his John Deere tractor. The hair on his right forearm was singed off. "David," he yelled from the cement floor. "Come on out! I got Brownie!" No reply other than the roaring of the flames and the crackling of the wood that used to be the frame of his house.

He scrambled to his feet, ran back out and around to the front of the house. He heard the lumbering fire trucks coming up the street, sirens blaring so loud it was hard to think. Flashing red lights played on the trees in the front yard casting strange shadows, lending a sense of unreality to the scene. The flames were spreading quickly to the second floor. He approached the front door, knowing that it was locked—Marie was a stickler for these things. He grabbed a key under the thick bristly doormat with WELCOME printed in bold letters on it. It struck him as absurd. Welcome to hell, maybe. He unlocked the door and opened it. Again a wall of flame greeted him. This time he was ready; he took two steps back, careful not to fall down.

"David!" he yelled. "I have Brownie!" He paused to listen— he thought he could make out a faint scream. But, from where? He was about to leave when he heard a peculiar, musical sound coming from the living room. Was that David playing the piano? Again, the unreality of the situation washed over him and for a split second he questioned his sanity. Then, just as quickly, he realized the piano wires were twanging randomly as the flames set them free.

He ran around to the back of the house, almost slipping on the dew-slicked grass, and peered in the kitchen window. The flames were not as intense here, but smoke was everywhere. He thought he could make out some movement through the smoke. Please God, protect him. Save my boy.

He tried the handle—for once it wasn't burning hot. It was locked and he didn't have the key. He kicked at the door, high near the lock. He heard cracking but the door held. He took several steps backwards, then ran toward the door and leapt off the ground. He hit the door squarely with both feet. The door and frame splintered, crashing inwards. He fell backwards onto the flagstone patio, smacking his right elbow. Smoke billowed out of the ruined doorway, but no flames.

As he made for the entrance, he was tackled from behind, knocking the wind out of him. "I can't let you go in there," came a deep voice of authority. He turned over and looked up at a large firefighter standing over him. The man was outfitted with all the latest gear, complete with air tanks strapped to his back and helmet; the firefighter resembled a cross between a spaceman and a sumo wrestler.

Painfully, he sucked air back into his lungs and pleaded hoarsely while climbing to his feet. "My boy's in there!"

Another fireman, smaller than the first, ran over and helped restrain him. The big one said, "Take it easy! If you go in there, you'll never come out alive."

"But my boy . . ." he said, his voice trailing off into an agonizing groan. He strained harder against them.

The firefighter put a hand on his shoulder and fixed him with kind, bluish eyes. "We have equipment—we'll go in and get him." Blue eyes turned and shouted, "Bill, bring the hose and gear around back here!"

He stopped struggling and the arms holding him relaxed a bit. Immediately, he broke free of their grip and ignored the cries of "Shit!" and "Don't be a fool!"

He ran through the doorway into the kitchen, his sneakers crunching on broken glass. "David—it's Dad," he called out. "I'm in the kitchen." Coughing spasms prevented him from saying anything further. The black smoke was so thick he couldn't see a thing. Breathing was a nightmare. He dropped to all fours, cutting his hands on the glass. Here he could breathe in little gasps and see his bloodied hands on the vinyl brick flooring.

"I'm coming for you, son," he yelled, his voice already raspy from the smoke. More coughing fits. Again, he thought he could hear faint cries coming from upstairs, but he couldn't be sure because the roar of the flames was so loud. He crawled into the foyer to the base of the stairway and began to ascend the stairs. As he went up, the heat quickly ratcheted up and the smoke thickened.

Coughs racked his chest. He wouldn't be able to breathe much longer. If he turned around now, he could probably make it out the way he had come, to the cool, fresh air outside. He groped for the gold cross dangling from his neck and squeezed it hard, saying a quick prayer. Then he heard the sound of his boy crying—no imagining this time—a horrible, high-pitched keening that pierced his very soul. He pressed upwards.

He paused halfway up the staircase and lifted his sweat-soaked T-shirt to cover his mouth and nose. He took several deep breaths through it, and then held the last one. He clambered to the top of the stairs. Although the smoke burned his eyes like someone had poured acid in them, he forced himself to look down the hallway.

What he saw filled him with a sickening dread. Midway down, the hallway was blocked by a hellish inferno. The heat pouring off the flames was roasting him alive. He put one hand up to shield his eyes. He clenched his jaw and advanced.

As he got closer, he noticed that the wall of flame wasn't quite as thick as he had first thought. There was a spot clear of flames at the end of the hallway, near David's room. His air hunger was becoming unbearable and his surroundings started to swirl as his vision dimmed. He ran toward the flames, but tripped on some unseen debris and went down hard. The air was forced out of him; reflexively, he sucked in a lungful of thick, burning smoke. He coughed painfully. It felt like his lungs were being ripped to shreds—soon the bloody remnants would spill out of his mouth. No air was getting in. The hallway dimmed again and he realized he would not make it. His last flicker of consciousness caught a glimpse of his boy through the smoke and flame at the end of the hallway. David was reaching out to him, crying out. "Dad, I'm here! Help me!"

28944436R00186

Made in the USA
Middletown, DE
01 February 2016